FRANKIE

FRANKIE

Shivaun Plozza

FLATIRON
BOOKS
NEW YORK

FRANKIE. Copyright © 2017 by Shivaun Plozza. All rights reserved. Printed in the United States of America. For information, address Flatiron Books, 175 Fifth Avenue, New York, N.Y. 10010.

www.flatironbooks.com

The Library of Congress Cataloging-in-Publication Data is available upon request.

ISBN 978-1-250-14299-3 (hardcover)
ISBN 978-1-250-14301-3 (ebook)

Our books may be purchased in bulk for promotional, educational, or business use. Please contact your local bookseller or the Macmillan Corporate and Premium Sales Department at 1-800-221-7945, extension 5442, or by email at MacmillanSpecialMarkets@ macmillan.com.

Originally published in Australia by Penguin Australia Pty Ltd.

First U.S. Edition: November 2017

10 9 8 7 6 5 4 3 2 1

For Mum and Dad

FRANKIE

One

"Don't tell him where you live. Don't give him any money. Don't trust a word he says." That's what Aunt Vinnie said about Xavier.

"How bad can a fourteen-year-old be?" I asked her.

That got a throaty "Ha! The kid says he's your brother, so wipe off four years and take a look in the mirror."

Touché.

Anyway, he's late. So I guess I can add *Don't rely on his time-management skills* to the list. Behind me, people dash in and out of Bean Me Up, Scotty, the smell of coffee calling me each time the door opens. But I wait. I search the afternoon crowd for "brown hair, gray hoodie, high-tops" because that's what Xavier said to look for. "I'll wear bright blue high-tops so you'll know it's me."

The 86 rattles down Smith Street. Sparks fly where the

tram's mechanical-arm thingy meets a crisscross of overhead cables and I jolt back into something warm and solid. Something that lets out a loud "Oi!" I swing round and get a dirty look from the old guy I've just bashed into: gray hair, dandruff-sprinkled jacket, expensive-looking brogues.

So, not Xavier?

The guy shuffles past, shaking his head and muttering. My middle finger itches, but I'm trying to cut down on obscene gestures: Vinnie says it's a sign of low breeding. "Not like you can't think of something colorful to say instead," she says.

I check my phone for the time. Again.

What's this kid going to look like, anyhow? Dark-olive skin like me? Short? No, he sounded tall. But he also *sounded* like a con-artist junkie. Maybe.

A young guy walks onto Smith Street from Gertrude: gray jacket, the hood flipped over his head. My gaze slides down his black skinny jeans toward his shoes, my heart kabooming the whole way.

He's wearing white Chucks.

My nails dig into my palms.

There's a voice behind me. "Got change, cuz?" I turn and see Homeless Eddie doing his morning rounds. Right now he's chasing a gray-haired librarian type. His hands are in a prayer pose as she's shaking her head, gripping her bag to her chest. She scurries away.

"Nothing for Eddie," he says, raising one arm high above his head—it's his usual tic. He jiggles his outstretched arm, his index finger poking all sorts of holes in the sky.

I'm just about to split when another voice stops me short. Male. Young. Right behind me. "Frankie?"

Cripes.

Okay, so running away is still an option, right? Grow a pair, Frankie.

I take a deep breath, swing round, and get a punch in the face.

No, not literally. What I experience is more like a bitch-slap from fate.

Brown hair, gray hoodie, high-tops, bright blue.

I look him over—this Xavier person, this boy who shouldn't exist. I look him over and it's like a sumo wrestler is bear-hugging my lungs.

"Frankie, right?" The kid blinks at me, half smiling, and all the while my lungs are collapsing into mashed-banana mush in my chest.

He holds out his hand, staring at me with wide-set, so-brown-they're-black eyes.

My eyes.

"You're Frankie?" His outstretched hand hangs between us. I don't take it. I give him a small wave: jerky and mechanical.

"I'm Frankie."

Well, duh.

"Cool," he says. He shoves both hands in his pockets and grins.

He's tall, broad-shouldered and pale, light-brown hair cut short back and sides, with a fringe flopping half across his face, all the way to his chin. More skate punk than junkie. No meth sores and all his teeth. That's a good start.

We stand in silence. Me and my brother. *Half* brother.

"Shit. This is awkward," he says in a voice deeper than it sounded on the phone. Raspier. And then he laughs.

Homeless Eddie laughs too, but I ignore him because right now I'm listening to my half brother laugh for the first time and it's . . . weird. Weird and cool. It's like when you get a whiff of some random chick's perfume and the smell drags you back to primary school and that teacher who cuddled you after the kids ganged up on you at the monkey bars because all your clothes were from the Salvos. So you want to chase the random chick down the street and hug her for reminding you of that moment. But you also want to slap her because it's not just Ms. Ng stroking your hair you remember, it's the name-calling, too.

Xavier chews on his bottom lip. He's not laughing anymore.

Maybe because I'm staring at him. Like a proper psycho.

I shift my weight, boots sloshing in a puddle. I nod at the café. "We could go in? I mean, if it's gonna be awkward we may as well overdose on brownies, right?"

"Cool," he says with a shrug.

Cool.

We got the call three nights ago. Vinnie answered and said nothing—just shoved the phone under my nose. I half expected it to be a cop or a nurse—someone saying, "Sorry about your mum. We did everything we could. It was just her time," blah, blah, blah.

I haven't heard from Juliet in forever, not since she dumped me at age four. Not since she pissed off to Queensland so she wouldn't have to worry about a kid cramping her style while she got high and ripped people off.

But it was a young voice on the phone. Male. "Are you Francesca Vega?"

"I'm Frankie. Who the hell are you?"

"Is Juliet Vega your mum?"

"Why are you asking?"

"Cos I'm Xavier Green. She's my mum too."

Bam, crash, ka-pow. Hell of a game changer.

It's those four words—"She's my mum too"—that loop through my head as I follow Xavier into the frosted, wooden Scandinavian-ness of Bean Me Up, Scotty.

We grab a table at the back and I inhale my brownie. Because eating equals mouth full equals can't talk.

In between mouthfuls I watch him, sitting there looking more like Juliet than I do. It's the long, thin nose and the straggly hair, I think.

There's a nervous, jangly energy about him. "This is cool, hey," he says.

I nod because if I open my big mouth I'll be honest and tell him this is 10 percent cool, 30 percent uncomfortable, and 60 percent completely freaking me out. Either that or I'll tell him there *are* words other than "cool."

He rips a napkin out of the dispenser, pulls out a fineliner, and starts doodling while I flag down the waitress and order a second brownie.

I tear my fingernails and watch him—his tongue at the corner of his mouth as he scribbles all over the napkin with the kind of fluid, easy movement of someone who knows what he's doing. He moves his arm so I can't see what he's drawing, but what I do see are the scrapes on his knuckles, the pen marks on his fingers, the dark stain on his hoodie, and the shadows under his eyes. And slowly I think I might be beginning to see Xavier.

On the phone he told me he's just turned fourteen; already he's a fair bit taller than me. I don't know if I'd call him good-looking, but I think girls would go for him. It's the dimples. Bet he gets away with murder.

He looks up. "You like music?" He points his pen at my Joy Division T-shirt.

"Some," I say. "Ian Curtis is a god."

"He's a wanker," says Xavier.

I stop wiping brownie crumbs from around my mouth. "You did not just say that."

He looks up at me and grins.

Dimples don't work on me, kid.

I lean forward and jab my finger at him. "Firstly, without Joy Division there would be no Smiths and without The Smiths there would be no Radiohead and without Radiohead there would be no music. At all. Secondly—"

"So that's how I get you to talk, hey?" Xavier flips the napkin over and slumps back in his chair. Still grinning.

"Insulting Ian Curtis is how you get on my bad side."

"Confession: I don't know who Brian Curtis is."

"Ian."

Dimples. "Exactly."

The edges of my lips twitch. It's a weird feeling. Almost like I might be about to . . . smile. I quickly cover my mouth with my hand.

Xavier leans forward on his elbows. "So you live with your aunt, hey."

I nod.

"I guess she's my aunt too. What's she like?"

What do you say about Vinnie? That she has three ex-husbands and two ex-fiancés? That there's nothing tighter than her skirts? That she took me in when no one else wanted me?

"Amazing. Basically the opposite of Juliet," I say.

He looks away, a little crease between his brows.

Way to go, Frankie. He was probably dumped in a cardboard

box on the doorstep of a convent and raised by sadistic nuns. The only thing keeping him going was the hope that out there, somewhere, was a fairy-tale mother who would ride in on a silver unicorn and rescue him. But now his ugly half sister is telling him his mum's the Wicked Witch.

Man, I need another brownie.

He taps his long fingers on the napkin and clears his throat. "What year are you in at school?"

"Twelve."

"Shit," he says.

I nod. I don't tell him I'm currently on "extended hiatus." I don't tell him that two days ago I was suspended indefinitely, until the school board meets and decides whether or not I'm kicked out for good. I don't tell him, because I am *not* talking about the Steve Sparrow Incident.

"You?" I ask.

"Eight. It's bullshit."

And it's like that, back and forth, firing off questions like we're ticking off a list.

He tells me he lives with his dad in Reservoir (but grew up in Townsville), only bothers turning up at school for Art, doesn't have any other siblings (that he knows about), obsessively plays some game called *StarCraft* (it's big in Korea), and his least favorite food is anything green. I have to answer the same questions and pretty soon we've covered all the key topics.

Except one. No one's mentioning Juliet. But it's fine. Got to know what this kid's favorite color/animal/holiday destination is before I broach the J-word.

"Got a boyfriend?" he asks.

"I'm taking an extended hiatus."

He looks at me, nose crinkled. "You like big words, hey."

"Big words, yes. Boys, not so much. They lie."

"Most people do."

Same eyes, same healthy dose of cynicism. No need for a DNA test, doctor. We're definitely related.

I lean forward. "What's your dad like?"

"Total prick."

"Just Juliet's type, then."

He frowns, a chipped front tooth digging into his lip. "You don't like her, do you?"

Hmm. Looks like we're having this conversation after all.

Diplomacy is not my strong point but I'm going to try. I pick over my words as carefully as a girl in combat boots can. "She never gave me much chance to like her. There's a lot I might have forgiven if . . . Well, she's not exactly bombarding me with phone calls begging for forgiveness, is she?"

Xavier's frown deepens, so I assume my little foray into diplomacy has sucked. If I were a country, I'd be North Korea.

World's shortest sibling relationship? I guess this is the end of what might otherwise have been the feel-good story of the year. No more Frankie and Xavier. You'll get your way after all, Vinnie.

The silence stretches all the way to Awkwardville. Xavier stares at nothing. All I can focus on is the tip of his pen as he raps it against the table.

And then he takes a deep breath, shoulders drawing down. "Dad says she should've never had kids. Not fit to be a mum."

"Your dad and I would get along fine."

He looks at me, the barest hint of dimple. "That's cos you haven't met him."

"Or maybe because he hasn't met me."

He laughs.

"Look." I lay my hands on the table, palms down. "I don't know how old you were when she dumped you but, believe me, she was doing you a favor. If I can give you one piece of sisterly advice it'd be to stay away from Juliet Vega. Unless you're a disappointment junkie. Then you should go right ahead. If you can find her."

When I'm done with my incredibly undiplomatic diplomatic speech, there's silence. Except for all the coffee orders, hipsters droning on about how drunk they were last night, plates and cups clinking, and whatever crappy dance music is pounding in the background. Actually, it's just Xavier and me who are silent.

"How long did she stick around?" I ask. "She must have got knocked up with you pretty soon after she left me."

No dimples now, more of a grimace. "I'm no good with maths . . . But family's family. Sometimes it's all you got, hey? And if you don't—"

He's cut short by a racket from his jeans' pocket: a thin beat, vinyl scratching—*wooka wook wook*—and some dude rapping with a nasally voice and a bad case of sexism.

He has Eminem for a ringtone? This is not going to end well for us.

He grabs his thigh with a jolt. "Shit," he says. His second-favorite word after "cool." "Sorry." He reaches into his pocket and pulls out the phone. "Got to take this." He swipes the screen and the racket ends—thank god. "What?"

Sheesh. Rude much? I rest my chin on my palm and try to look fascinated by the lunch menu.

"Nah, dude. Not for like an hour or something." Xavier's eyes keep flicking between the floor and me. He angles his body to the side, his phone ear completely hidden from view.

The waitress appears. "Anything else?" She eyes my plate with the mounds of brownie crumbs.

Don't judge me, bitch. This is a high-stress situation. I shake my head. "We're good."

The waitress flicks me a half-arsed smile and walks away. Xavier ignores her.

"You for real?" He glances my way, so I try out a smile. He shifts farther around in his chair. "What the fuck, Nate? Why does it have to be now?"

Vinnie's number one hate is when people come into her shop and order while still on the phone. "Yeah, I'll have a—what do you mean you won't be able to make it by six?—kebab with— well, then you'll have to pick up Madysin and Jakwelin from bal- let lessons—but no garlic sauce, 'kay?" Those kinds of people get the special sauce.

So what would Vinnie make of Xavier? Looking so much like Juliet would be a massive black mark next to his name in the Book of Vinnie. He didn't thank the waitress when she brought him his Coke—another big no-no—but, having met the wait- ress in question, I'd argue that in this instance it's a gray area.

I reckon if Vinnie were here she'd be kicking me under the table, telling me to get the hell out. She doesn't have a lot of time for Juliet Vega–related things; I'm the one and only exception.

But I'm not sure what *I* think about Xavier. Junkie? Prob- ably not. Liar? Thief? Not enough evidence. The jury's still out on how far this apple fell from the tree.

He hangs up and pockets his phone. "Something's come up. I'm real sorry, Frankie, but I gotta go."

No, wait—jury's in: the kid's a bastard.

I push my plate into the center of the table and stand, chair scraping. "Yeah. I got to go too. Busy, busy, busy." I rummage through my bag for cash. Why can't I ever find anything in this stupid jumbo-size backpack? Is there a vortex at the bottom of it?

"It's my mate," he says. "I owe him. He's calling in a favor so . . ." He frowns at the napkin and keeps blinking, like he's got dust in there. It's weird watching my eyes doing stuff in someone else's face. "But we should do this again, hey."

"Sure." Not a chance.

Xavier places two fingers on the napkin and slides it across the table. "I really would like to see you again, Frankie," he says. "We never got to . . . Well, maybe I could swing by your shop? Meet Vinnie? You can shout me a kebab, hey."

I dump a twenty on the table.

I'm not sure what I was expecting from this meeting. It isn't like a date, but then it kind of is. I wanted to be funny, intriguing, intelligent. I didn't want to accidentally spit brownie on him or trip and face-plant the pastries. I wanted him to call me later and say, "Hey, I had a good time. Let's be brother and sister. Let's fight over the remote. You can call me Pus Face and I'll call you Sarcastitron, Her Royal Bitchiness, and we'll moan about what a fuckup Juliet is and no one will understand just how fucked up but us."

I wanted to be impossible to walk away from.

"How 'bout it?" he asks.

Looking into those black-brown eyes, I get that feeling again. Weird and cool at the same time. And then I look down at the napkin.

It's a girl. All delicate, swirling lines and feathery shading and eyes that you'd swear were real, that you could stare at for hours just waiting for them to blink. It's so raw, so good. And it's hard to tell the wrong way up, but I'm pretty sure it's a drawing of me. A nice me, though. A happy me.

Kaboom.

What's that sound? Oh, nothing. Just my heart exploding into a million pieces.

When I look up, he's watching me. Waiting. With dimples.

"Okay," I say.

Bouncing to his feet, he reaches into his back pocket and pulls out a few crumpled notes, dumping them on the table next to mine. "Cool," he says, and thrusts out a hand for me to shake.

This time, I take it.

Two

Ten minutes later I'm back home at the unfashionable end of Smith Street. Terry's Kebab Emporium: where kebabs go to die. I'm greeted by the familiar crack that spans the front window. It's like the shop front is giving me a sleazy, toothless grin.

I walk in and Vinnie's leaning against the front counter, flicking through a magazine. She's calm, not a bleached hair out of place. You'd never guess she'd spent the past couple of hours having a conniption about me meeting up with Xavier.

"Morning, sweetheart," she says.

I collapse against the counter with a groan. "*Afternoon,* Vinnie."

Vinnie licks her finger and flicks over another page. Her nails are painted the same shade of red—Vixen Rampage—as her lipstick. "Is it afternoon already? Well, I never."

There are a couple of people in the shop, all of them too busy stuffing their faces with kebab to worry about the drama unfolding in front of them. Or maybe they're locals, used to looking the other way.

Vinnie's still got her head down, and I'm not telepathic so I can't get her to look up simply by thinking it. And I'd *really* like her to look at me so I can launch into a detailed account of *everything* and ask her what she thinks. Is Xavier for real? Is he after money? Is he likely to sell me to sex traffickers for a pack of smokes?

"I'm starved," I say instead. "Do we have any food? I could score us some *banh mi*."

"Nice try, honey, but you're going nowhere. You're still grounded. It's not my fault you wasted your *one* get-out-of-jail-free card meeting up with God Knows Who."

Finally, she closes her magazine and looks up, giving me the Nonna Sofia: eyes narrowed, lips pursed, a single hand on a cocked hip. We don't live with Nonna anymore, not since she lost her marbles and had to go live at Peaceful Pines Retirement Home, but I can't escape The Look.

"Whatever," I say. From the bar fridge under the counter I grab a tub of Vinnie's emergency supply of low-fat yogurt, rip off the lid, and lick it clean. I grab a spork from the canister on top of the bain-marie. "You could have had it so much worse." I spork runny globs of yogurt into my mouth. "You could have—"

"Don't speak with your mouth full."

"—been lumped with a spider-fancying, cockroach-eating serial killer in the making. So you got a niece who gets expelled from school. Big deal. You've met Steve Sparrow. Tell me *you* don't want to slap his face with the collected works of Shakespeare. I just did what everyone wished they could do. It's called poetic justice."

She pushes the magazine away. "I love you more than life, honey, but I swear to god there are times when I could serve you on a spit." She jabs a pointed nail at me. "And you only got suspended."

"Suspended indefinitely. Don't call us, we'll call you."

It's been two days since the Steve Sparrow Incident and I'm already bored, stuck at home with nothing to do except think about how the "Steve Sparrow Incident" would make an excellent band name and how maybe I should learn an instrument so I can form that band. I don't think being able to play "Three Blind Mice" on the recorder counts.

Vinnie shakes her head and starts tossing the bowl of lettuce with a pair of tongs. We both know she's not really pissed off about what I did to Steve. Well, she is. Majorly. But right now she's more upset about my meeting with God Knows Who.

"Xavier got dumped, too," I say. "It's not his fault she's his mum." I stir the yogurt. "He's nice. Clean. Paid his half. Didn't kill me."

"Who's been looking after him, then?" She tries keeping her voice casual. She fails.

"His dad, I think. In Queensland."

"You going to be seeing him again?"

I do have a plan. I'm applying the rules of dating. If he contacts me in the next twelve hours I'll know it's a scam—too eager. If he waits twenty-four hours, then it's okay to meet up with him again, but not if he takes longer than three days to text me. Then he's a jerk who doesn't deserve my time.

"Maybe—maybe I'll see him again."

"Well, it won't be tomorrow," says Vinnie. "We're busy."

Tomorrow is The Meeting—my meeting with Principal Vukovic.

"Let's not go, Vin. We could skip the firing squad and get doughnuts instead."

I get a laugh. Which is a bonus.

"Not on your life," she tells me. "This meeting is important. I'll-kick-your-arse-if-you-mess-it-up important. We'll sort this out, and you'll be back at school before you've missed too much of your final year."

So, no pressure, right? I'll just walk into the principal's office, "explain my actions," and all will be forgiven. Then we'll all go unicorn riding.

I put down the yogurt and grab Vinnie's magazine. "Is making up crosswords a job? I could do that."

"You need to finish school before you can get a job," she says. She tries running her fingers through my hair but her nails get tangled in the knots. "And university. Didn't you always want to go to uni?"

I shrug. "Uni's overrated. Ian Curtis didn't go and he's, like, the most important human being. Ever."

"You've got to focus, Frankie. This is your future we're talking about . . ."

I concentrate on the crossword. The first couple of clues are easy. "Progress in Greece initially inhibits four-legged animal." I scrawl "pig" in the little boxes.

"Believe you me, you do not want to be working in this dump forty years from now."

"I am the crossword goddess, Vinnie. Goddesses do not need to finish school."

She snorts. "You're the goddess of being a pain in my bum, is what you are."

We both look up as the bell jangles. Speaking of pigs . . .

Detective Inspector Eric Marzoli spills in, shaking off the rain. Now I can play my favorite game: How Long Before Vinnie Threatens to Shove Something up a Cop's Arse? I check the clock above the drinks fridge. And your time . . . starts . . . now!

"It's crazy out there," he says. "Just saw a Mercedes almost collide with a tram."

Vinnie glares at the puddle forming around Marzoli's feet. "Everybody drives like a moron as soon as the weather gets nasty. Course, you being a cop and all, I guess you could do something about that."

Ten seconds and counting.

Marzoli runs his hand over the top of his head—thin wisps of hair clumping together in the wet. "That's for uniform to sort out." He looks up at the menu and chooses the Smith Street Gonzales. "What the wife doesn't know," he says to Vinnie with a wink. Half his face has to collapse to make the wink happen.

There's no way this guy has a wife.

"Nice choice, Detective," says Vinnie. She smiles. It's thin but passable.

Twenty-three seconds.

Vinnie does a shimmy as she hitches down her skirt and starts on Marzoli's order—lamb, no onion, extra jalapeños.

Marzoli turns my way; his eyes lock onto me like a pit bull's jaws around the neck of a shih tzu.

"Shouldn't you be in school?" he says.

"Isn't that for uniform to sort out?" I drop my gaze to the crossword. "Five across. Four letters." I tap my pen against my lip. " 'Eject backward first before cutting work in half to make preserved meat.' "

The electric knife roars to life as Vinnie starts shaving lamb off the spit. "Beats me," she says. "Spam?"

"Second letter's an *e*."

Vinnie doesn't bother with gloves, just starts piling on lettuce, tomato, and way, way too many jalapeños.

Thirty-five seconds. She's doing well.

"'Fraid I'm not just here for the excellent food," Marzoli says. He pulls out a little black notebook from his coat pocket. "We're canvassing the neighborhood. There's been a spate of burglaries in the area and we're checking if anyone has seen or heard anything suspicious."

"Burglaries?" Vinnie keeps her back to Marzoli.

"Yup."

Forty-two seconds.

"And seeing as though we're open all hours you thought we might have seen something?"

"Sure," says Marzoli. "That sounds about right."

"Pure chance you walked into this shop to ask us questions?" says Vinnie.

Fifty-one seconds.

Vinnie swings around and dumps Marzoli's kebab on the counter. "Your Smith Street Gonzales, Detective Inspector. And would you like a stiletto up your arse with that?"

Stop the clock.

Fifty-six seconds being civil to a cop. That's a new record.

Marzoli picks up his kebab. "Still a charmer, Lavinia," he says and takes a bite.

"Nobody calls me that, *Eric*. Now get out of my shop."

"How about you, Frankie?" he says. "You seen anything?" A thin strip of lettuce hangs from the side of his mouth. He sucks it up. "Anybody behaving oddly?"

"This is Collingwood," I say. "Define 'odd.'"

He smiles. "Pity," he says. "Still, we'll get the guy. We always do." He takes another bite and turns back to Vinnie. "Which reminds me: How's your brother, Terry? You manage to get to Port Philip much these days?"

I squeeze the spork in my grip. The reason Uncle Terry is behind bars is standing right in front of us, stuffing his face with *our* kebab. If I were Vinnie I'd have jumped the counter and spiked his eyeball with my Louboutin knockoffs.

"He sure is lucky he had you to take care of the family business," says Marzoli. "Picking right up where he left off."

My spork snaps in half. "Jerk."

A jalapeño drops from Marzoli's open mouth and plops onto the counter. "What'd you call me?"

"Five across. 'Eject backward first before cutting work in half to make preserved meat.'" I pick up my pencil. "J. E. R. K." I fill in each letter. Slowly. Smoothly.

A smile spreads across Marzoli's face. He shoves the last of the kebab into his mouth, wiping his hands down the front of his jacket. "If you remember anything," he says, removing a business card from his pocket and dropping it onto the bench, "number's on there."

Marzoli ducks through the front door with a *jingle-jangle-jingle*. "Always a pleasure," he calls over his shoulder.

I turn to Vinnie. "A stiletto up the arse, Vin? I thought you told me not every situation needs to be resolved with violence."

She shrugs.

"What was that about? Why's Marzoli suggesting we're involved in a bunch of burglaries?"

"Just the usual cop bullshit. Something happens in this neighborhood and we're the first port of call. You ought to know that by now. But maybe we should be more careful about lock-ing up. Collingwood types and all that."

I laugh. "Says Her Majesty, Queen of Collingwood."

Vinnie plants a Vixen Rampage kiss on my forehead. "Princess."

Three

I sneak into the backyard; early-morning dew clings to my boots as I trample through the patchy grass. I've got an hour before we're due at school for The Meeting.

Vinnie's Persian cat sits at the back gate, face like somebody rammed him into a brick wall. Which, ironically, is what I fantasize about doing to him every time I discover he's left a "surprise" in my boots. I hiss at him and he hisses back before squeezing his fat arse under the gate.

I grab a trowel and at the back fence I drop to my knees under the willow. I could easily dig with my hands because the earth is soft, but last time I did that there was dirt under my nails for days and Vinnie kept asking questions.

I drive the trowel in hard and cut a worm in half. "Shit."

I part the dirt with the tip of the trowel and scoop up the two halves, placing them on my thigh. They don't both wriggle off like I expect them to. I guess it's a myth that cutting a worm in half makes two worms.

I dig a small hole just to the left and bury the worm, trying to match up the two halves as I lay the little guy in his grave. I grab a willow leaf and a piece of bark shaped like a cocoon. I poke the leaf through the bark to make a cross, which I push into the ground for a headstone.

Then I get back to digging.

The whole point of a time capsule is you bury it and leave it. Well, that's what Daniel, my shrink, said when he came up with the dumb idea to help "curb my aggressive tendencies." You dig it up when you're divorced, fat, stressed, lonely, and thinking about a nip-and-tuck. So far I've dug this thing up three times, and I only buried it a week and a half ago. I keep finding things I want to bury.

The trowel hits wood so I scoop the mud away, slowly uncovering the pencil box I made in Year Seven woodwork.

When I slide the cover back, globs of dirt fall on top of the freezer bag inside. I shake off the dirt and open the bag, revealing the photo on top: the only picture I have of my father.

I think he's my father. Vinnie said he is, and he was living with Juliet when she had me, so he could be. It's not a great photo; he's half cut out. But you can see a bit of his arm and half his face. He has a nice smile. He has my dark-olive skin and my slightly hooked nose.

I don't remember anything about him.

According to Vinnie, Juliet left me with him once when I was a baby. She went to the shops to get diapers, but she didn't come back for a couple of days, and when she did he'd overdosed. I was in my cot, my diaper falling off because it was so full. I almost died.

I pull the napkin out of my back pocket and shove it on top of the photo. I figure something that reminds me of the first time I met my half brother is something that should go in a time capsule. I don't know if Xavier saw me slide it off the table and into my back pocket yesterday. I hope not.

My phone buzzes. The screen's smashed, cracks webbing in the top right-hand corner, but I can see Cara's message: *Good luck today, babe. No pressure but do NOT stuff this up. I NEED YOU BACK HERE.*

Thanks, Cara Lam, oh wise and beautiful BFF. Because I need to be reminded of The Meeting. I *so* want to blab on for hours to Principal Vukovic about why I'm such a psycho.

Especially as I don't plan on telling her the truth. All I want is to forget, forget about what happened in the corner of the library. I want to forget Steve's Dorito-smelling breath and what he said to make me so crazy angry, angry enough to slap him with the fattest hardback I could lay my hands on. A fat book for a fat head.

I get a sick taste in my mouth. Guess I can joke all I want but the closer it gets to The Meeting the harder it is to laugh. Because I know what I did to Steve was bad. Out-of-control, out-of-my-mind, out-of-this-world bad. Not that I remember much: anger does that to me. Red inkblots smear across my vision. One minute Steve's shooting his mouth off and the next there's blood and an ambulance and . . .

No. Stop thinking about it.

I slam the lid shut and dump the pencil box back into the hole. I shovel dirt from all around and pile it on top; I accidentally unearth the little worm's grave.

"Sorry, dude," I say.

I give him a second funeral. This time I give a speech. I tell him how all his little worm friends will miss him. I tell him that the backyard just won't be the same without him. I say how tragic it is that his life was cut short, but that's a bad choice of words.

Covering his poor little body with the last of the dirt, I tell him I'm sorry for giving him such a shitty funeral. I can't find the headstone again.

I push myself up, wiping the muddy earth from my jeans. It just rubs deeper into the fabric.

"Frankie?" shouts Vinnie from inside the shop. "Where the hell are you?"

Busted.

I hurry inside, letting the wire door slam shut behind me. "I'm taking out the garbage."

"Garbage is still here."

Okay. So not such a good cover.

"I know," I shout back. "I'm taking it out now."

That's what you get for lying, Frankie. Bin duty.

Four

Vinnie slaps my hand. "Stop your fidgeting."

"I'm allergic to this skirt." I adjust the waistband of my winter uniform; the prickly fabric is made from sheep that rolled around in thistles.

"Don't start that now." Vinnie checks her watch again. "I closed the shop for this."

It doesn't matter how often Vinnie checks the time, we're not being let into the principal's office until we've stewed. It's how Vukovic rolls.

With an armful of *Romeo and Juliet*s, my former English teacher, Mr. Tran, scuttles through the office foyer. When he spots me, he gives a curt nod and keeps heading to the door.

I slink down in my chair. "Why don't we just—"

"This is important, Frankie," says Vinnie. "You'll go in there, tell Ms. Vukovic what happened, and everything will be fine." She pats my knee. "You just have to tell the truth."

Over by the front entrance, Mr. Tran lifts one leg, balancing the stack of books on his thigh to free a hand for the door. His corduroy pants sag around his arse. He teeters and the top few books fall to the ground. When he bends to pick them up, the whole stack topples.

Ha. It *almost* cheers me up.

"Won't be long now, Francesca," says the school receptionist. Except she says: "Fran-chess-caaaaar."

I don't know her name; I only know her as Sponge-Bum Square-Tits. She's addicted to sniffing Wite-Out and has the worst dress sense. The jacket she's wearing today is the color of cud. Seriously, it's like a cow vomited on her.

"Francesca," calls Mr. Tran. "Help me with these. Please."

I sink lower in my chair.

Vinnie nudges me. "Get," she says.

Mr. Tran waits, hands on hips, while I drag my feet over to him.

"Just grab those couple," he says.

I crouch and gather books. There's a drawing of Romeo and Juliet on the covers. It's mostly black-and-white but there's red where Juliet stabbed herself. I don't remember reading this copy when we studied it—ours had a photo from the movie. Stupidly attractive teenagers giving gooey eyes to each other. Maybe they kept this version out of my class because they were afraid it would give me ideas.

"So are we getting you back anytime soon?" asks Mr. Tran.

I blow the fringe out of my eyes and shrug.

"I hear you inflicted quite a bit of damage. Of course, not

the way I intended for you to use Shakespeare. Did Steve bite his thumb at you?" Mr. Tran laughs as he straightens up.

Shakespeare humor. Awesome.

I hold out the last book, one hand wrapped around my wrist to control the trembling.

"Shove that on top there, please. And if you could . . ." He motions to the door with his chin.

I push it open. He steps into the drizzle, eyes to the heavens.

Does writing out a new menu for the Kebab Emporium count as English homework? I should have asked Mr. Tran. I could totally drop that into The Meeting.

"Keep the door closed, Fran-chess-caaaaar." Square-Tits waves the Wite-Out brush under her nose before daubing it onto the page in front of her. "We want the heat to stay in."

I drag my feet back to Vinnie and slump in my seat. "It's already quarter past eleven. Vukovic's on a power trip."

"*Ms.* Vukovic," Vinnie says out the side of her mouth. "And I swear, if you act up in that room I'll make you clean out the meat tray for the rest of your life."

Shudder.

Two giggling Year Sevens hurry past, delivering a note to the office. Square-Tits takes it from them and smiles. "Hurry back to class, now," she says.

When the girls pass, one of them goes wide-eyed and leans in to whisper to her friend. They both look over their shoulder at me and laugh, collapsing into each other.

"Let's just go home." I pull the neck of my sweater over my chin and mouth.

Vinnie's bracelets tinkle as she checks her watch. "Not a chance. We're fighting this."

She gives me an encouraging smile. The kind you give the scrawny nerd with two left feet as he's running onto the football field.

"What's the point?" I say, sinking lower in my chair. I'm practically in nap position. "I'm a Vega so I'm cursed to be a screwup. Nonna says so, remember?"

Vinnie glares at me.

"Ms. Vukovic is ready for you now," says Square-Tits. She points down the corridor. Like I don't know where the principal's office is.

"Thank you, Doreen." Vinnie stands, smoothing out the creases in her skirt.

I stay where I am. "Do we have to, Vinnie? Let's have a girls' day in. Let's prank call Marzoli. I'll clean my room."

She answers with a look. It's not Shakespeare but it's effective.

With a grunt of effort I push myself to standing, untucking my shirt on one side, making sure it's hanging below my sweater line.

Vinnie grabs my underarm and drags me along. "Check your attitude at the door, Francesca Madalina Vega," she whispers. "Or I'll check it for you."

A clipped voice summons us.

Vinnie fluffs her curls and fixes a smile to her lips (Red Bloody Murder is her color of choice today). "Principal Vukovic. Thank you so much for seeing us."

Well, she gets the first four words out.

My jaw drops as I take in the room and its occupants. Breakfast thinks real hard about making its escape. This was not what I was expecting.

First things first. Vukovic is all angles—wiry hair, pointy nose, thin lines. She's thin on humor, too. She's dressed in grays and browns. Judging by the photos on the wall behind her, she's had the same haircut since the seventies. That, and she really likes horses. But none of that's new.

"Take a seat. Please." Vukovic points to two available seats. I say "available" because there are actually five seats in the room. "Do you know Fred Sparrow?" she adds, waving a hand at a man with salt-and-pepper hair sitting in one of the unavailable seats.

With a quickly reapplied smile, Vinnie steps forward and offers Fred Sparrow her hand.

Unlike my crappy winter skirt, the sheep that gave its wool for Fred Sparrow's suit did a lot of rolling around in candy floss and cotton wool. It ate caviar and went to the opera. His suit looks so soft and luxurious I have a weird compulsion to nestle my cheek against it.

I don't (obviously).

"We haven't met," says Fred Sparrow, flashing a chemically whitened smile as he stands, "but since your niece rearranged my son's face, we were bound to run into each other." His hand's in Vinnie's for a billionth of a second before he whips it away and takes his seat again. "I have another meeting at twelve so I'd really like to—"

"And Steve, of course," says Vukovic, still smiling at Vinnie.

I don't know what Vinnie does, whether she shakes Steve's hand or not, because I'm *not* looking at Steve Sparrow. I untuck the other side of my shirt and sit.

"I didn't know this was a group meeting," says Vinnie.

Vukovic takes a seat behind her enormous eighteenth-century handcrafted mahogany desk and it's like the desk eats half of her.

"This is an informal meeting, Ms. Vega," she says, smoothing her palms in circles across the desk's surface. "I'm hoping we can work this all out."

Fred Sparrow clears his throat. Loudly. "You mean sweep it under the carpet."

He has the same eyes as his son, but other than that they look completely different. If it wasn't for the eyes, Fred Sparrow would need to be asking his wife some uncomfortable questions—where Steve's bright orange hair comes from would be top of that list.

"You agreed to this meeting, Fred," says Vukovic.

"Did I have a choice?"

Vukovic turns to Vinnie. "I want today to be an open conversation. I honestly feel that—"

We don't get to hear what Vukovic honestly feels, because Fred Sparrow goes off on a tirade, lecturing Vukovic for letting a "psychologically disturbed girl" into his son's school. Then he spends five minutes banging on about the "irreparable damage" I caused. He even brings out X-rays and a doctor's report. Mostly what we learn is that Steve's dad is the chief executive officer of one of those businesses that are all names: Proctor, Lloyd, and Hanson. Parker, Chan, and Davis. Larry, Curly, and Moe. How do I know this? Because he finds a way to wedge it into every sentence.

Well, Vinnie's the CEO of Terry's Kebab Emporium so we're all on the same level here, dude.

"Can I remind you," says Sparrow—he's talking to Vinnie

but he's looking at Vukovic's desk—"that your niece assaulted my son? Give me one reason why this shouldn't be a criminal matter."

Before I can say anything, Vinnie grips my knee, her nails digging in.

All right, so I won't answer the nice man's question.

"Putting aside the fact that your son provoked my niece . . ." says Vinnie. Sparrow opens his mouth but Vinnie shuts him up with a Nonna Sofia. "Putting *that* aside, there are considerations to be taken into account here. Frankie has been through a lot in her young life. She's just found out she has a brother and that has really brought up a lot of—"

Oh hell no. She did not just say *that*. "Don't bring Xavier into this."

Vinnie turns her Nonna Sofia on me. "I'm just saying—"

"I know exactly what you're saying."

She snorts. "Well, I'm sorry, but this kid calls you up out of the blue and the next day you're getting suspended for fighting? I don't think that's a coincidence, do you?"

"Do you hear this, Leona?" Sparrow leans back in his chair, shirt buttons straining. "You bring trash into the school and then wonder why it stinks."

This time I have to grab Vinnie's knee.

"Frankie," says Vukovic. She's looking at me; her expression says *I care* but it's like someone conducted market research into what a caring expression should look like and came up with constipated.

"We haven't heard your side of the story yet. I'm not going to lie; we've had our issues with you, but I've never known you to act without provocation." Steve snorts, but a look from Vukovic silences him. "It's time for you to explain your actions."

Vinnie is watching me side-on. There's nothing forced or market-researched about her expression. She's willing me to open my mouth and defend myself.

Of course she is. She's Vinnie.

Fred Sparrow throws up his hands. "Look at my son, Leona. What more do you need to know?"

Vukovic shifts in her chair, her hands palms down on the desk. She doesn't say anything, because even though Fred Sparrow is a tool, there's no denying he's right.

All you have to do is look at Steve Sparrow.

Simple.

Just look.

Look.

I start with the floor. It's parquet—diamonds, scuffed from years of school shoes and high heels.

Up.

Steve Sparrow is wearing Vans. They might have been white once but now they're puddle gray.

Halfway up his trouser leg there's a grass stain.

Higher.

He taps a beat against his thigh—fingers stained a pale red. Marker, maybe? From the lame tags he scrawls around the school?

Higher.

His phone is half out of his pocket and white earphones snake up and around the back of his neck, hanging over his shoulder down the opposite side.

All the way.

Oh shit.

Steve Sparrow has bruises under each eye, deep purple and mottled—it's been a couple of days and they're already a little yellow round the edges. There are scabs of dried blood, both his cheeks are swollen, his jaw's bruised and *apparently* cracked. There's a splint on his nose, so I guess I broke that, too.

All I can do is look away. Like a coward. Like the kind of psycho freak who goes around hitting guys in the face with massive hardback books.

Vinnie squeezes my leg. "Go on, honey."

Vukovic's thin lips are pressed tight and she's leaning forward, ready to leap over the desk and drag the words out of my throat. I guess she'd really like a reason to stick it to Fred Sparrow.

I would too, but I can't stop thinking about whether Steve's nose will be crooked forever. Because of what I did. You see people with their noses bent to one side or maybe with a bulge in the middle or a flat section. Juliet had a guy with a nose like that—I don't remember his name but he was a boxer. Not professional, just in the kitchen with Juliet.

Is that what Steve's going to look like now? Did I do that? I look down and my hands are balled into fists. I have to work hard to unlock them.

Boxer-guy used to say he was sorry. Used to feed Juliet excuses mixed with blame.

So what's my excuse?

Vinnie's leg brushes against mine. "Frankie?"

"Told you she's a psycho," says Steve. "She just went mental. I didn't do nothing."

Vinnie grips my knee a little tighter. "Frankie?" Her voice breaks. Just a little.

Just enough.

I swallow. But I don't open my mouth, because I haven't got anything to say. For once.

"I'm so sorry," Vinnie says, shifting back to face Vukovic. "She's been seeing that psychologist like you wanted. She's really trying, I swear—"

Fred Sparrow stands, his chair screeching along the floor. "This has been a complete waste of time." He grabs Steve by the arm and hauls him up. "You'll be hearing from our lawyers."

Steve shuffles behind my chair, dragging his Vans, screamo buzzing from his earphones. I wait for the door to close, seconds that seem to drag on and on and . . .

Slam.

The whole room breathes again.

Vukovic leans back in her chair, shaking her head. "That was pretty stupid. Even for you, Frankie. We give you an opportunity to apologize and nip this whole thing in the bud and you throw it back in our faces."

"Stupid and selfish, downright idiotic," says Vinnie. I rub the red marks on my thigh as soon as she removes her hand. "Why can't you just tell us what happened?" She turns to Vukovic. "She won't even tell Cara."

"Listen." Vukovic brushes nonexistent dust from the surface of her desk. "I'll speak to Fred. When he's calm I should be able to talk him out of legal action. You'll need to pay for the medical bills, but maybe I can keep the police out of it."

"What about finishing school?" Vinnie glances at me. "She was supposed to go to uni."

"I wonder if you could wait outside for a minute, Frankie," says Vukovic. "Your aunt and I have a few things to discuss."

My chair screeches but not as loudly as Fred Sparrow's. It teeters and then bumps against the back of my knees. Vinnie clicks her tongue. Who knows what at—there's a pretty long list.

I open my mouth but Vukovic beats me to it.

"You had your chance to speak, Frankie. That moment has passed."

All I see of Vinnie is the dark roots of her hair and the nibs of her shoulder blades jutting out as she hunches forward.

"I'll wait outside," I say.

Vukovic nods. "And tuck your shirt in."

Five

I'm waiting outside the office. Two magpies are clashing over bin scraps. They've pulled out chip packets and mandarin peels and are squawking like a couple having an argument out in front of the Kmart.

One magpie charges the other. *Squawk, squawk.* The other beats his wings and lifts off, settling on the ground a foot away, picking at a stolen apple core. I shove my earphones in and crank up The Horrors for a therapeutic dose of wailing rockabilly punk.

I'm pretty sure when Vukovic told me to wait outside she didn't mean *outside* outside. But I don't care.

I check the time but drop my phone as I'm wrapped in a hug from behind. Cara squeals into my ear; her turquoise-dyed hair falls across my arm and tickles my skin. I yank out my earphones.

"Why didn't you message me?" she says. "I saw you from the library. Told Dunbar I've got period pain to get out of class."

Cara gives the best hugs if you're not into breathing.

I untangle myself but she won't let go of my hands. She swings them side to side. "So, what happened?"

I pull a hand free to pick up my phone. It's hard to tell if I've done more damage. "Ouch," I say when Cara pokes me in the gut.

"Open your mouth and speak to me, minion," she says.

I wipe the screen clear of grit. "Steve was there."

"Was he messed up? I heard he was back today but I haven't seen him. Speak!"

"I broke his nose. His dad reckons he's got post-traumatic stress or whatever."

"You broke his ego. His nose, you probably improved."

Cara's got this way of jutting out her chin. It makes her look aggressive—like you'd want to keep the collected works of Shakespeare out of her reach too—but really it's because she's five foot nothing and has to look up at everyone.

She's been my best friend since the start of high school. The first week of Year Seven she stapled this other kid's hand when he tried to copy her answers. She got in shitloads of trouble, but no one ever copied her work again. We met in the office, both of us waiting to be told off by Vukovic. The name Sponge-Bum Square-Tits was born that day and so was our friendship— how could I not fall in love with a girl who thinks stapling is a martial art?

She's got flowers and hearts drawn in blue ink all over the back of her hand. She does it when she's bored. I used to come home with vines growing halfway up my arm.

"Did you tell them that Steve asked for it? Cos he did, right?"

"When's the bell gonna go?"

"About five minutes. Are you allowed to stick around for lunch?"

"Doubt it."

My phone beeps and I pull it out. One new message from Xavier: *I'm starved. Craving a kebab ;)*

I grin. Longer than twelve hours, less than three days. We have a winner. I text back: *No can do little bro. Stuck at school. Rain check.*

Cara peers over my shoulder. "Updating your profile? 'Emo-for-Life, hashtag YOLO'?"

"I'm texting, nosy cow." She knows I shut down my entire online life after the whole #FrankieVegaIsAFuglySlut thing. And the rest.

She nudges me. "Then who's your boyfriend?"

"No one. Don't make me hurt you. It's Xavier."

"Yuck. Still can't believe you went through with that. If I had a chance not to know my brothers I'd take it."

Cara's got four brothers—Will, Paul, Aaron, and Lawrence. She calls them: Nine Mill, Machete, Gas Leak, and Dagger. "Cos that's how I'm going to kill them," she says.

My phone beeps again: *Cool. But now you owe me two. And chips.*

I wipe the grin from my face when I catch Cara watching me.

"You know it's not normal to like your brother, don't you?" she says.

I pocket my phone. "I just met him—I'm not sure if I like him or not."

"Let's just hide on the oval." Cara spins me around. "I'll

split my bagel with you and by the time they find us lunch'll be over."

She gives me puppy-eyes, but I shake my head.

Then, from behind Cara's head, I spot the Greek version of Ryan Gosling sauntering toward us. Three skinny boys are circling him like dogs waiting to be fed. "Shit," I say.

At the exact moment I tell Cara not to look, she does.

She pinches my side. "Ex-boyfriend alert."

"That's kind of what I meant when I said 'shit.'"

I look around for somewhere to hide. Behind the garbage? Pretend I'm a magpie? I grab hold of Cara, tugging her sweater. "Let's—"

"What's up?" calls Mark.

Hey, that's cheating! He's well out of the conversation zone. I totally had time to run. But once a cheater, always a cheater, right?

I pull Cara close. "Keep all sharp objects out of my reach."

Mark Argyros always smells of chlorine. If you opened his pencil case you'd find a secret stash of moisturizer because the pool water dries his skin out. Everybody says he's going to the Olympics. Everybody except Mark. "I just want to be someone who doesn't get up at four a.m.," he told me. He did have his hand up my top at the time, though, so maybe he wasn't thinking straight.

"Who let you wander round the school without a police guard?" Cara juts out her chin.

"Alveraz dismissed us early," says Mark. "What's your excuse?"

"Period pain," says Cara, loud enough for the whole school to hear.

The boys all groan. "Rank," says one. I don't know his name—he's a PopAsia boy-band wannabe. But he gives Cara an approving once-over. I catch her giving him the same. Please god, not another one.

Mark is working overtime to catch my eye. "Hey, Frankie."

"It's Paul, right?"

He smiles. He's got perfect teeth. "Nah, it's Mark."

I give myself a face-palm. "Right, knew it was an apostle. So, which one of these dudes is Jesus?"

I look from one scrawny sidekick to another, but all I get back from them is a collective "Huh?"

"Hey, aren't you that chick who beat up Steve-o?" says boy-band dude.

"Is your brain constipated, dumbarse?" Marks snaps. He steps up to me and chlorine fills my nostrils. It brings on a brain full of *Hey, remember that time you and Mark (censored)*. He's changed a bit since we dated—taller, black hair clipped short, jawline sharper. I usually make it a point *not* to look at the guy, so I haven't been keeping tabs on the good things puberty's been doing for him. But he's also kind of the same. He's Mark. And for some reason we're talking again.

"I wanted to call," he says. "When I heard about Steve. You okay?"

I meet his eyes for zero-point-three seconds. I haven't been this close to him in approximately one year, two months, five weeks, four days, three hours, and thirty-seven minutes. Approximately.

I drop my gaze to my boots, frowning. "Well, this has been an awesome reunion but I really need to get to my AA meeting."

Cara swats my shoulder. "You know that'll be around school by fifth period."

"Fran-chess-caaaaar?"

Everyone spins round: a Year-Sevens-caught-behind-the-shelter-sheds-smoking spin. Square-Tits is poking her head out the glass doors. She crooks a finger. "Inside, please."

I wonder if the adults think I'm contagious.

"Now," she adds, ducking back in. Presumably for another hit of Wite-Out.

"Stay," says Mark. He grins, lightly tapping his folder on my arm. "Stay and tell me what Collingwood's Most Notorious has been up to."

I thought I'd trained Mark not to talk to me, not to look at me, not to be nice and trick me into forgetting why we broke up. But no, looks like someone needs a refresher course in Stay Out of My Life 101.

I step away from his reach. "I've mainly been killing. Mostly I do it to appease His Dark Lord—he's such a demanding master, it's all blood and gore and sacrifices and orgies—but sometimes I do it just for funsies."

Only Mark laughs. Cara rolls her eyes.

"Sounds cool," says Mark. "Maybe you can invite me along sometime."

Vinnie reads these romance novels and the guys in them are always "smoldering"—their eyes burning into any unsuspecting girl, like they're fitted with lasers or something. Obviously Mark's been reading the same books as Vinnie because he shoots me his best smoldering gaze. Maybe his current girlfriend, Ava, is into the laser eyes but it does nothing for me. It makes me think about Year Eleven and what happened behind the science block. And Ava's online hate campaign.

"Well, I'm sure your girlfriend would love that," I say. My voice is extra perky, like I have a cheerleader stuck in my throat.

"Maybe Ava can come too and we'll take turns basking in your glorious company. Apparently I'm okay with sharing."

It could be the cold or maybe it's a wayward spark from his smoldering eyes; either way, Mark's cheeks flush red.

Yeah, that's right, jerk. I haven't forgotten.

"She's not my girlfriend," he says, an out-of-control inferno raging in his cheeks.

"Does she know that?"

He opens his stupid mouth to stutter a response but doesn't get the chance.

Steve Sparrow comes flying toward us, jumping onto Mark's back. "Swim Boy!"

"Piss off, dickhead," says Mark, pushing him away.

"Sorry, mate," says Steve. "Hope I haven't wrecked your shot at Olympic glory."

Cara leans into me. "Oh yeah," she says. "I can see how traumatized he is."

"Dude, check out your nose," says one of Mark's sidekicks. He tries to jab it, but Steve dodges him.

"Yeah," says Steve, "some bitch broke it."

"Oh, I'm sorry, was that a dig at me? It was so subtle I almost missed it."

Cara grips my arm, but she's overreacting. There aren't any heavy objects around. Not a Shakespearean tome to be found.

I give Cara a reassuring smile and mouth, *It's fine.*

Apparently Mark is not as Zen as me, though. He steps up to Steve. "You call her a bitch again and I'll break your nose a second time."

Mark's mates "ooh" and "ahh" and backhand each other across their chests. "Dude, it's on," says one of them.

Steve holds up both hands. "Settle down, Swim Boy. Didn't know you and Freakie were still a thing."

My Zen smile is fading fast.

Mark digs the corner of his folder into Steve's chest. "I just don't like you calling her a bitch, okay?"

"Not my fault, mate," Steve says, grinning. "It's scientific. It's what you call a female dog. Look it up in the fucking dictionary."

Clearly Mark's friends aren't as dumb as they look. It takes them a split second to grab Mark by the shoulders, a split second quicker than it takes Mark to swing at Steve. Steve snorts as Mark's fist connects with air.

"Why don't you look up the definition for 'prick'?" says Mark, struggling in his mates' grip.

Steve laughs. "Why? Am I gonna find a picture of you?" And that's when he pulls the most dickhead move imaginable.

He punches Mark in the gut while Mark's arms are pinned behind him.

I don't owe Mark anything. Really, I don't. But I figure I owe Steve. And that's why I grab hold of his shirt and thrust him against the office wall.

He tries shrugging free, reeling off insults at me—inventive stuff like "stupid bitch."

I tighten my grip. "Oh please, *please* give me a reason to remove your balls and bequeath them to the Museum of Really Tiny Things."

Someone grabs me around the waist and yanks me back. I kick out, my feet pedaling air—I lose my grip on Steve. I'm wriggling and yelling and digging my nails into whoever's got me wrapped up. There's a lot of noise and movement I can't make out.

Except for Vinnie.

I can see her.

Watching me with an open mouth.

Turns out Red Bloody Murder was an appropriate choice of lipstick today.

"Get her off school grounds," shouts Vukovic. "Now!"

Vinnie grabs me by the arm and wrenches. I think it was Mr. Tran who had me by the waist, because I glimpse corduroy as Vinnie yanks me toward the school gates.

Steve points at me. "She just attacked me for no reason. Psycho bitch."

Cara's yelling but I can't make her words out.

Vinnie yanks me along, my wrist burning under her grip.

"I'm sorry," I say, but I don't think she hears me. Maybe I only say it in my head.

Six

When Vinnie gives the silent treatment it's hard to ignore. It leaves a hole, which is kind of what silence is. A gap where something used to be. Laughter, chatter, noise. Love.

A Vinnie-size hole takes up the entire flat.

It fills the Emporium.

The drinks fridge hums extra loud to try to cover the silence. Not even the electric knife can cut through it.

Two days I have to wait until she speaks to me again.

"Pass the milk, Francesca," she says.

It'll do.

Later that night she comes into my room and sits on the end of my bed. "Princess? *Mia principessa*?"

I didn't speak Italian when I first moved in with Vinnie and Nonna but I soon learned. I worked out what *questa maledetta ragazza* meant. It meant that my nonna apparently didn't think much of me.

I don't like Italian.

"*Mia principessa*? Why won't you tell me what that boy did?"

I pretend to be asleep, in my own little black hole.

"Did he say something nasty to you?"

A cocoon. I bet caterpillars don't hear anything wrapped up like that.

"Did he try to hurt you?"

Vinnie's psycho cat, Buttons, starts meowing from the corridor.

Two days of nothing and now it's noise, noise, noise.

"Talking about it will help," she says. "Doesn't Daniel tell you that?"

Daniel, my shrink, tells me lots of things. Sometimes he just watches me, and waits for me to talk. "How does that make you feel, Frankie? Did that hurt your feelings? You can't bottle everything up, Frankie. How much room do you think you have in there?"

Vinnie stands. "We'll talk about this tomorrow," she says. "A serious talk."

I roll over, twisting in the sheets.

I'm an astronaut in deep space, where no one can hear anything.

Seven

It's late when I hear the first knock. I ignore it because I'm lying under my comforter with Joy Division blaring and my nose stuck in one of Vinnie's romance novels. There're plenty of bulging man parts and sighing ladies. If I'd stolen the vodka from under Vinnie's bed and played the euphemism drinking game I'd be dead by now.

Actually, even if I wasn't living vicariously through trashy romance fiction I'd still ignore the knocking. It can't be Cara, because I'm grounded and on my "last, last, *last* warning" to behave myself. I'm not even allowed to call Cara because she's grounded too and, according to her mum, it's my fault. What Cara chooses to do with a compass and Steve Sparrow's penis is totally on her. Besides, she only *threatened* to do it. And how can that be my fault if I wasn't even there?

So it has to be Vinnie with another one of her you-better-be-doing-your-homework speeches. The only reason Vinnie is still talking to me is because I've got another chance to stay at school. In two weeks' time the board is meeting to decide whether or not to expel me and I have to front up and explain why I should be allowed to stay. She's got the date circled in the calendar, the one with cats dressed up in scenes from silent-era films. Every time I look at the dreaded date I see a Persian tied to a railway track.

Irony's a bitch.

So basically I'm suspended for an extra two weeks during which I have to catch up in all my classes, earn back Vinnie's trust, and write a stirring speech to present to the board— I have a dream, ask not what Collingwood can do for you but what you can do for Collingwood, we shall fight them on the tram lines, blah, blah, blah.

Too easy.

There's another quick succession of taps. I'm ready to shout at Vinnie to go away when it dawns on me that what I'm hearing is tapping at my *window*. My window on the second story of Terry's Kebab Emporium.

I lay the book flat on top of my bed and silence Ian Curtis.

There's a long pause, a very long pause, and then—*tap.*

I edge off the bed and scurry across the floor like a proper spy. When I reach the wall, I slowly peek my head over the windowsill until I can see outside. A soft spray of light spills from the Emporium's back window, illuminating the alley beside the shop.

I recognize him by his bright blue high-tops and skinny frame.

I straighten and open the window, cursing as it creaks. I stick my head out and whisper-shouts, "What the hell, Xavier? You could have broken my window."

He's wearing a peaked cap under his gray hoodie and skinny jeans so tight they have to be for girls. His arm is raised, poised to throw another rock. "Throw down your hair?"

I try not to grin. I do not want to get sucked into this. Vinnie's told me, in no uncertain terms, to keep away from God Knows Who. And I'm so far out of Vinnie's good books as it is. I already sent him a text saying I couldn't meet up, so what's he doing here? And how come he knows this is my window? *I* didn't tell him I lived here. Dimples or no dimples, I'm still watching this kid for signs of demonic possession.

He juggles the rock. "So what's up?"

"Grounded, bored, pissed off, and hungry. The usual. How about you? Just passing through the neighborhood?"

He shrugs. "You coming down or what?" He drops the rock. I can tell he's grinning. He clasps his hands together in a prayer pose. "Aw, c'mon, you're not going to make me beg, are you?"

Sigh. "Five minutes," I tell him. "I'm already in the shit."

"Aren't we all?" he says with a laugh. "And hurry up. My balls are freezing off."

Nice.

The gate clicks shut behind me. Xavier leans against the brick wall, tapping his foot.

"Most people call first," I say.

"Do most people bring dumplings?"

He stoops to pick up a plastic bag and grins. "Might be cold now, hey."

That is definitely the way to my heart.

I grab the bag out of his hands and slide down the brick wall. We sit there, freezing our arses off in the alley, eating cold dumplings. I could get used to this.

I last four and a half minutes of small talk before I ask, "Are you going to tell me how you know where I live?"

He picks at a loose thread on his jeans. There's less of that nervous, jangly energy to him this time but he still can't seem to quit fidgeting. "What do you want me to say? I followed you?"

I stop chewing, mouth full of pork dumpling. "Wow."

He grins. "Kidding. You told me you worked at the shop with the worst kebabs in Collingwood and, according to the internet, this is it. So I hung out front for a bit, but Vinnie was inside and I didn't want to talk to her because she looks scary. I came round here for a smoke and saw you through the window."

"You smoke?"

"I'm quitting." He yanks the thread clean off. "Why are you grounded?"

"There might have been an incident. I might have lost my temper."

He laughs. "Like that, is it?"

"Almost always."

He shoves a dumpling in his mouth. "Last year I got suspended for punching some dickhead on the football field. Teachers have got zero sense of humor, hey."

"Exactly. They shove a violent book like *Macbeth* down our throats but then get all antsy when you break a dickhead's nose with it."

He almost chokes. "You did what?"

"The details aren't important. The point is, I can categorically say that the pen really is mightier than the sword."

He laughs. It starts me off too. Pretty soon we're snorting dumplings and trying not to choke with laughter.

And I have to admit it feels pretty good. Not the choking part. That's kind of uncomfortable. But the part where I get to trade stories with someone who gets where I've been and why I am the way I am. Because he's that way too. That's the really cool part.

Actually, the *really* cool part is that Xavier's head hasn't spun 360 degrees this whole time, so I doubt he's possessed. Yay.

Behind his unpossessed head is a high brick wall separating the alley from our neighbors. It used to be a Victorian terrace. Now it's four stories of yuppies living in dog boxes. Someone named "Jackknife" has staked his claim on the wall, writing his name in bright red paint, sloppy lettering, and zero artistic skill. There used to be graffiti of a woman there: purple skin, large brown eyes, hair fanning around her in wild Medusa snakes of green, blue, orange, and pink. I see glimpses of her beneath the red.

"That's a shame," I say.

He follows my gaze.

"Used to be a really cool painting there before Jackknife painted over it. They should make it so you have to get a license to do graf."

"It's illegal, Frankie. They can't give out a license to commit a crime."

Aw, bless his moral little heart.

"So I got something else for you," he says.

"Dessert?"

He pulls a white plastic bag out of his satchel and hands it to me. More cuts and scabs on his knuckles this time. "It made me think of you."

Whatever's in the bag is thin but square. Like a big square of cardboard. I slide the plastic bag down and pull out something worth more than gold.

The picture on the front is black and white, maybe a print, maybe a drawing. A chisel-featured young man in shorts and a shirt has his arms raised, captured right in the middle of beating the large drum he's got strapped to his chest. The name of the band is written in gothic lettering along the top. The name of the record, *An Ideal for Living*, runs vertically down the right-hand side, like it's dripping from the *n* in the band's name. I'm holding in my hands the debut EP from Joy Division. Released all the way back in 1978, not long after they changed their name from Warsaw. Twelve minutes and forty-seven seconds of pure fuzzy punk beauty.

It's gorgeous. Perfect. I'm certain it's ridiculously expensive.

"No way." I stare at the black-and-white drummer boy with my mouth open. I've been drooling over this exact record in the Vinyl Underground for ages. Phil, the guy who runs the shop, kicks me out for wasting his time on a regular basis. One time I worked up the courage to ask him how much it cost. He said, "More than you can afford, kid."

"S'posed to be rare or something," says Xavier. He lifts his cap to ruffle his lank hair. "Just a piece of plastic as far as I can tell."

"Are you kidding? They only pressed, like, a thousand of these so it's ultra rare. Still bleeding it's so rare. How the hell did you afford it?"

He looks down at his knees, hugged to his chest. "Nah," he says. "A mate had it. He picked it up at some garage sale. Don't reckon he knows how much it's worth cos he traded it for four Eminem CDs. What a dickhead."

I flip the vinyl over. It's not like I don't already have these songs, but this is different. It's a seriously awesome musical moment forever cast in vinyl goodness.

"Your friend's going to be pissed if he ever finds out how much this is worth. I mean, it must be hundreds."

"We could listen to it," says Xavier.

"I don't have a player."

"Then I guess I know what I'm getting for your birthday, hey." He's watching me, shyness in the tilt of his head.

My birthday's in December, months away. I try to picture what Xavier and I will be like by then. Once the newness has worn off and we start acting like real siblings—fighting, swearing at each other, dobbing each other in, arguing over trivial shit. I might actually enjoy it.

"What?" he says. Because I'm staring at him.

I pull out my phone and hold it at arm's length. "Just smile."

"Hate photos," he says, but when I lean closer, our shoulders pressed against each other's, he doesn't flinch or move out of shot.

My phone makes a fake camera noise and flashes.

It's not a great photo—too dark and Xavier's eyes are kind of half-closed—but then family photos are supposed to be crappy.

I show him.

"Great," he says. "I look like a serial killer."

"You look like Uncle Terry."

"Cool," he says.

I laugh. He doesn't know that Uncle Terry's a lowlife armed robber.

"What?"

I shake my head. "Nothing. I mean, thanks. For the dumplings and . . ." I hold up the vinyl and wiggle it. "I mean it. Thanks."

He grins. Dimples. "No problem. I mean, you do kind of owe me four Eminem CDs, but . . ."

I elbow him. "You seriously need a musical overhaul."

He laughs. It brings a grin to my face.

Being grounded isn't so bad after all.

Eight

Daniel Awolowo watches me with his fist pressed into his neck, just below the ear. He taps his pen against a notepad on his knee. It's one of those four-colored pens. As if anyone uses the green ink.

A burn scar runs the length of his forearm; I asked him about it at our first session but he said it was nothing I needed to hear about. I had to tell him how I got the cluster of five-cent-piece-size scars on my forearm—how come there's a different rule for *him*?

He's been waiting for me to speak for five minutes now. I've forgotten what he even asked. I doubt it was important.

He's got a serene, sleepy look on his face, though. I almost want to break my vow of silence to ask how come he looks so happy when I'm being a total cow.

If I'd met Daniel in the real world I'd probably like him.

I can actually picture him dropping by the Emporium, sitting at the front counter, a Scrabble board between us, him getting a triple word score with "xebec." I think he'd order the falafel, extra garlic sauce, and he'd have his chips with sweet chili aioli. He'd drink Coke; not Diet, not Zero. Coke. Vinnie would wear her blouse, the black one that's see-through, and she'd flirt with him. We'd talk about stuff. Stupid stuff that only he and I would get.

But I met him here, and there's no chance to laugh about stupid things. We're not going to take turns making up silly stories about passing strangers. We're not going to argue about the etiquette of double-dipping a chip. This sterile office in the university's psychology department is where an underpaid psychologist-in-the-making is trying to get me to open up about my *feelings*. The walls need painting, there's a dead plant in the corner, stained cups on the desk, an egg timer in the shape of a chicken, and dusty venetian blinds. One of the cups says *You don't have to be crazy to work here, but it helps*, with a picture of a cross-eyed monkey eating bananas. Someone thought they were the life of the party giving that as a Kris Kringle.

I'd be in a better mood if it weren't for Vinnie having another go at me this morning. It's all because she doesn't like Xavier and reckons I shouldn't see him. "You need to keep out of trouble, stay on top of your schoolwork, be on your best behavior, blah, blah, blah." So I asked her, how does she know Xavier will get me into trouble? Is it because he's Juliet's? "Cos if you think her kids are nothing but trouble then you should just chuck it in with me," I told her. She didn't like that. And she didn't like finding out I've seen Xavier three times she didn't know about: first the dumplings, then an arcade to play *StarCraft*, and then yesterday we took a train into the city and I showed him the National Gallery because I figured he might be into that stuff.

"Don't think much of that landscape shit but some of the people ones were cool," he said when we stopped to get take-away coffee. He was wearing his skinny jeans and a sweater with holes in the sleeves where his thumbs poked through.

"You might have something in a gallery one day," I said and he blushed all the way to the ears. "Wish I had something I was good at."

We hugged our steaming coffee cups between our palms and crossed the bridge, headed for Flinders Street Station.

"You're smart," he said and I laughed.

"I'm a smart-arse," I said. "There's a difference."

He looked at me, sidelong and with a little crease between his brows. "You make me laugh." There were only a few little blotches of red on his cheeks by then and maybe they were because of the cold. I watched as his eyes flicked from my face to over my shoulder and to the ground and back to my face. "There's nothing better than that, hey?" And he smiled.

I guess I could tell Daniel about Xavier.

"I'm bored," I tell him. "Can I go now?"

Daniel takes a sip from the monkey cup. "My mother always told me there was no such thing as boredom; just boring people." He smiles. I wonder how he gets his teeth so white.

"Did your precious mother say it was rude to call people boring?"

Sleepy smile and only a minor shoulder adjustment. "You're easy to anger today. Anything upsetting you?"

"These questions."

"Aside from my questions."

I glare at the chicken.

Whose idea was therapy? I don't mean for me specifically, because I already know it was a harebrained scheme cooked up by Vinnie and Vukovic. I mean in general. Like, who invented it? What idiot thought it was a good idea to have someone sit in a crappy little room divulging all their deepest hurts and fears to a total stranger? How did they manage to keep a straight face selling that idea? Because everybody knows that talking about things only makes them worse. It's way better to push your worst experiences deep into your subconscious and then shovel a whole heap of shit on top of them to make sure they never surface again.

I'm going to invent anti-therapy. I'll make millions.

Daniel crosses his legs. "Did you at least do the time capsule like I recommended?"

"No. I told you that was a dumb idea."

"I remember. You were vivid in your description of how dumb it was."

"My Grade Four teacher said I was verbally gifted."

"Did you like it when she said that? Did it make you feel good?"

"I'm not sure. She also said I was a pain in the arse. Not in front of me. I was listening at the door of the teachers' lounge."

"And how did that make you feel?"

"No big deal. It was easy being a pain in her arse because it was such a massive arse."

Daniel doesn't say anything. He scribbles in his notepad and smiles when he catches me watching him. "Sorry. I know you hate me taking notes."

Despite the apology, he keeps writing. He marks the full stop at the end of his sentence by twisting the pen into the page. He doesn't ask me another question.

Fine. I can ignore you too, Daniel. I pull out my phone and scroll through the news. There's been a bad car accident on Alexandra Parade. Gippsland is flooding. A meth-head has had a showdown with police, locking himself in his house and screaming about being allowed to see the emperor. Some politician was accused of lying, a rapist got off on a technicality, and a footballer got drunk and peed in a public fountain.

The usual, basically.

Except for the boy.

There's a big picture of him on every news site. He's probably my brother's age, even though he's one of those kids that puberty hasn't gotten around to yet. It's a school photo—you can see his lips are partway through "cheese." It's the kind of photo that haunts twenty-first birthdays—zits, braces, bad haircut, hunched shoulders, half-closed eyes.

Missing, reads the headline.

"So let's talk about what happened between you and Steve. He made you angry, didn't he?"

Shush, Daniel. I'm reading.

I'm reading about . . . Harrison Finnik-Hyde?

Jeez Louise.

His parents talk about him like they're recommending him for a job: accelerated learning program at school, soccer star, always does his chores, eighth-grade violin. "Harrison is a good kid," his dad tells the reporter. "We want him home with us."

There's a picture of the parents standing outside their leafy Malvern home. The dad's got cropped gray hair and eyes that are too close together. The mother is short; hair like a shampoo commercial. Her skin is soft, line-free, even though she's been crying. She's holding a bunch of tissues to her nose and mouth.

No one's seen him since Friday morning, when a neighbor spotted him talking to a man—late fifties, fair, short.

And then he didn't show up at school.

"Frankie? Are you listening to me?"

I sigh loudly and look up from my phone with a well-practiced scowl. "What?"

"I asked why you think Steve made you so mad."

"Do you find it hard not to judge people?" I ask. "Do you analyze your wife? Your kids? The checkout chick? The plumber? 'Oh look, he picked up his coffee cup with his left hand even though he's right-handed—he's sexually repressed.' Is that what you do?"

He leans back, both hands behind his head. "You think I'm judging you?"

"I'm just interested. I think I'd find it hard to switch off. If I knew stuff. If I knew what it meant when someone pulled on their earlobe or shifted in their seat or licked their lips when they spoke about their mother."

"Do you want to talk about your mother?"

"Why, did I lick my lips?"

"No. But you brought her up."

"I brought up a generic mother. A hypothetical mother. A fantasy."

"Is that how you see your mother? As a fantasy?"

"You're pissing me off, Daniel."

He laughs. It's a warm sound. Makes me hate him even more. "Then I am not earning my fee, am I? I'm supposed to make you feel better, not worse."

There's a second desk in the room so maybe Daniel shares this office with someone. I bet the other person killed the plant.

I tried growing flowers in the back garden once but they all died. It's so much easier to kill a plant than help it grow.

I slide my phone into my pocket and sink down in my seat. I wonder what Harrison Finnik-Hyde's mother is doing right now. I've seen the films. Men in suits with silver briefcases, poking around the house dusting things while the parents sit by the phone and wait for the kidnapper to call in a ransom. She'd be crying into a wad of tissues just like in the photo. She's probably never left the house before without her hair and makeup done, but today she'd still be in her pj's and dressing gown. She'd have red, puffy eyes and her hands would be shaking.

Because she's so distraught.

Because she can't think of anything worse than something happening to her violin-star baby.

Because she cares.

I sit forward. "You want me to tell you about Juliet?"

Daniel doesn't say anything, just watches. I wonder how much talking goes on in his house. I bet they do nothing but talk—a big, messy, warm family and all they do is talk about their day, what they did, what they're going to do. And I bet they laugh a lot. He's got laughing eyes.

"When I was four, Juliet took me to the Collingwood Children's Farm. There was this guy she'd been dating. I don't remember his name. He had really thin hair and it was fair, too, so you could see his scalp underneath; I remember that. He was tall. And about the same size wide. Juliet got big eyes around him and she was always hanging off him. We walked to the farm and she kept saying, "We're going on a family outing, just the three of us." I liked it there. They had those fluffy rat things— they're not rats, they're . . . I don't know. They're cute, and we all sat in this barn and they passed the rat things around and we petted them. There were lots of other kids. And I saw chickens and pigs and horses and goats. Guinea pigs, that's what they're called. I liked them best. They were soft and really fragile and the lady—the woman who worked at the farm—said I had soft hands, that I knew how to hold the guinea pig without hurting it. I was proud of myself for that. I turned around to tell Juliet but she wasn't there. I asked the lady where my mum was, but she didn't know. I handed her the guinea pig and went outside. I looked. I called for my mother.

"The lady sat me in the office. There was so much wood. I remember that: wood floor, wood walls, a wooden desk, wood chairs. The police came; they asked me what Juliet looked like. 'Snow White,' I said. They took me to the station and I waited there for ages. I colored. I ate. I slept. I talked to the police officers. I couldn't remember my last name. I couldn't remember my mum's name. Then they found a note in my jacket pocket. It had a number to call: Vinnie's. She came and took me to her home and then that's where I lived. With Vinnie and Nonna Sofia. And no one talked about Juliet. For ages I thought she was dead, but then Vinnie told me she'd moved to Queensland and that's why I couldn't see her again."

Daniel's sleepy smile is gone. He's just looking at me. Blank.

"Are you going to ask me how I felt about that? How Juliet abandoning me made me feel? Maybe I should be grateful that she left me where there were cute animals to distract me. It was pretty considerate of her, you know. She did much worse things to me than that."

Daniel's chair creaks as he shifts.

"But I don't feel grateful. It makes me so damn angry I want to hit people over the head with the collected works of Shake-speare."

The egg timer goes off. Instead of ringing, the chicken clucks.

I stand. My chair wobbles but doesn't topple. "So we're done, right?"

Daniel shifts forward, like he's about to stand. He doesn't, though. "You should—"

"Do you know what a 'xebec' is?"

A frown spoils his smooth forehead. "A kind of ship. I think. Why don't you—?"

"No, Daniel. The chicken has spoken."

I pick up my bag and walk out. He doesn't call after me. He can't because my time's up.

Nine

When I first moved in with Vinnie she had her fruit and veg delivered. But when the handsome Greek guy who did the deliveries became ex-fiancé number two, Vinnie started dragging me to the Queen Victoria Market on Saturday mornings for a special kind of torture.

I hear the stallholders shouting the second we stumble from the tram, me wrestling with our old-lady trolley and Vinnie digging into her handbag for a cigarette.

I punch the button at the intersection and wait. I punch it again.

Then over and over.

The green man starts flashing at me. About time, dude.

I fight a gang of Vietnamese ladies as we cross the street, the wheels of their trolleys bashing into my ankles as we jostle for space. Old-lady trolley racing is a blood sport.

The second we're under the market's corrugated tin roof, I'm immersed in noise—kids screaming, ladies haggling over the price of bananas, stallholders shouting over the top of one another, pigeons cooing from the beams, and the off-key wailing of the busker who sings Korean love songs even though he's Croatian.

And it stinks.

Nothing beats the stench of rotting fruit, Spanish doughnuts, pigeon poo, baby vomit, and hairy-guy body odor.

"This way," says Vinnie, tucking her handbag under her arm. She butts out her cigarette on a post before we enter the massive market. "Remind me to grab some pet mince for my baby."

Baby. Yeah. Baby dragon, more like.

Buttons is a fussy eater. He'll eat my socks (and piss in my shoes) but won't go near tinned cat food.

I ram the trolley into the back of a slow guy's legs. When he turns I look the other way. This is a contact sport, mate. If you can't handle it, quit.

Saturday morning is the worst time to come to the market. Vinnie says coming on a Saturday is tradition. I say it's child abuse.

But not today I don't. Today I smile and pretend I'm loving it. Because I'm trying to stay on Vinnie's good side, mostly so she doesn't give me another ear bashing about Xavier and school and The Meeting. It's best to just smile and even better not to tell her who I was texting this morning (spoiler: it was Xavier).

I don't know how she does it, but Vinnie carves a path through the mass of heaving, sweating people, even in six-inch heels. Me and my combat boots have to elbow our way through, never once coming out the other side without a stomped-on foot, a bruised rib, a finger caught in a trolley, or the slimy feeling of having been gawked at by a bunch of hairy, apron-clad, middle-aged men.

The call goes up around us: "Get your tomatoes! Granny Smith apples! Two ninety-nine a kilo! Potatoes! Get your potatoes here!"

"*Bella!*" Sergei calls as Vinnie marches up to his stall. He reaches down and brings up a box of vine tomatoes. "I keep these aside. Just for you, my *bella*."

She doesn't even look at the fruit. "Half price, I assume."

Sergei looks at her like she just flopped a dead rat onto his table. "No, no, no. How I live?" he asks, hands imploring. "How I feed my son?"

"I've seen your son," says Vinnie. "He could skip a meal or two."

Sergei sighs loudly. "Is true." He leans forward, pushing the box into Vinnie's arms. "Half price for my *bella*." He winks.

Somehow Vinnie always manages to strike the perfect balance between flirting—"Why, you have the biggest plums, Sergei"—and haggling—"Who would pay full price for these? They look like they've already been eaten."

So much I need to learn. Teach me, oh masterful one.

"Now," says Vinnie, eyeing the other veggies, "how about those cucumbers? They look a little limp."

I stand to the side, tighten my scarf around my neck, and people-watch.

There's an older woman wearing pearls and a powder-blue cardigan. She's stuffing a bag of something red into her trolley with her face scrunched up. Retired secretary, divorced, small dog. She spies on her neighbors. Hasn't spoken to her only daughter for twenty years. Bitch.

A guy walks past. Late thirties, green-rimmed glasses, carrying a giant bag of almonds. I don't even bother because it's just too easy.

The stallholder opposite is arguing with a woman who wants to pay a third of the marked price for spring onions. I reckon he's married to a woman who wears floral dresses. Puts onion in everything he cooks because he needs an excuse to cry. Has a total disappointment of a son. A son who still lives at home even though he's forty and collects science-fiction toys and never—never—takes them out of the packaging.

"Frankie?"

Vinnie is holding out a bag of cucumbers; she shakes the bag at me until I grab them.

"Are we planning a girls' night in? Face masks, cucumbers on the eyes. I'll let you braid my hair."

"I'll braid your tongue," she says.

I stuff the cucumbers into the bottom of the trolley. When I look up, the stallholder opposite is throwing his hands up in exasperation and I wonder how long he's been doing this job.

I read somewhere that the average person has seven jobs in their lifetime. Vinnie used to be a secretary for an accountant; that's how she met husband number two. After he got done for fraud and the firm went bust, Vinnie burned their wedding photos in the backyard and went to work as a cleaner. After that she was a barmaid, then a cleaner again, and then an Avon lady. When Uncle Terry went to jail, she started making kebabs.

But what if this is it for me? What if I get stuck sweating it up at Terry's Kebab Emporium for the rest of my life? If I make kebabs for long enough will I start smelling of garlic sauce?

The woman walks away from the stall, shaking her head. The guy gives her the finger and swears in whatever language he speaks.

My phone vibrates in my pocket. I pull it out but I don't know the number flashing on the screen. Maybe Xavier calling from home?

Vinnie shoots me a look.

"What? It's Cara," I say.

"Thought she wasn't supposed to talk to you."

"I'll tell her." I move away, holding the phone to my ear.

"Are you Frankie?" It's a guy's voice. Gruff like Marzoli's, but deeper.

"Who are you?"

He laughs. "So you inherited your mother's charm. Real polite."

"Do I know you?"

"Where's Xavier?"

I push past a hugging couple. She's standing on tippy-toes to kiss him, and the stallholder is waving them aside, trying to let paying customers in.

"Tell me who you are or I hang up."

"Bill. Bill Green."

Ah.

I don't know much about Xavier's dad—only what Xavier's told me, which is that he's an arsehole. If Juliet hooked up with him, that's a given.

"Why are you asking me where he is? You're his dad."

Bill laughs like a smoker coughs. "Guess you don't know Xavier very well."

Down, hackles, down.

"I've only met him three times, Bill. Pity you're not my dad. Then I could have inherited my charm from Juliet and my intelligence from you."

"Well, if I know your mother then I've got as much a chance of being your father as the rest of Collingwood."

I stand in the center of the walkway with my teeth clenched and my hand balled into a fist by my side. People push past; I push back.

"Just tell that shithead brother of yours to get his worthless arse home," says Bill. "The prick owes me money."

The line goes dead before I can tell him to fuck the fuck off.

It takes me a minute to get my breathing under control. I grip the phone tight, staring at the cracked screen. I wait for the red blots to clear.

I remember the first time I felt like this. Not long after I moved into Vinnie's, she was taking me somewhere. The doctor, probably. I was pretty sick for the first little while.

Vinnie led me out the front door and the neighbor leaned over the fence. "That her?" she asked. All I remember of the woman is the pink floral blouse she wore with a big frill around the neck. Like a posh frilled-neck lizard. Vinnie turned. "This is my niece, yes." The neighbor sized me up. "Looks like trouble," she said. "She's got her mother's mouth."

The red blots descended. Later, I cut the heads off the flowers in her front garden. It was the only thing that helped draw the red away.

Since Xavier materialized, it's been shitting down memories. Things I haven't thought about in years. Things I didn't think I remembered.

I pull out my phone and dial his number. But what am I even going to say?

The call goes to voice mail: "I'm not around so leave a message. Probs won't call you back, but, yeah. Beep."

I hang up and slide the phone into my back pocket.

Xavier owes his dad money. No big deal because (a) Bill is a prick who deserves to be swindled and (b) I owe Vinnie heaps—well, I will after she pays Steve's medical bills. It's a child's duty to owe their parents money. So it's no big deal.

When I finally get back to Vinnie, she shoves a box of lettuces into my arms. "Put these—you look pale. Are you sick?" She grabs my chin.

I shake her off.

I hate that little crinkle between her brows; I hate when it's there because of me.

I grab the lettuce and stuff it into the trolley. "I saw an Ian Curtis lookalike. I'm still swooning."

She laughs, shaking her head. "What am I going to do with you?"

"I take her off your hands. I have son," says Sergei. "Short but clean. Good match."

Vinnie laughs. "For her, maybe. Not such a good deal for him."

Ten

As punishment for the Steve Sparrow Incident, Vinnie has given me a list of crappy jobs. First on the list: bin duty.

I drag the garbage across the tile floor of the Emporium, ignoring the trail of bin juice. I push open the shop's back door with my butt and lift the bag into the alley. The gate swings shut behind me.

Rain is falling steadily, the kind that covers you in a soft film of dampness the second you enter it.

Rain and bin juice; it's like that sometimes.

As I drag the garbage along the cobblestones, a siren cuts through the rumble of traffic from Alexandra Parade. One of my earliest memories is of a siren. I can't remember who Juliet was living with then, but I can picture his boots as the policeman marched him out the door. He'd wrapped the laces several times around the top before tying them. Juliet was crying, louder than the siren.

I lug the bag to the Dumpster but a noise behind stops me short. My whole body tenses. I don't know karate but I'll damn well give it a go.

I drop the garbage and swing round, fists raised.

Black jeans, black hoodie, bright blue high-tops.

I grab my chest and fall against the Dumpster. "Holy crap, Xavier. You scared the shit out of me."

He stares wide-eyed like I'm the last person he expected. Which is stupid because this is where I live *and* work—it'd be no fun playing *Where's Frankie?* in this part of the world.

"Wha—?" He drags his fingers through his hair and laughs: a nervous splutter. No dimples. "What the fuck, hey?"

"Who were you expecting?" My heart is still trying to parachute out of my chest. "And don't say 'fuck.'"

He laughs again. A little less nerves, a lot more dimple. "You've been my sister for a week and already you're telling me what to do?"

"It's in the DNA, bro. Wait till you meet Nonna Sofia."

He flicks a cigarette onto the ground and grinds it under his boot. There's a scattering of butts at his feet so he's obviously been here for ages. Why is he standing around in the rain? It's freezing.

"Thought you were going to quit," I say.

"I did. Just then."

"So you're here because . . ."

"Came to see you, didn't I? What else?"

It'd be easy just to slip into the banter, keep it light and fluffy. But I frown at the graveyard of cigarette butts and blurt, "Your dad called me."

He rubs the back of his neck. "Yeah?"

"Said you owed him money."

He wets his lips with his tongue. "Who hasn't swiped a twenty from their dad's wallet? Told you the guy's a prick."

Exactly. Perfectly sound argument.

He looks over his shoulder at the brick wall, at the purple-skinned girl hidden beneath Jackknife's shitty tag.

"So it's nothing, right?" I say.

He nods, rubbing his hands on the front of his jeans and flicking his eyes between the wall and me. "Dad's a tight-arse."

Okay, so this isn't exactly like the last meeting we had at the gallery. No giggles, no easy smiles, no playful punches. Am I going to have to give him a homicidally themed nickname after all?

"Then I guess you're here for that free kebab," I say. "Sorry, *two* free kebabs."

His eyes grow big and he takes a step back. Maybe I over-sold the "worst kebab joint in Collingwood" line. Clearly the kid thinks he'll get the salmonella special with a side of gastro.

"Nah. It's cool. I should probably get going, hey." He looks at Jackknife's tag again but doesn't move.

"Oh. Okay. Well, I'm drenched. Plus, hanging out here makes us look like we're up to no good. There's this cop who already thinks I'm robbing the neighborhood. I hate to break it to you, Xavier, but our family is no stranger to the wrong side of the law. Our uncle's in prison for armed robbery. And then there's Juliet."

Xavier mutters something I can't hear. So I lean forward, hoping he'll repeat himself, but we end up just staring at each other.

He looks down at his high-tops, gnawing on his bottom lip. "Sorry, but I'm—"

He doesn't get to finish because a black blur lands with a heavy thud just behind him, a guy jumping down from the brick wall.

Because *that's* normal.

The first thing I notice about him is his jacket. If Ian Curtis and Lou Reed had a love child who grew up to run a vintage clothing shop on Sydney Road, that jacket would be somewhere in the back of that shop. It's textured black velvet. If you brushed your hand along it the wrong way it would send a shiver down your spine.

The second thing I notice—and I really should have seen this first—is the balaclava the guy's wearing.

Paging DI Marzoli, I have your burglary suspect on line one.

He whips off his balaclava and I get an eyeful of the bluest damn eyes I've ever seen. He's stupidly hot, if you're into that indie-boy punk look with the unkempt hair and I-live-on-cigarettes-and-coffee physique. But even though he looks rough round the edges, he still seems put together. He's taken a lot of time and effort to look this just-rolled-out-of-bed cool. Like his tattered jeans are actually brand-new and his hair, a bramble of black, loose curls, is really a well-manicured, artfully arranged bramble.

In other words, he's a poseur. An art-school dropout, musician-wannabe, Kerouac-reading ponce. Who steals.

He stuffs the balaclava into his back pocket, blue eyes calmly assessing everything but me as he swings his oversize duffel bag onto his shoulder and faces Xavier.

"You call *this* keeping a lookout?" He flicks a hand in my direction.

Apparently I'm a "this."

Xavier shrugs. "Told you it was a bad idea coming here, Nate."

So poseur-boy is called Nate. He points to the duffel and grins. "Yeah? Cos I reckon it was a brilliant idea."

I'm five or more steps behind everyone else but as I'm looking between my brand-new baby brother and this black-clad skinny guy I'm connecting the dots. Suddenly my brother's incessant brick-wall staring is making a whole lot more sense.

My jaw drops. "Shut the fuck up."

Xavier shoots me a sheepish grin. "Don't say 'fuck.'"

Nate's duffel bag makes a loud clatter as he adjusts it higher on his shoulder. "If you're done with your mothers' club meeting maybe we can split?"

"Are you serious?" My voice is high-pitched and squeaky. But Xavier won't look at me.

Nate rolls his stupidly blue eyes. "It's not exactly the done thing to hang around for a chat after—"

"Oh I can tell you're an in-and-out kind of guy," I say. "Done in three seconds."

The duffel bag slips off Nate's shoulder as he steps toward me. He's centimeters from my face and way taller than I first thought. Maybe not so scrawny, either. I back up.

"What are you inferring?"

"I'm not inferring anything; I'm implying it."

"What's that mean?"

"Steal a dictionary and work it out for yourself."

"If I were going to steal a dictionary it would be to shove it up your—"

Xavier grabs Nate's arm. "That's enough. This is my sister."

"Like I give a shit who she is." Nate shrugs free. "Just make sure she keeps her mouth shut."

He stands there, framed by Jackknife's logo. It's like some sort of crazy aura.

"Well, I care who *you* are. Xavier's just turned fourteen and you're dragging him along on a felony. Who does that?"

Nate covers his mouth with a gloved hand, eyes wide. He looks like a puppy that took a dump on a brand-new carpet. For a second, anyway. "You mean I missed his birthday? Now I feel *awful*."

Give the man an Oscar.

"Grow a brain," he says. "You think I had to twist your brother's arm?"

I glare at Xavier. I wouldn't exactly call his expression "innocent." I'd go for "guilty as sin." Or "Jesse James's got nothing on me."

"We should split," Xavier says. He's backing away, tugging on Nate's arm. He couldn't be in a bigger hurry to get out of here. It might have something to do with the whole being-in-the-middle-of-a-burglary thing or maybe he just doesn't want to have "the conversation" with me. The "Oh, didn't I mention I'm a criminal?" conversation. The "Well, you can't fight genetics" conversation. The—

The penny drops. It falls from the bloody Eureka Tower and lands on my head. "Oh my god. The vinyl."

"Frankie . . ."

"You didn't swap it for four Eminem CDs, did you?"

Xavier runs both hands through his hair, slick with rain. "I swear I bought it, Frankie. Legit."

"Swear? On our mother's life?"

He winces. "Honest, Frankie. I bought it from that shop. The one on Smith Street. Paid heaps."

"Then why did you tell me your mate swapped it?"

"Cos I didn't want you to know how much I paid for it."

"Why?"

"Because then you'd think I was desperate for you to like me!" His voice echoes through the alley, the sound as cold and as sharp as the air. He rubs his face, both hands. "I mean, shit. How lame is that?"

I swallow. *Don't believe him, don't believe him, don't believe him* . . .

"It's the truth, Frankie. Honest."

The duffel bag clatters. "Can we go, X? This chick is boring me."

Now I remember. The café. The phone call from some guy called Nate. The "favor."

I face Nate; the guy is sneering. I mean genuine, silent-movie-bad-guy sneering. This pathetic excuse for a punk is Fagin to my brother's Oliver Twist. This guy is going down.

"Well, how about I grab Uncle Terry's baseball bat? It's perfect for playing Pin the Jackass with a Right Hook."

Nate leans forward, challenge in his eyes. "Sure. Like to see you try."

I feel the red descending, a surge of biting, blinding rage. I lunge forward, but Xavier grabs me and hauls me back. "Shit, Frankie," he says, breathless. "Calm down."

"I'll calm down after Hamburglar takes his skinny arse back to whatever butt crack he crawled out of."

Nate scowls. "If you were a guy you'd be flat on your back right now. I'd have hit you so hard . . ."

"And if you were a guy I'd be impressed." I kick out, aiming squarely for Nate's balls, but Xavier holds me back again and all I get is air.

Then Xavier shoves me. Not hard, but enough. I stumble, crashing into the Dumpster. I'm too shocked to say anything.

Xavier runs his hands through his damp hair as he starts walking away. "I'm sorry, okay, but you don't know shit about it. I didn't have a choice. I'm in way over my head and I . . . Screw it." He turns his back on me, hunching his shoulders and digging his hands into his pockets. "It's not my fault, okay?"

I open my mouth but nothing comes out. Just a cloud of foggy air. My back stings; funny how bashing into a Dumpster feels like taking a knife in the back.

Nate grips the duffel bag and hoists it over his shoulder. "Pleasure to meet you," he says, and salutes. Then he gives me the finger as Xavier drags him round the corner.

When they're gone, the alley is silent and I'm breathing hard. I think about punching the wall, right between the two *k*'s in "Jackknife."

A pigeon picks at a rotting tomato that's fallen out of the garbage bag.

"Piss off," I tell it.

The bird grips the tomato in its beak and flies away.

Eleven

I perch on a stool in the front of the shop and lean my forehead against the glass. The crack running the length of the Emporium's front window might look like it's giving Smith Street its sleaziest grin, but I'm giving it one hell of a scowl. My breath fogs up the glass.

"Are you going to mope around this place all day? You're scaring off customers." Vinnie's on her knees, filling up the drinks fridge.

There's only one couple in the shop, eating their magpie kebabs in silence (no actual magpies were harmed in the making of the kebabs—just don't ask what happened to the chickens).

I draw a frownie face in the huffed-up glass. Maybe I will stay here. Maybe I'll never leave. Ever.

"Do your homework. Didn't I pick up a heap from school just the other day?"

"Done it."

The fridge door slams shut. Vinnie grips the handle to pull herself up. "I'm not even going to act like I believe that."

Outside, a tram rattles uphill, cutting through the rain shooting down at an angle. People walking past hold their umbrellas out in front and duck their heads.

Vinnie's got nothing to worry about. I've been totally productive this morning. I made a list: "Xavier's Pros and Cons."

> Pro: He brings me dumplings.
> Con: He lied to me about the vinyl.
> Pro: He's the only other person who knows what
>   it means to be the spawn of Juliet Vega.
> Con: It looks like he might have inherited some
>   of her less desirable traits.
> Pro: He's a stupidly talented artist.
> Con: He might also be a stupidly talented con
>   artist.

And that's the rub, that's the stick-a-knife-in-my-back-and-twist of it all. Because he didn't just steal, he lied about it. Lied to my face. And I've already had one blood relative lie and lie and lie her way through my life. I know how it ends for me and I don't need that. Not again.

A dark gray sedan parallel parks in front of the outlet across the road. The driver has to back in and out three times before he gets it right. I'd laugh but my one and only driving lesson ended five seconds after it started; apparently driving instructors don't like it when you fail to indicate and then call them a "dog's arse" for ticking you off.

I press my nose against the window, squishing it up like a

pig's. A guy stops to peer at the menu pinned to the window and doesn't see me right away. He jolts when he does, his eyes bulging and his hand gripping his chest.

I laugh—now isn't that much better? He flips me the bird before walking off.

"Get away from the window, Frankie."

"Why? Are you ashamed of me?"

She lugs the empty boxes to the counter and tosses them over. "You get in fights, get suspended from school, shoot your mouth off every chance you get, and stiff me with thousands of dollars' worth of medical bills, and I still love you. What do you reckon?"

I lean my elbows on the bench. She forgot to mention God Knows Who.

Sigh.

Four Eminem CDs for a record probably worth hundreds of dollars? Of *course* it was stolen. No one swaps a rare vinyl for four shitty CDs. How gullible can I get? That's "stupid" in all caps, underlined, bolded, and in some weirdo font that makes it look like the title of a horror film.

But do I believe his revised version of events? He *did* seem pretty embarrassed when he admitted why he'd lied. *But* he's clearly not averse to stealing: just ask my neighbors. *Although*, he didn't actually steal anything—that was all Nate. *However*, is being a lookout just as bad?

Man, morality is so blurry.

Vinnie walks up behind me, planting a kiss on the top of my head. "You know, honey, there's a Frankie-shaped tumor in my head but I love you anyhow. Course, if you want to tell me why I'm paying for some rich brat to see a plastic surgeon about his nose, that'd make me real happy. I just don't understand—"

"Isn't that Marzoli?" I point at a guy climbing out the passenger-side door of the badly parked sedan. It looks like him: same tan trench coat and potbelly. He walks the length of the car, inspecting the park. The driver gets out and starts waving his hands around.

Vinnie presses my arm down. "It's rude to point."

"You reckon he's coming here?"

"Sooner or later Marzoli's going to realize this is a legitimate business now. Either that or he'll get sick of me busting his balls every time he sticks his ugly face into my shop. He can search this place all he likes; he's not finding a bloody thing."

Search?

Shit. Can I go to prison for being gullible?

Double shit. Can they arrest me for profiting from a crime?

Triple shit. What if they think *I* stole the record?

The bell jangles as our only customers finish up and leave, their table a mess of wrappers, drips of garlic sauce, and used napkins. The sound sends a shiver down my spine—any second now Marzoli's going to come in here and that *jingle-jangle* might as well be my death knell.

Vinnie sighs and heads to the counter. She grabs a cleaning tray. "Just keep away from the window."

Marzoli and his partner hover on the other side of the street, looking for a break in traffic to cross.

I pull my phone out of my pocket and rest it on the bench. No new texts, seven missed calls since yesterday, all from the same number: he who shall not be named.

As soon as a white Volvo passes, Marzoli grabs his partner by the arm and drags him halfway across the road. They wait for a stream of cars to pass before they jog the rest of the way. I wonder if I can make a citizen's arrest for jaywalking.

On the curb outside the Emporium, Marzoli pulls out his notebook and starts flipping through. The other guy opens an umbrella, holding it over Marzoli more than himself. Marzoli flips through his notebook for a while and then looks up, like he senses being watched, and stares straight through the front window of the Emporium. At me.

Cripes.

"Get a hobby if you're bored," says Vinnie. "Do kids knit these days?"

Marzoli and I stare at each other. Like a high-noon stand-off, except it's three p.m. He lifts a hand and holds it just out in front of his face in a frozen wave.

I lift mine, too, but I'm too confused to know what to do with it once it's up there. I think we're waving at each other.

Me and a cop. Waving.

I lower my hand. Marzoli does the same thing.

"How about you take up ballet again?" says Vinnie.

I remember the day they arrested Uncle Terry. I never liked the guy, if I'm honest. I was always wriggling free of his hugs. "Give Old Terenzio some sugar," he'd say, stabbing a finger against his stubbled cheek. He wasn't a total perv, just handsy. When I was eleven he moved into the Hoddle Street house because he'd gotten into some kind of trouble. Vinnie wouldn't tell me—she just said "shush" whenever I asked. He bunked in my room and I slept on the sofa with the cats.

He was never home much, which suited me, but it made Nonna and Vinnie yell at each other in the kitchen. "He's your son," Vinnie would yell. "*È tuo, questo figlio buono a nulla!* Sort him out." Nonna would just get hysterical and start wailing. She said he was cursed. "Vega men are no good," she'd say. "*Siamo tutti maledetti!*"

Just the men? So how do you explain Juliet, Nonna?

They came in the middle of the night. Makes it sound like an alien invasion, doesn't it? It actually felt like it. Men with guns, torches attached to the ends, the light strobing through the house as they dragged Uncle Terry into the living room. They handcuffed his arms behind his back and shoved his face into the carpet. There was so much shouting, Nonna loudest of all.

And then Marzoli arrived, complete with tan coat and stained tie. He came in right at the end when Uncle Terry was crying into the carpet and the men had lowered their guns. Vinnie kicked Marzoli in the shins and called him a lowlife but he didn't arrest her. He just shouted for someone to get Terry into the back of the divvy van and that was that. Fifteen years for multiple armed robberies.

I pick up my phone and type: *I'm still mad at you but keep away from Smith Street. Someone left the gate open and the pigs are loose. I repeat: the pigs have left the farmyard.*

Send.

". . . and you looked so cute in your little pink tutu. Frankie? You listening?"

I'm leaning so far forward I almost fall off my stool. Marzoli and his minion are still standing out in front of the shop, not looking at me in a looking-at-me kind of way.

"Ballet," says Vinnie, her bangles clunking against the tabletop as she wipes. "I really think you ought to give it another go."

Oh god. I've got zero explanation for why I have a possibly stolen, rare, and incredibly awesome vinyl in my room. I can't take the risk.

"Are you listening, Frankie?" Vinnie stops swishing the cloth back and forth and stands straight, giving me her most concerned look: the full brow collapse and the downturned mouth. "Do I need to worry about you? More than usual, I mean? Maybe we ought to have that talk."

I slide off the stool and grab my jacket. "If it's about the birds and the bees you're a little late on that one, Vin. We had this guy come to school and he had a bag of bananas. Plastic ones, and when you pulled off the skin it was actually a penis and we practiced putting condoms on them and he showed us pictures—who knew the female reproductive system looked so much like a ram's head?" I hurry to the back stairs, the ones that lead to our flat.

"Where are you going?"

"Ah . . . nap time."

"Don't forget your shift starts at four."

"It's seared into my memory."

The door closes with a bang.

The alley is empty. It only took me a couple of minutes to grab the vinyl. And then a couple more to change my mind, change it back, then hug the vinyl to my chest, cursing my shitty luck for forcing me to part with this most awesome of things. But with Marzoli and his minion no doubt already inside the Emporium, waving their warrant under Vinnie's nose, I don't have a choice.

I hurry to the bins; they're overflowing and reeking like a classroom of Year Seven boys on a stinking hot day. No cops in sight.

In case Marzoli gets all CSI with fingerprinting and shit, I wipe the record with my sweater. My heart squeezes tight as I lower this beautiful piece of musical history into the bin; I can't let go, my trembling fingers gripping tight. But it's evidence of a crime and a glaring reminder that my brother's shit seriously stinks, so I reluctantly slide it under a bag of rotting tomatoes and meat juice and step back.

Goddamn it.

Shit.

I wonder if Marzoli's already in my room, rifling through my life. If he is, I'm going to kick him in the shins. And then I'm going to set Buttons on him.

I turn when I hear voices. Male. Piglike. Down the other end of the alley.

Why aren't they in the shop? Good Frankie wants to run, put some serious distance between me and the evidence I just dumped in the bin. Bad Frankie sees a perfect chance to snoop and find out what the cops know.

I'm already in the "majorly screwed" basket, and spying on a couple of cops is not how I claw my way out of this shitty predicament. Not when I'm supposed to be kiss-arse-ing my school and rehearsing my "I didn't do it/it wasn't my fault/please give me a second chance" speech. But I need to know exactly how much trouble my brother is in.

Bad Frankie wins.

A voice wafts up the alley. An unhappy-neighbor voice. "I've already told those other cops. What more do you want?"

It's coming from the house behind the block of yuppie flats. A crumbling semi that must have the developers drooling. My shoulder scrapes the bricks as I crouch low and edge closer.

"Sure," says a familiar gravelly voice. "But we've got a few more questions. Won't take long."

"I'm not inviting you in."

I think the woman's called Marlee. I've seen her around—she's Collingwood through and through. "I've had it up to here with you lot. Some prick robs a flat and you're all business. But I got complaints about those students two doors up with their *doof doof* music and their beer cans on the street and you reckon you're too busy to do anything about it."

I shuffle to where the wall is low enough for me to peek over the edge and . . .

Bingo. Two cops and a grumpy neighbor.

There's about four steps leading up to a weatherboard porch, white paint peeling back to the pink underneath. A half-dead jacaranda takes up most of the front yard; Tibetan prayer flags hang faded and ripped along the gutter.

Marlee's in her dressing gown, sucking on a cigarette. She's got reddish-brown curly hair and nails so sharp they ought to be illegal. She'd never get through airport security with them.

Marzoli's partner holds up a glossy piece of paper. "You know this kid, ma'am?" His voice is nasally, words-dripping-with-snot kind of nasally. "Seen him round, maybe?"

She squints into the sky. "Nope."

"It'd help if you looked at the photo, Ms. Ganan."

I screw up my face and squint but can't see shit. I'm too far away and he's got it angled toward Marlee.

"Two youths were seen near here on the afternoon your neighbors were robbed," says Marzoli. "The one in this picture has a criminal record as long as my ex-wife's credit card bill. Don't you want us to catch the . . ." He consults his flip book. ". . . the 'prick' who robbed your neighbors?"

I don't know Marlee well—just enough to grunt "hey" if I pass her in the street—but I know her type, and I know the

Marlees of this world do not respond well to middle-aged-cop sass.

The porch groans under her shifting weight. "I want you to do your job and quit trying to get me to do it for you." She plucks the half-spent cigarette from her mouth and throws it at Snot Guy's feet. "I got a hair appointment so maybe you two want to piss off and do some actual work. Like sorting those students out."

The wire door slams shut with a squeak, then a twang, then a thud as she thunders back inside her house.

You just made my list of awesome people, Marlee Ganan.

Snot Guy turns to Marzoli. "What the hell do you call that?"

He's holding the picture angled farther round toward me now, enough that I can see the guy in the photo has brown hair. Could be Xavier, could be anyone.

"I call that Collingwood." Marzoli does an about-face, trundling down the steps. "Keep moving, Peters. We're going to get that kid one way or another." They walk up the path to the next house.

Okay, so two things. One: I seriously hope Xavier's not the guy in that picture. I'm still mad at him but I guess I was hoping he wouldn't be carrying on the family tradition of spending more time behind bars than not—he didn't even grow up a Vega so he had the best chance of the lot of us. Or maybe Nonna was right and he's cursed. Maybe he never stood a chance.

But, more important, two: Holy fuck! I dumped *An Ideal for Living* for nothing? They weren't coming for me and my stolen record after all? Fuckity fuck.

I run back up the alley to the bins and dig through a week's worth of Emporium garbage, praying there's a how-to-remove-bin-juice-stains-from-a-vinyl-record tutorial on YouTube.

But it turns out there's no need for the tute because the record's not there.

Five minutes.

That's how long it took in this classy neighborhood of mine.

Five minutes for some bastard to steal my record.

Fuck.

Twelve

Cara and I are sitting by the river on top of the old Dights Mill turbine house, our legs dangling over the edge of the platform. It's heritage-listed, but it's really just a slab of concrete, three brick walls, and a nest of rats. We're stuffing our faces with churros and coffee (the breakfast of champions). It was Cara who insisted we come, the climax of her I-never-get-to-see-you-anymore rant. And I like to sleep in as much as the next girl, but I also need a distraction from the kebab, lecture, kebab, chores, kebab, spill garlic sauce down my top, lecture, kebab-ness of my life right now.

Cara's got goose bumps up and down her bare legs. She hates the winter school uniform and wears the summer dress year-round. It started in Year Eight when I made a bet that she couldn't do it; I lost my best New Order poster that year.

I wipe the sugar crumbs off my jeans. "America. Your turn."

Cara shakes her head. "I know what you're doing. And it's not happening."

I try looking at her with a mix of confusion and indignation, but her don't-even-try-it glare trumps mine.

"I told you everything already. Quit bitching." I've just spent the past half hour blabbing on about Xavier—what more does she want? "It's a straightforward story: Girl meets long-lost brother, brother turns out to be a thief, girl attempts to kick brother's criminal mate in the balls. The end."

"Nuh-uh," she says. "You told me facts. The second I ask you something that involves *feelings*, you stuff your face with a doughnut, and voilà—suddenly we're playing the countries game. If you were a superhero, you'd be Distractacon."

"Well, you'd be my sidekick, Nag Girl."

She chucks half a churro at me. "You're disappointed Xavier turned out to be your mum's mini-me."

She's right, of course, but if I keep talking about it then how am I going to bury it way down deep and pile the shit on top?

God Knows Who has left tons of messages but I haven't listened to any of them. Well, when I say tons I mean seven, and he hasn't called today. Or yesterday. Guess seven's the limit.

I've been thinking I might call him back. Just to yell at him.

Or he can explain everything and I'll be able to breathe easy because he's not Juliet's mini-me at all. I'd really like that.

"Cut Break-lines," says Cara.

I look sideways at her, frowning. "Huh?"

"That's what you can call him," she says. "Cos that's how you're going to—" She slices her throat with her finger, tongue rolling out the side of her mouth, eyes crossing.

I laugh and make a mental list of the things I'm grateful for: churros.

Coffee.

Cara.

Not necessarily in that order (but sometimes totally in that order).

I'm glad Cara's mum decided to stop being a cow and finally let my girl out for our morning ritual. I'm nothing without the three most important C-words in the world.

"Albania." Cara rocks to her right, bumping my shoulder. "Your turn."

Distractacon strikes again. I lift the lid on my takeaway coffee and peer inside. "Armenia." I upend the cup and out dribbles the last of my latte.

"Stop with the frigging A's."

Early-morning joggers pass on the track behind us, talking, panting, thudding.

I push myself up and then head down the steps. The entire west wall is missing; you can see through to Dights Falls, which aren't really falls. Not in the Niagara sense of the word. They're more like stumbles. A bunch of rocks and man-made concrete walls that the water sort of trips over in a slightly embarrassed way.

Above my head, iron beams crisscross. I reach up and brush my fingertips along one of them. Rust comes away, falling onto my face like diseased snowflakes. Gross. I brush down my sweater with fingers stained rust red, like they've been dipped in henna. "How many drug deals do you think have happened here?"

"And how many infectious diseases have been passed on?" Cara brushes past me. She heads to the edge of the slab and leans against the railings. "How many cherries . . ." She sticks her finger in the side of her mouth and pops.

"Cross."

"This is what happens when you live in a house full of boys." She pulls her hair into a topknot. "Afghanistan."

"Nigeria."

"Screw you. Argentina."

I lean against the brickwork. Right over some guy's tag—*Jonza* in bright yellow and purple paint. I reckon if you're going to deface something then at least make sure your art doesn't look like some toddler ate a liter of paint and vomited it up. Like the purple-skinned girl in the alley. That piece was good.

There are voices above us, someone walking out on the concrete platform on top. Cara and I stay silent until they leave. We listen to them complain about the cold.

"Azerbaijan," I say.

"Sorry. Did you just sneeze?"

"Don't be racist. It's a legit country. And it doesn't end in *a*, so be thankful."

"Oh shit," says Cara. "I almost forgot. I've got the best story." She bends back over the railings, swinging like she's on the monkey bars at school.

"I was in Specialist Math, which is currently in the portables near the tech building. You know that splashy science center the school got a grant to build? Well, it means we get shunted to Antarctica—I'm talking distance from anywhere *and* temperature—and we get the awesome soundtrack of grinders and jigsaws screeching all lesson. I swear, Dunbar is one hacksaw away from a mental breakdown. Oh. Norway."

"Y. Great. Last time I gift you, bitch."

She smiles. "So last Friday, Dunbar left us on our own—he had to go to the staff room for his afternoon medication break.

But it's cool because there's only eight of us and we're all pretty focused. Plus, we love not having a teacher eyeballing us—why can't they all be high-functioning alcoholics?

"But this time, Mark—yes, I said Mark—chose to sit next to me. That's weird because Mark normally sits next to Eden Kyles-Tewolde because she's the smartest chick in school. I'm good at maths too but I'd stab my pencil through his cock before I gave him my answers, you know?"

I laugh. I know.

"As soon as Dunbar splits, Mark starts talking to me. First it's all, 'What did you get for question eight,' 'Why did I even take the top-level maths,' 'Are you going to Truc's party this weekend,' blah blah blah, bullshit bullshit bullshit. I can tell he's got something he wants to ask me because he never talks to me. So I say, 'Spit it out, Mark, what do you really want to ask?' And he's all like, 'What, can't we just have a conversation?' So I'm like, 'No, actually, unless you're keen to explain why you cheated on my best friend.' So he gets all sulky and stops talking to me and I'm like, 'Suits me fine because now I can get on with my work.' But after five minutes he finally spits it out. Wants to know if I've heard from you. 'She's my best friend,' I tell him, 'of course I've heard from her.' And he's like, 'Well, what's up with her? Are they going to kick her out?' And I'm like, 'You just saw her the other day,' and he's all like, 'I didn't really get to talk to her, did I?' So I tell him you've joined a cult, and he laughs and says, 'No, seriously,' and I'm like, 'Seriously, she's joined this cult and she's only allowed to wear hessian and they worship a turtle god who carries the world around on his shell and they can only eat peas. Frozen peas.' And he looks at me for a second like, 'Really?' And I'm like, 'No, you dick, she still works at her aunt's kebab shop and if you want to know how she is and if she'll go out with you, then you know where to find her.'"

Cara swings back over the railings. When she pops up again her cheeks are flushed with the blood rush. She's grinning. "So the moral of this story is that lover boy still has a thing for you."

"Maybe he's one of those people who gets all revved up over criminals." I jab at the dirty concrete floor with the tip of my boot. "You know, they write letters to people on death row. Maybe he figures I'm a good one to bet on."

"Even in Texas you wouldn't get the death penalty for breaking a dickhead's nose with a book."

"Yemen," I say. "It's in the Middle East."

"I know where Yemen is. I'm not a total dummy."

I inspect my rust-stained fingertips. "So what about Ava? I thought her and Mark were all sucking face and sunshine."

"I think they just hook up. Apparently it's you he's all happily-ever-after about."

"He cheated."

"True. And then he apologized about fifty gazillion times and talked Square-Tits into playing your favorite song over the loudspeakers at lunch and wrote you a gag-worthy poem and got all puppy-eyed whenever you walked past. So I guess he tried to win your forgiveness."

The bricks are cold as I press against them. I frown deeply; Cara watches me with her know-it-all eyes. She's catlike in her intensity. The kind of intensity Buttons reserves for his surprise attacks on my bare feet. "You think I should forgive him?"

She tilts her head. "As if. He's a bona fide douche. The question is: *Could* you forgive him? I don't think you know how to forgive."

"I take it back—you're not Nag Girl, you're Bitch Girl."

"Says Queen Bitch-Face of the Bitchi-Bitchi tribe of Bitchlandia." She blows me a raspberry and then checks her phone. "I got to go. School's almost starting. If I get another detention for being late, Mum will flip. Nepal. Walk me?"

We run up the steps, two at a time.

"I'm not really allowed near the school."

"So wear a hessian bag over your head. People already think you're in a cult that only wears hessian. It's karma. No, I mean fortuitous. Do I mean fortuitous?"

My phone vibrates. "Wait up." I hang back a couple of steps from the top. The screen is cold against my ear. "Yeah?"

"That shit turned up?"

Ugh. Bill Green.

Cara waits at the top of the stairs, looking down at me. Her dress is so short I've got a good view of her pink knickers from here. She motions for me to hang up.

"How much does he owe you, Bill?"

"He's my son. I'm concerned about his welfare."

"Oh yeah, you sound all broken up."

"You'd be all broken up if someone stole your credit card and maxed it out at some bloody record store you'd never heard of."

And there it is. A hot, niggling sensation deep in my chest. The same feeling I got when I hid beneath the cubby house eating Gregory Vu's lunch because he'd laughed at me for being relegated to the stupid table in maths. He deserved it, but those spring rolls sure tasted bitter.

I grip the railing. "Record store? You mean Vinyl Underground?"

"How'd you know that?"

Shit, shit, shit, shit.

Cara is giving me big eyes and even bigger hang-up-the-phone charades. I wave at her in a way I hope approximates *I'm coming—take a chill pill*. She gives me the finger.

I hold a hand over my mouth and the phone, and turn away. "I just . . . I mean, when you say 'maxed out' you mean . . . ?"

"Four and a half."

Shit. "Hundred?"

"Try thousand, little girl. So you can tell that shit-for-brains kid of mine I'm going to wring his bloody neck when I see him. And he'll be paying me back every cent."

Beep.

I stare at my phone, chest and throat burning.

I think there's another C-word I might be about to use.

"Who was—?"

"Latvia." I wonder if my face is as flushed as it feels. I hurry up the last couple of steps.

I mean, "holy shit" just doesn't cover it.

Cara wiggles her eyebrows at me. "Latvia? That's an expensive call."

I give her a weak smile.

FOUR AND A HALF THOUSAND? Did he mean Australian dollars or some foreign currency where four and a half thousand is equivalent to five cents? Now I want to take a sledgehammer to my brain and punish it for being stupid enough to think Xavier was an innocent kid who'd been led astray by poseur-boy Nate.

Four and a half thousand.

That's an overseas holiday.

That's two MacBook Pros.

That's a whole wardrobe of fancy clothes with change left over for about a hundred churros.

That's Juliet Vega.

"Are you listening?" Cara tugs on my arm. "I'm going to be late. Do you want me to get a detention? Oh, and Algeria."

I let her pull me along but I can't even fake a smile right now. I've got four and a half thousand reasons why not.

Thirteen

I'm *not* talking to Xavier. If I was, I'd tell him what a dickhead he is. Stealing his dad's credit card to buy me a gift I don't need, then shoving me against a Dumpster and walking away with that smug bastard Nate instead of dropping to his knees and begging me for forgiveness.

I am *not* speaking to the thieving little bastard, but if I was I'd tell him he can forget about his free kebab. He can forget about me, about dumplings, about a total musical overhaul. He can rot in musical purgatory for all I care.

I slam the door to my room; it rattles in the frame. I turn up Joy Division: the clanking drums and fuzzy base and yearning, violent wails of "I Remember Nothing" flood my ears and soothe my soul. I collapse onto the bed.

I am not speaking to him. *Ever.*

I am going to focus on sorting out my own shitty mess:

it's going to be homework every night and I'm going to volunteer for a charity or read to sick kids or something. And I'm going to be a good niece and do the laundry like Vinnie asked (demanded). I'm not going to spend another second searching through the bins looking for that stupid, ridiculously expensive record because (a) someone has definitely stolen it, and (b) bins are gross.

I slide my phone out of my back pocket: no new messages. Seven unplayed messages.

I might have something to say to Xavier if he left me four and a half thousand messages, but he hasn't called for the past two days. Not even after my more-than-helpful stay-away-from-Smith-Street warning text.

I curl onto my side and squash the pillow under my head. I let out an angry sigh.

What is it with Vegas and monumental mistakes? Shakespearean nose-breaking, armed robbery, stealing, drug addiction and dumping your kids, marrying the wrong guy (three times). Robbing your dad to buy a gift for a girl you just met because . . . I don't even know why.

Why?

I roll onto my back and glare at the star stickers all over my ceiling. They're not glowing—it's daytime—but I can see the outlines and they're pissing me off. So cheery and pretty and meaningful. Stars—I hate the bastards.

I push up to seated and stare at the floordrobe that is my room. No wonder Vinnie threatened me with extreme physical violence if I didn't get my laundry done pronto.

I slide down the edge of the bed and onto the carpet, and when I'm on my arse I start dragging clothes toward me. Sniff-test time. I get four pairs of socks, a T-shirt, and one pair of jeans into sorting before my mind drifts. Four and a half thousand. Why hasn't he called? Vinnie's going to kill me if I get expelled. Yuck, this sweater stinks. I'm starved. Four and a half *thousand*. Wish I'd kicked that thief Nate. What if Cara finds a new BFF because I'm not around enough at school? Four and a half—but why? Why steal for *me*?

Of course, I could just *listen* to his voice messages. I'm not going to call him back, so there's no harm in *listening* to the little shit's groveling messages, is there? Besides, if he's got an explanation, then I'd like to hear it.

I could do with the laugh.

I wedge the phone between my shoulder and ear, freeing my hands for laundry duty. "You have seven new messages," says the voice-mail lady in her robotic tone. "Message received on the tenth at one seventeen p.m."

How do you get to be the lady who does these stupid voice recordings? Easiest job in the world. Just talk slowly and put a weird emphasis on every fifth word. I *really* want that job.

"Frankie?" Xavier sounds like he's outside. Like he's in a wind tunnel or something. "I'm sorry, okay? Call me back. I'll tell you everything."

Beep.

The robot lady intros the next message. Four hours after the first one.

"Frankie? Did you get my message? I know you're mad but call me back."

Beep.

I'm not getting an overwhelming sense of pity for the guy. Where's the poetry? The badly sung forgive-me ballads? The I-have-so-much-groveling-to-do-I'm-going-to-get-cut-off-trying-to-leave-it-all-in-one-mess—*beeeeeep.*

The next three are pretty much the same. "I'm sorry. Call me back." "Me again. Please call me back." "Frankie? Call me back. Please."

I close my fist around the T-shirt in my hand. Is it light or dark washing? Does it matter?

The sixth message starts with a heap of background noise. Lots of voices. Shouting, swearing, laughing. Someone is singing the blues.

"Frankie," he says, voice covered with static. "I messed up, hey. But it's not my fault." He breathes heavily, like he's moving. A door closes and suddenly it's quiet. "I owe money. Heaps, but I'm going to pay it back. I'm not bad. Swear it. I don't do really bad things. Sometimes you've got to make a choice though, hey. To fix things."

I look down at the T-shirt in my hand. It's black so it doesn't take a rocket scientist to know which pile to dump it in. I let my head roll back, still gripping the damn T-shirt.

"I'm really in the shit, hey. I don't even know if you're listening to these messages. Maybe you're just deleting them. Maybe you've written me off. Don't blame you if you have. But I'm going to make it up to you. You'll see. I've got a plan. Don't give up on me, hey."

Beep.

I toss the T-shirt across the room. The phone is getting hot against my ear. Clammy.

"Message received yesterday at nine ten a.m."

I chew on my thumbnail, my legs jiggling. Xavier's voice kicks in. No blues this time but he sounds breathless. Like he's been running.

"I did it, Frankie. I got the money." He sounds like a kid at 4 a.m. Christmas morning. "And it was easy, too. Can't believe

I didn't think of it already. Dickhead won't even know what's hit him. I'm going to pay back Dad and sort out some other stuff and there'll even be some left over. I can get that record player, hey. Legit. We can listen to the vinyl and maybe I'll let you change my mind about Brian Curtis." He laughs. I hold a hand over my chest, gripping the fabric over my heart.

"I fixed everything," he says. "I told you I would. So call me back. I'll be at Dad's for the next bit but anytime after, hey. I'll wait."

Beep.

I drop the phone into my lap. I don't need to replay the message because it's seared into my brain, on a loop. *I got the money. Dickhead won't even know what's hit him. There'll even be some left over. I fixed everything.*

I'm sitting there with four and a half thousand questions burning a hole in my brain, chief of which is how do you make five grand or more in under a day? Short of doing something very illegal, something very bad?

I close my eyes, cover my face with my hands. A familiar mix of dread, fear, and shame burns in my chest—I haven't felt it for, oh, I don't know, say, fourteen years?

Hell, Xavier, what have you done?

There's the rotting carcass of a Holden Commodore in the front yard of Bill Green's house, the only B. Green in the phone book living in Reservoir. Long grass grows around and up through the rusted heap. I hover by the front gate—wrought iron, painted undercoat-pink. Why couldn't Xavier have just answered his damn phone? I'm way out of my natural habitat here and it's not like I even owe the kid but . . .

There's always a "but," isn't there? The same "but" that used to keep me pressed to the window, heart in my throat, waiting for Juliet to come home.

Anger and worry all mixed up.

Next door to Bill's house, an old lady dressed in black is leaning against her low brick fence. Her garden is a slab of concrete. She stares at me.

"Do you know Bill Green?" I ask.

She straightens and steps back, shaking her head. *"Non mi parlare. Io non so niente."*

Italian—damn it. I look around but there's no one else on the street. "Is he in? *Conosci l'uomo che abita qui? Sai se c'è?"*

She waves her hands at me, a black lace handkerchief in one hand, and yells, *"Che alleva un cobra muore avvelenato. Aiutati che Dio t'Aiuta."* She flicks the handkerchief at me several times before the rant lets up.

And here was me thinking they broke the mold after Nonna Sofia.

"I'll just knock." I push the gate as far open as it will go. Which isn't far at all.

I squeeze through the tiny gap and into the front yard. I try walking on the surviving chunks of concrete path and it's like I'm jumping from rock to rock in a river. Almost fun.

The old lady in black watches me with narrowed eyes, emitting a quiet hum of disapproval.

I make the front porch with an impressive leap. When I land, I teeter but manage not to fall on my arse. I look back at the lady but instead of applauding me she starts ranting again. Some people are hard to please.

I step up to the front door but the glass panels are impossible to see through—beveled and covered in prehistoric cob-webs.

I bash my fist on the frame and wait.

Four knocks later there's a lot of banging and thudding from inside and eventually I see the outline of a figure nearing the door. When it opens I get a flash of something big, hairy, and almost naked.

"*Un cobra!*" shouts the old lady. "*Che alleva un cobra muore avvelenato!*"

The big almost-naked hairy guy pushes past me and spits on the ground. "Fuck off back to Greece!" he shouts. Same voice as on the phone.

The old lady crosses herself. Bill Green gives her the finger. "Stupid old bitch," he says.

My shoulder clips the wall as he pushes me aside again. "Excuse me?"

He pauses in the doorway and deigns to look at me. I rub my shoulder and glare back.

Xavier's dad is wearing blue Y-fronts. And that's it. He's got a heap of bad tattoos, scars, and coarse hair all over his body. I think he's part yeti. I also think—and this is the jaw-dropping part—that he's the thin-haired guy. The guy from the Colling-wood Children's Farm. The guy Juliet was seeing when she dumped me.

He's fatter and has next to no hair on his head now. But there's a lump in my throat and a quickening of my heartbeat to confirm it.

This prick was more appealing to my mother than me. She dumped me so she could run off with *this guy*.

He adjusts his Y-fronts. "It's not my birthday," he says with a gap-toothed smile.

"Frankie Vega," I say. His smile vanishes pronto; hey, I'm a magician.

His eyes are red-rimmed and cloudy, like somebody ran a hot bath in his head and steamed them up. He peers at me a little closer and I get the feeling I'm only just coming into his vision now.

He nods. "Yeah. I remember," he says. "You've grown but you're the same. Still look like you just sucked on a lemon."

What a touching reunion. Somebody call Oprah.

"What do you want, anyway?"

"I want to see Xavier."

"The little shit's not here. I called you this morning, didn't I? Told you I was looking for him."

He grabs hold of the door, ready to slam it in my face.

"But he came by, right?"

"What?" Bill's not even looking at me anymore.

"He came by. Two mornings ago. With your money."

"Little girl, two mornings ago I was at the doctor. And there wasn't any money waiting for me when I got back."

"When did you last see him? A week? A month?"

He shrugs; his man-boobs jiggle. "Not my fault if he doesn't want to be found."

He tries to close the door, but I shove my combat boot in the jam and press my palm against the frame. "And that doesn't bother you? He's fourteen."

Bill lets the door fall open and adjusts his package again. Am I sheltered or do they really require that much maneuvering?

"Course it bothers me," he says. He treats me to another coin-slot grin. "He owes me four and a half grand."

"He really hasn't paid you back?" I pull out my phone, flipping through screens to play back Xavier's message. "He said, I mean, his message, it said he was . . ."

Bill's cloudy eyes wander down to me. "Look, kid," he says. "I haven't heard from him because he knows if he shows his face around here without my money, I'll rearrange it."

In Year Ten the level coordinator told me to imagine shoving my fist in my mouth in moments like this. Apparently it's to stop me from shooting my mouth off—or worse. It doesn't work (ask Steve Sparrow) but I imagine shoving my fist down Bill Green's throat, and that kind of helps.

None of this makes sense. Xavier said he had the money and was going to pay his dad back. So what stopped him?

A cold hand grips my heart.

"Do you have any of his friends' numbers? I want to make sure he's okay."

"Don't know any."

"There's one called Nate. Bit older than me. Hair like a tumbleweed."

Bill shakes his head.

"Well, what school does Xavier go to?"

"Something High."

"Well, you've just been a wonderful help." I imagine my fist smashing into his teeth—that's even better.

Bill itches his chest. Before he closes the door in my face, he says, "Do yourself a favor, kid. Forget about Xavier. He'll drag you through the shit and rip you off on the other side. He learned that from your mother."

The door slams, glass rattling.

"*Aiutati che Dio t'Aiuta!*" shouts the old lady.

I'm trembling as I walk the path out of there. No jumping

this time. Unless you count the pulsing beat of my heart, close to jumping out of my chest.

I bend to pick up a palm-size stone from next to the gatepost. I think it might be a chunk of old path.

I weigh it in my hand, giving myself a few deep breaths and a count of ten to change my mind.

I don't change my mind.

"This is something *I* learned from my mother." I hurl the rock at the front door. It crashes through the beveled glass.

As I run down the street, the old lady claps her hands. "*Bravo,*" she shouts after me.

I pause long enough to bow.

Fourteen

The bowels of the Collingwood police station open up, eject-
ing two uniformed officers arguing about football. They don't
look at me as they pass. No one's looked at me.

Last time I was here they gave me coloring books and
lollipops. Of course, back then I was four and newly dumped.
Now I'm a soon-to-be-expelled miscreant worried about her
missing, thieving half brother.

Still, the service has really gone downhill.

It's been thirty-seven minutes since I spoke to the officer at
the front desk, a policewoman who rolled her eyes before saying someone would be down to take a statement "real soon."
Guess I missed the sarcasm.

I thought people made a big deal about missing kids. I
thought they cried on TV and offered rewards and made public
vows to never stop searching. It's what Harrison Finnik-Hyde's

parents are doing. I watched a clip on my phone—tears, hiccups, scrunched-up faces, pleas.

I tried picturing Bill Green weeping into a hanky on TV. Not likely. And I called Xavier's school. Actually, I called every high school in Reservoir until . . . jackpot. "Haven't seen him for a week," said the coordinator. "I'd be more surprised if he actually showed up."

What the hell? Some Malvern kid doesn't show up to school for one measly day and we get a statewide manhunt, but my brother goes AWOL for a whole week and no one gives a shit?

I shove my head between my knees and run my fingers through the long strands of hair swaying in front of my face. Buttons does this thing where he sits over the back of the chair, grabbing at his tail like he doesn't know it belongs to him. I can't pretend the hair's not mine, because it tugs whenever my fingers get caught in a knot.

Why doesn't Xavier just call? "Hi, it's me. I don't want to be found but you should know I'm okay." That would take, what? Five seconds? I've left enough messages on his phone today for him to know I'm freaking out.

Unless he can't call.

A bear-hand clamps down on my shoulder.

I flick my head up: cheap polyester, coffee breath, stale cigarette smoke, and a sparse comb-over.

"What are *you* doing here?" I sneer. I'm all charm.

Marzoli doesn't even blink. "It's a police station. I'm a cop. You do the math."

"I failed maths."

"Shall we head to the interview room? I need to take a statement from you."

I stand and he grabs my arm, steering me toward a nondescript door to the right of reception. "In here." He guides me into a windowless room painted mental-asylum green.

"Sit," he says, pushing me into a chair.

I freeze. I can't even breathe.

It's the same room.

They haven't painted the walls of this room for fourteen years—and they were scuffed and dirty back then. It's smaller than I remember and the ceiling is lower. The light flickers and hums.

I leave my life up to fate for a few minutes and look what happens. If karma's a bitch then fate is her psychopathic cousin. You know, the one no one invites to family reunions because she makes the little kids cry.

I shove the tip of my thumb into my mouth and start chewing the nail.

Marzoli plonks a manila folder stuffed with papers on the table in front of me. The cover is stained with two coffee rings overlapping like a Venn diagram. Papers in different shades of white are stuffed inside, their edges curled, torn, manhandled. The words "Xavier Green" are scrawled in pencil across the top right-hand corner.

Shit.

He closes the door and takes a seat.

"The PC on the front desk said you think a young gentleman by the name of Xavier Green is missing." He drags the folder across the table and into his lap, loosely crossing his right leg over his left. "What makes you think that, Miss Vega?"

He begins to flick through the folder. Slowly. It's a pretty thick folder for a fourteen-year-old boy.

I shrug. My stomach is cramping and, despite the icy temperature, my face is burning.

"What's a DI doing taking a missing-kid statement? You short-staffed or something?"

"How do you know Xavier Green?" Marzoli doesn't look up.

"He's my half brother."

"Didn't know you had a brother."

"Half. And neither did I."

"When did you last hear from him?"

"He left a message on my phone two days ago. I've called him a gazillion times and he's not answering."

"Any particular reason why you think something's happened to him?"

I give him a were-you-dropped-as-a-baby look followed by a well-duh voice. It's a classic combination. "No one has seen him. He's missing."

"But why do you think he's missing and not just a runaway?"

Okay. First off, "just a runaway"? Stellar empathy there, Marzoli. Second, the answer to Marzoli's superb question is actually: because he stole over four grand from his dad, maybe even more from someone else, and then did something possibly more illegal, possibly more stupid, to get the money back. But that's not an answer I can give.

"Because, Detective Inspector, he didn't have a reason to run away. He was happy."

Marzoli sighs and then rattles off more questions, scribbling notes the whole time. Missing person's full name, date of birth, description? Any scars, tattoos, birthmarks, distinctive jewelry, clothing? What kind of car does he drive? (He's fourteen, dipshit.) Credit card details, favorite places to hang out, friends, contact details for friends, medical conditions, medications, GP? Blah, blah, blah.

I'm able to answer two and a half questions—the rest get a shrug. God only knows what Marzoli is scribbling.

"When did you see him last?"

"Thursday."

"You two have a fight? Maybe said things? I know you're not the type to blow up at someone and say stuff you later regret but . . ."

I glare at a stain on the laminate table. Probably some suspect's brain matter from when Marzoli roughed him up for a confession.

"He's missing," I say. "What are you going to do about it?"

Marzoli picks at the corner of the folder. "Have either of his parents seen or spoken to him?"

"I don't know. I'll just go ask Mummy dearest. Oh wait, I can't. She's missing too."

"His dad?"

I shake my head.

Marzoli scans the folder, pursing his lips like he's reading a bestseller. "Did you know Xavier's run away before?" He pulls out a single page, holding it at arm's length to read. "He's been in trouble with us a fair bit. Done community service. Currently on probation."

"He's missing. You forgot to add that to the list. Missing and only fourteen."

"I'm just putting it out there that maybe—*maybe*—he's not missing. Maybe he's run away. Again."

"Did you give the Malvern kid's family that line?"

He doesn't look at me. Just the stupid folder. "That's not my case, Frankie."

Of course it's not his case. They'd only have the best for Harrison Finnik-Hyde.

"Just say you'll look into it."

It takes him a second longer than it should to answer me. "Of course we'll look into it."

He can't meet my eye. So I figure that by "look into it" he means "throw the report into the bin the second I'm out of here."

This was the worst idea ever.

Fuck you, brain. Fuck you very muchly.

He clears his throat. "Rest easy, Frankie. I always get my man."

"Is that your line on Tinder or are you trying to comfort me?"

His lazy smile says *hardy-har-har* but his eyes say *I'm going to stand over your dead body and cackle.*

"Listen, Frankie—"

"Forget it, Detective. We all know the son of a junkie prostitute doesn't get a front-page spread so let's just call this what it is—a waste of everybody's time, mostly mine—and move on with our lives. You obviously have a Tinder profile to update and I have kebabs to make." I stand, and my thighs bash into the edge of the table, ramming it into Marzoli's crossed leg. He swallows a curse and drops the folder, pages spilling all over the floor. One of them is a mug shot.

The dimpled smile is there. And so much of Juliet I want to puke.

I push straight past Marzoli and burst into reception, everything blurring around me.

"Frankie, wait."

No chance.

I'm so busy thinking about how the hell to get out of this place that I don't see the guy until I've face-planted into his chest.

It's Nate.

"Hey," he says. "Watch where you're . . ."

I figure the point that his voice trails off is the point at which he recognizes me. And boy does he recognize me. It's the look of horror and all-consuming anger that gives it away.

He doesn't say anything, though. Neither do I. We just do the whole open-mouthed-stare thing for way too long.

Under his cooler-than-cool jacket he's wearing a—gasp— Smiths T-shirt. His dark hair falls messily across his face, al- most hiding a purple bruise circling his right eye. Guess I'm not the only one Nate has pissed off.

"Excuse me, miss," says the cop behind him. It's Peters, the snot-nosed guy from Marlee's. "Need to get past."

My gaze travels down to where Nate's got his arms pulled behind his back and Peters is gripping Nate's handcuffed wrists.

"Didn't you hear the man?" says Nate. "Get lost. VIP com- ing through."

"By VIP you mean 'vulgar impotent pig'?"

"Careful with the name-calling. I might have to start call- ing you 'snitch.'" Nate jiggles his arms, handcuffs rattling. "You just like hanging round cop shops, do you?"

"Whoa. I'm not here to—"

I smell Marzoli's cologne before he opens his mouth. "Nate Wishaw," he growls from right behind me.

"Detective." Nate grins. Long-lost friends, apparently.

Marzoli stands like the sheriff facing an outlaw at high noon: hands on hips, pushing back his trench coat, slightly bowed legs, narrowed, wizened eyes. "You don't get frequent flyer points round here."

I get squeezed out of the way as he steps up to Nate and they have a stare-off.

"Ask Mr. VIP where my brother is. I bet he knows."

Marzoli chuckles, rubbing his stubble. "You mean Nate Wishaw and Xavier Green are mates? Why doesn't that surprise me? A match made in heaven."

Nate throws me a look, something halfway between a smile and a grimace.

Interesting. Looks like Mr. Unflappable is getting a teensy bit flapped.

"Green's missing," says Marzoli to Nate. "Know anything about it?"

"Nate was the last person I saw Xavier with. Of course he knows something."

Marzoli looks at me like I've just dumped a million dollars into his lap. "You saw Wishaw on Thursday? What time?"

Nate is staring at his boots, jaw set firm.

As I glare at him, I mentally run through everything I know. I know Nate and Xavier robbed my neighbor's house Thursday afternoon. I could easily tell Marzoli everything. I know Marzoli's investigating the burglaries, and he's positively salivating at the idea of sending Nate down for it. I know it's a crime to lie to the police but I also know pinning Nate for this crime dumps my brother in the shit too. Which he deserves. But Vegas don't snitch.

I know Xavier owes a heap of money. What I don't know is what Xavier did to get the money back, where he went instead of delivering it, and how I'm going to find him.

And if I can't find him, how can I make sure he's okay and then beat him over the head with Uncle Terry's baseball bat for being the second blood relative to skip out on me?

But maybe Nate knows the things I don't.

And he can't tell me anything if he's rotting in jail.

"Five p.m.," I say. Which isn't a lie.

Marzoli licks his lips. "And where did you see them, Miss Vega?" I think he's already planning a victory party. Would Marzoli do the conga?

"Inside the Emporium."

Marzoli turns his pit-bull stare my way. If he was doing the conga in his head then he just tripped and fell on his lei. "Repeat that, please."

Breathe, Frankie.

"My brother came for dinner and he brought Nate with him. We played Scrabble. It was fun."

I look at Nate. He looks at me. There's a lot of looking. Those eyes are *very* blue.

Nate swallows hard. "Got a triple word score with 'indebted.'" For a second he looks genuinely thankful. Sincere. Humbled.

Then he winks.

And we're back to normal transmission. Do not adjust your TV sets.

Marzoli's jaw twitches. "Are you sure about that, Miss Vega? It's really important you're sure."

I glare pointedly at Nate. "They stayed until closing— one a.m. He's lying about the triple word score, though. He didn't make a single word bigger than four letters all night."

Nate shrugs. "There are plenty of good four-letter words."

"You know it's an offense to lie to the police, Frankie?" Marzoli is going to grind all the way through his teeth and into his jawbone if he's not careful. "You're sure this kid was with you the whole time? He didn't sneak out for a cigarette?"

I fold my arms across my chest. "I'd remember if he left; I'd have noticed how much less annoyed I was."

"Well, that's me in the clear." Nate jiggles his wrists. *Rattle, rattle, clink.*

"We've still got questions for you, Wishaw." Marzoli waves Nate toward the interview room.

"But I've got an alibi." He goes stumbling as Peters shoves him forward. He wriggles around in Peter's grip to face me. "Airtight."

He laughs as I give him the finger.

Marzoli bashes his fist against the wall. "Shut him up, Peters."

The door to the interview room slams shut on Nate's grinning face. Can't believe I just helped that guy. Hope I don't live to regret it.

Speaking of which . . .

Marzoli leans over me, his coffee breath testing out my wobbly stomach. "If I can prove you're lying," he says, jabbing his finger at me, "I'll have you thrown in jail."

I hold my ground. "Just make sure you ask him about my brother."

Marzoli snorts. "Get out of here." The tail of his coat flaps as he swings around. It's a little bit superhero-like. Well, it would be if he weren't such a massive arsehole.

The door to the interview room slams shut for a second time.

Fifteen

In Year Eight, Mark read this book about some dude who went to Antarctica and nearly died. It's all he talked about for weeks: he kept saying how the guy ate his dog and how his feet were so frostbitten, bits kept falling off. He totally had a hard-on for the guy. Right now I'm so cold that bits of *my* feet are probably falling off, but I don't think I'll write a book about it because no one gives a damn about a girl who makes kebabs all day long. The dog barking at me from behind the fence next door better watch out, though.

I jiggle up and down on the spot, eyes on the glass doors of the police station. I've stopped checking the time because I don't want to know just how late it is and just how much trouble I'll be in from Vinnie for not being tucked up in bed. But I need to talk to Nate.

Luckily I don't have to wait much longer. Nate's in reception, hunched over the desk with a pen. He keeps "accidentally" brushing his hand against the policewoman's arm and grinning. Marzoli is leaning against the door frame of the interview room. He looks about twenty years older than usual.

I shuffle to the right, out of Marzoli's view. I think I've worked my way onto his Christmas card list. Only it's the list where people get a horse's head instead of a card.

Finally the glass doors swing open and Nate runs down the steps, two at a time.

I'm not sure what I'm going to say to the guy but I'm pretty sure he'll have a few words for me. First, he's going to grovel. He'll beg me to forgive him for being such a jerk. Then he'll say he owes me. I'll tell him to think nothing of it; we juvenile delinquents need to stick together. And that's when he'll nod and say, "You're so wise, Frankie. Let me tell you everything I know about your missing brother."

He walks right past me.

"Oi! Girl who saved your arse standing here."

He comes to a stop. I can practically see the stupid grin on his face through the back of his head. "If you hung around for a reward, Vega, you're out of luck. Unless it was me you were after." He turns to face me. Yup, stupid grin. "Back to mine?" He arches a single brow.

Really? Six percent of people can arch a single brow and he, *he* can do it?

I ignore him. And remind myself that, yes, he's hot, but he's also a prime example of the species *Jerkus arseholeous*. "You were the last one I saw Xavier with so I want to know if—"

"I've just spent the last hour breathing in Marzoli's coffee breath so I'm all out of small talk. But thanks for the alibi." He salutes, winks, and walks away.

Dickhead.

There's no one else around because it's (a) freezing, (b) late, and (c) really fucking freezing. The only light comes from the train station, the platform high up to our right. Nate heads down a walkway under the tracks. And I follow, boots clomping.

"I can easily go back to the station and withdraw my statement," I say as I catch up. I'm already out of breath. Frankie Vega does *not* run. "And then they'll lock you away. You'll have to get a teardrop tattoo."

"That could happen," says Nate. "Except you'd be admitting you lied to the cops and they'd arrest us both." He points to my shoulder. "You can get your tattoo right there."

Damn it.

I follow Nate out of the walkway and into an empty parking lot, which is basically a block of dusty earth ringed by a high wire fence. There are streetlights around the perimeter. It's lit up like a football stadium. Nate cuts toward a row of double-story Victorians.

"I'll say I was confused." Hop, step, jump. "That I thought it was Thursday but really it was Friday." Jog, stumble, wheeze. The guy has giraffe legs, I swear.

"Then you'd be alibi-ing me for Friday."

"Don't you ever take a night off?"

"Sure. I do yoga on Tuesdays."

We pass through to the other side of the parking lot and out onto the street, the row of Victorians looming. We're nearing the edge of my comfort zone—I am not on Smith Street anymore.

As soon as a car with way-too-bright headlights zooms past, Nate jogs across the street.

I hurry after him. "Wait, were you with my brother on Friday, too?"

He lifts an overhanging branch, holding it high as I walk under. "What did I tell you? I'm all questioned out. Go home and drool over Ian Curtis."

"I don't drool. Anyway, how do you know I like Ian Curtis?"

He stops again but only so he can give me another eyebrow raise. "Seriously? Have you looked in the mirror?"

"Have you?"

"Whatever. Didn't your mother warn you against talking to strangers?"

"My mother taught me jack shit. And if you're after a matching pair for your black eye, ask me about her again."

I stare him out.

"Look." He points at the wooden fence we're standing in front of, palings wonky and rotted. "You want to know about your brother? Look right there."

I look at the fence. I look at Nate. I look at the fence.

Maybe this is some weird-arse version of that diversion trick people play. Look! A fence! But when I turn back Nate hasn't run away. And he's looking at me like *I'm* the idiot.

He waves his hand at the fence. "Are you blind?"

"Are you mad?"

He jabs again at the wooden slats. "X Marks."

The fence is covered in graffiti. Mostly tags and mostly shit but there's one piece that's really good—it's right above the little red *X* Nate's pointing at. It reminds me of the purple-skinned girl from the alley, except this one's an angel. Not just any angel, though. She's riding a skateboard and her golden wings are giving the finger.

The slats wobble as Nate thumbs the fence. "X marks the

spot. X for, I don't know, maybe 'Xavier'? Do I have to spell it out?"

I doubt he can spell, but he doesn't have to.

The angel grins at me. The kind of grin that makes you jealous because whoever smiles like that knows the secrets of the world. I hold a hand up to the fence, palm flat against the angel's shoulder.

Wow.

My brother: dimpled thief, fond of dumplings, talented artist. I guess it makes sense—I've seen his drawing; it's buried in my backyard. But this is like seeing the Taj Mahal when all you've ever laid eyes on are mud huts. I don't know how to describe art but I know how it makes me feel looking at Xavier's angel: all tangled up and breathless and drunk and hopeful. My little brother, the kick-arse graf artist. Warmth shoots through my body. Either I need to pee or . . . oh my god, is this what pride feels like?

"It's incredible," I say.

Nate brushes a finger along the angel's wing and smiles like he can feel it too. "Yeah. It is." My smile matches his but when he catches me looking at him the scowl returns. Tenfold. "Heaps more around," he says. "Just look for the X. Show's over."

He shoves his hands in his pocket and jogs across the road, not even checking for traffic. I take a final look at the angel. She's oddly familiar. Like a grown-up version of someone you used to know as a kid—new and familiar at the same time.

The angel grins at me, eyes twinkling, middle finger saluting me. She's beautiful. There's no way anyone who can paint like this is an evil criminal mastermind.

When I turn, Nate's not only on the other side of the street, he's about halfway up the block, his giraffe legs whisking him—and whatever secrets he's keeping from me—far, far away.

As I give chase I ask myself: How shit is my life right now that this douchebag is my only hope? But the angel spurs me on.

Nate glances over his shoulder as I come spluttering and stumbling up to him. "I thought we were done," he says.

I can't have a heart attack and be a smart-arse at the same time, so I reserve my mouth for breathing purposes only. He rolls his eyes and walks faster. We're in a different postcode now. Abbotsford (I think).

After about another minute of jogging/walking he stops in front of the creepiest, most decrepit-looking bungalow I've ever seen. It's set a little ways back from the street, lurking in the shadows. It's squat, brown, and ugly—like a giant cane toad. Half the front gutter has pulled away, dangling onto the porch. All of the windows are boarded up and paint is peeling away from the walls, like the house has terminal skin cancer. I can hear the river flowing somewhere in the near distance.

Nate faces me. "This is where I tell you to piss off."

"You live here?"

"No. I'm just bored with you following me."

I did not run—in public—to be dumped outside a crack den. "Suck it up, Nate. You *owe* me."

"Then you have a problem."

"I've got ninety-nine problems but your bitchy attitude isn't one."

"That's cute," he says. "You're real funny. I'm guessing it's your sense of humor that brings all the boys to the yard."

"Screw you. I'm calling the cops." I reach into my coat pocket but my hand slides in way too easily; I think it has something to do with my phone not being where it should be. I pat my other pockets. Nothing.

"Can I help?" Nate lowers his face in line with mine. "I owe you a favor."

He's holding my phone.

Son of a kleptomaniac!

I make a grab for the phone but he holds it out of my reach.

"Give it to me."

"Or what?" He grins, his crooked smile promising trouble with a side of trouble and a little extra trouble for dessert. "You going to make a citizen's arrest? You going to handcuff me?"

And that, Mark Argyros, is how you do the laser-eye thing properly.

Nate might be hot, yes (oh god yes), but not enough to distract me from all the stealing.

I hold out my hand, flicking my fingers.

He waits for ages, grinning like the cat that got the native bird, before he finally lays the phone in my palm. "See? I'm a nice guy."

"You're a tool."

He laughs. "You don't have a filter, do you? I mean, you'd call the pope a dick in a dress to his face, wouldn't you?" I guess I get a look on my face, because he holds up both hands. "Hey, never said that was a bad thing. In fact . . ." He leans forward with an impish grin, sending an unexpected shiver down my spine, a bolt of heart-stopping electricity that fizzes in my fingertips and causes a catastrophic meltdown in my brain. Reboot! Reboot! "Maybe I'm telling you it's the opposite."

Did Nate Wishaw, tough-guy burglar and pickpocket, just hand me a compliment?

He sets a playful smile on his lips but what gets me is the

little crease in his brow. The tiniest flash of self-doubt and vul-
nerability and truth. "I've never met anyone like you, Vega," he
says.

I have to admit I get more than a little lost in the blue-eyed
laser show—seriously, I'm only human—but I'm also a realist.
So I'm pretty sure Nate Wishaw is taking the piss. Because
the alternative is . . . too confusing.

"Nice try, buddy, but your pickup lines are about as convincing as your I-didn't-do-it-officer act. Just tell me where my
brother is."

He pushes his curls out of his eyes. "Look. You're worried
about Xavier. I get it. I don't know where your brother is . . ."
He tilts his head as he looks at me with all the sincerity he can
muster—a surprising amount. "But I do have your neighbor's
fifteen-year-old scotch and a milk crate with your name on it.
So if you want we can head inside. And talk." He shrugs at me
like he doesn't care either way.

I wonder if there's a school for guys like Nate to hone their
Prince Charming acts. With classes like "Perfecting a Lopsided
Smile" and "Using Booze and Compliments to Distract Girls
from Asking Questions about Their Missing Brother and Dis-
covering You Know More Than You're Letting On." Nate would
have graduated with honors.

And, yes, part of me *is* tempted. But the rest of me knows
that when Nate says "talk" he doesn't mean about Xavier. Hell,
he doesn't even mean "talk."

"I thought you said you didn't live here." I look at the creepy
house and remind myself that this boy spent the afternoon in
the Collingwood cop shop. That I met him robbing a house.

I look back and he's smiling, a raw and imperfect smile
that did not graduate from the University of Prince Charming.

It's the real kind: goofy and awkward and shy. The kind that dances on the edge of beautiful.

But still: burglar, liar, jerk.

Walk away, Frankie.

"I'll pass."

There's a flash of something dark in his look before he clutches his heart and laughs. Nice-guy act over. "Ouch. You don't like being hit on, do you?"

"I love it. It makes me ecstatic."

"Then you should know that your 'ecstatic' face and your 'angry' face are exactly the same."

I think about kicking him in the balls. Apparently my *I'm going to kick you* face is different enough from my *"ecstatic"* face, because he takes a quick step backward.

"You've been a big help," I say. "And when I say 'help' I mean 'arsehole.' Why won't you tell me about my brother?"

"Whatever." With a salute Nate saunters off toward the house. "Go home and quit wandering down dark streets—all kinds of bad people about."

"You ought to know," I call. But it's too late; he's gone, sucked into the darkness. I can't even tell if he went inside or somewhere down the side of the house. All I can hear are his footsteps, fading slowly.

Sixteen

My alarm Monday morning is Vinnie slamming every door in the apartment, vacuuming, rearranging the living room, turning up AC/DC way too loud, and renovating the bathroom. At least that's how it sounds to me; I'm operating on a couple of hours' sleep. And not just because I got home late; it's more the verbal spanking I scored from Vinnie when I slunk in after midnight and found her waiting up for me, worried sick.

I groan and unwrap the sheets twisted round my body. I want desperately to get back to dreamland but I can't switch my brain to Zen setting. I try counting sheep but the sheep are giving me filthy looks as I force them to jump the fence again and again.

About five past nine, Vinnie slams the front door and heads downstairs to the Emporium, and peace and quiet finally descend. I wrap the comforter over my head and close my eyes.

Sleep. Please? Sleeeeeeep.

I'd be in first-period English right now if I was at school. That would put me to sleep. Or maybe not, because Cara would be drawing vines up and down my arm and telling me about Greg or Jackson or Nathan or whichever idiot boy she was currently crushing on and maybe I would tell her about Nate, about how infuriating he is but also how I kind of want to know more, like why does he steal things and where does he really live and does he have a family and where did he get that amazing jacket from?

I toss and turn and wrestle with the comforter. No sleep for Frankie.

So I get up and make breakfast. I chomp on each mouthful like it's cat food and glare at the kitchen. Everything is offensive to me today: the chrome toaster is too perky. The fridge is humming: arsehole. Even though it's winter there's actual sunlight streaming in through the kitchen window. Great, who knew weather could be sarcastic?

Buttons is staring at me from his perch on top of the kitchen table, his mushed-in Persian face judging my every move.

"What?" I say.

He flicks his tail.

"Same to you, Smoosh-face."

I pull out my phone and text Cara, telling her I'm bored and that she should entertain me immediately before I realize it's unlikely she can answer until class breaks. Ugh. So I check the news online and there's nothing about Xavier. Where's the full-color spread? The million-dollar reward? I pull up my gallery and look at the picture I took of us. Awkward poses, neither of us grinning, too dark, blurry. Wouldn't look great on the front page of a newspaper, I guess.

For some reason I decide calling Marzoli is a good idea. Why not? What else am I going to do? Homework? I grab his business card from beside the microwave, where Vinnie shoved it with the stuff to go out for recycling.

He answers on the fourth ring with a bark. "Yeah?" he says.

"It's Frankie Vega."

"You going to retract your statement from last night?" His voice goes high-pitched with hope.

I'm about two seconds away from saying, "Why, have you found Xavier already?" when I realize he's talking about Nate.

"Sure," I say. "I mean, if you want me to lie."

Sigh. "Then why call?" Less hope, more suspicion.

"Missing brother, worried sister. What's happening?"

"I'm looking into it."

I wait for him to elaborate on account of that being a crappy answer. He doesn't. "What does 'looking into it' mean?"

"It means I do my job, you do yours. Whatever that is. I'll call when I know something."

Soon as I hang up I dump his business card in the rubbish. I scoop my unfinished, soggy cereal on top of it and I only just stop short of cleaning out Buttons's kitty litter tray to scoop that on top.

I tidy, shower, dress, grab a block of chocolate (yay, Vinnie went shopping), and head downstairs to the Emporium. I have a plan. It has nothing to do with stressing about Xavier or school or anything else. And it doesn't involve blue-eyed burglars who can't decide if they want to hit on me or piss me off. I'm going to comfort-eat, suck up to Vinnie, and watch mind-numbing TV.

I tell myself Xavier is okay, because what else can I do? I've told the cops, and I've called all the hospitals and his school and left a billion messages on his phone. I've faced up to Bill Green. I've been brushed off outside a crack den.

I've done all I can.

But I can't forget that stupid angel on the fence. In my head she's no longer grinning, she's glaring at me, wings folded, accusation in her brown eyes.

When I get downstairs to the shop there's an old guy shoving a kebab down his throat. He looks like an off-duty Santa with a permanent red sheen lacquering his nose and cheeks. He waves at me like he knows me, and I guess maybe he does look a little familiar, but all these old men look the same to me.

At least there's a witness so Vinnie can't kill me.

She emerges from behind the counter, slinging her dishcloth over her shoulder. "Looky looky what the cat dragged in."

It's not so much what she says but how she says it that makes me certain a night's sleep hasn't improved her mood. It's not even the Nonna Sofia she's giving me. It's her original creation: the Vinnie. The difference is in the eyes: you need a whole other level of hellfire burning in your eyes to get the Vinnie just right.

"Before you say anything . . ." I whip out the chocolate from under my sweater and plonk myself on a stool. I slide the block along the counter until it's directly under Vinnie's nose.

"No good," she says. "Not going to work."

She hoists herself onto the stool beside me. I breathe in stale smoke, White Diamonds, and Cedel hairspray.

"I'm going to eat it, of course." She breaks off a square of chocolate and hands it to me. "But it's your last meal."

I grab the TV remote and turn it up. It's some kind of game show. I try answering "pineapple" to every question the slick-haired host poses.

"What's the capital of Romania?"

"Pineapple."

"What was the name of Henry the Eighth's second wife?"

"Pineapple."

"Finish this famous line from Martin Luther King's speech: 'I have a . . .'?"

"Pineapple."

I laugh. Vinnie frowns. "I think it's high time we had that talk," she says. The Vinnie is getting worked overtime.

"Cara's mum gave her this picture book," I say. "*Where Did I Come From?* So I already know that babies sort of magically come along nine months after a man and woman get married, but that doesn't explain Eden Kyles-Tewolde."

"Eden Kyles-Tewolde?"

"Smartest girl in school. She has two mums. It also doesn't explain Cara, who has no dad. Or me, who had too many dads." I get an elbow to my stomach. "Ouch."

"You know full well that's not the talk we need to have."

I say "pineapple" ("The chemical composition of water is one part oxygen to two parts what?") before turning to face Vinnie. "If it's about me coming home so late last night, I already explained that." I break off a line of chocolate and shove the whole thing in my mouth. "Pineapple." ("How many players make up a netball side?")

"No, you went on some tirade about people who can raise one eyebrow and then something about your brother not calling you back. I know you think I'm nagging you for no reason but I don't think you're taking this seriously. You could be expelled."

"A famous landmark in Woombye, Queensland," says the TV host, "is called the Big what . . . ?"

We look at each other before bursting into pants-peeing laughter. Who would have thought a giant fiberglass pineapple would one day come in handy?

"Better get a lottery ticket," Vinnie says, wiping her eyes. "Apparently you're a lucky lady. It'll help pay for that kid's nose." I can't help rolling my eyes, so she grabs my chin between her thumb and forefinger. "I say this with the utmost love for you, Frankie," she says and sighs. "Pull your finger out. Who do you think is going to give a job—a good job—to a high school drop-out? What are you going to do while Cara's flitting about uni and you're still here stinking of garlic? Sleeping in, disappearing half the night, talking back when you should be groveling—it's got to stop. Or I stop it for you."

Man. Happiness is like sugar, isn't it? The ride up is totally awesome but then you have to watch for the crash on the other side. And we were having so much pineapple.

Vinnie doesn't do subtle. Not in the sheer blouses and tight skirts she wears, not in the burning of her ex-husbands' things, not in her screaming matches with Nonna Sofia. So I know full well that when she says she'll "stop it for me" she means she'll bury me six feet under in the back garden. With the worm I killed and my stupid time capsule.

"Okay?" she says, squeezing my chin.

I nod and it wins me a smile. Not a big one, but an I'm-thinking-about-forgiving-you-give-me-a-minute smile. A reluctant curl of the lips. It's a massive win.

I get to lollop in my happiness bubble for all of three seconds—the exact time it takes the game show to make way for the news and a stern-faced news anchor to introduce the lead story: the missing kid from Malvern.

Am I to assume that the report on Xavier will be up next?

Can I expect to see Bill weeping and Marzoli pleading for information?

I reach for the remote but Vinnie wrenches it from my hand. "I'm watching this."

The old guy shuffles up behind us, dumping his dirty wrapper on the counter. "Isn't that just horrible," he wheezes. He's a loud breather and he stinks of pee, mustiness, and wet knitwear.

The news anchor throws to a reporter standing on some leafy street, reminding us where Harrison was last seen. They've got some kind of police caravan on the street corner, with officers handing out posters plastered with Harrison's face and information. There's even a dummy dressed in identical clothes to what the kid was wearing the last time he was seen. They're offering a $100,000 reward for information. And here's me with ten dollars and seventy cents in my pocket. Maybe I could talk Vinnie into stumping up a year's worth of free kebabs as a reward for information on Xavier.

Actually . . .

I stand, mind buzzing. "I've got to go."

"Hold up," says Vinnie. "We haven't finished."

I don't stop. I can't. I've just had the brain wave of the century. "I'm late. I've got to meet Cara."

"What did I just tell you? Pull. Your. Finger. Out. Not go hang out with Cara."

"Exactly! She's going to tutor me. In maths. You know I suck at number things. Ask me what five plus five equals."

"Frankie—"

"Eleven."

"It's the middle of the day, Frankie. Cara's in school."

"She's got a free period." I stumble as my foot catches the

leg of a chair. Can't believe I didn't already think of this. Who says you never learn anything from TV?

"Really?" says Vinnie. "So if I call the school—?"

"I wouldn't trust Square-Tits; she's high on Wite-Out."

Vinnie jabs her cigarette at me. "Keep away from that school, Frankie. You're on suspension."

"I'm not meeting Cara there. I'm not stupid."

I blow her a kiss. She catches it.

"I'm not so sure about that," she mutters, stuffing my kiss into her fake Chanel handbag. "You're a Vega, after all."

Seventeen

I arrive while classes are running so I don't have to dodge teachers in the yard, but it also means the computer labs are in use so I have to wait for lunchtime to put phase one of Operation Find Xavier into place. We've got a computer at the Emporium but no printer. Besides, like everything in that place, it was cutting-edge around the time Jesus was marveling at the technology behind sandal making.

I check my phone but Cara hasn't returned my text. She's obeying the stupid no-phones-in-class rule.

I loiter near the bike racks. From there I only have to duck between the garden shed and the art block before I'm at the back entrance to the computer labs, where Cara can sneak me in. It also means that when the bell rings, the only students I'll have to dodge are the smokers—most of whom are too

cool, too stupid, or too preoccupied with gang warfare to notice me.

Everything's coming up Frankie.

I sit on the damp concrete and press my back against the
shed.

My coat is still wet from the weekend's rain. It wraps around
me, heavy and damp like Nonna Sofia's hugs. Vinnie always
warns me not to say anything about the wet spots on Nonna's
trousers when we go to sit with her at Peaceful Pines. "That'll
be you one day," she says. You first, Vinnie.

I send a text telling Cara where I am and sit back to enjoy
the little bit of sun that's poking through the clouds. My eyes
get all droopy and my head keeps rolling forward—I guess that
whole only getting a few hours' sleep thing is about to catch up
with me. With no other choice than to wait, there's not much I
can do but sit, daydream, and . . .

"—think she's doing here?"

"I heard she got kicked out cos she killed Vukovic's cat in a
Satanic ritual."

"Didn't she head-butt Steve?"

"Yeah, but it was the cat thing that got her expelled."

Crap. How did I fall asleep?

I keep my eyes closed and wait as my mind slowly claws its
way back to consciousness. The cold pricks my skin; the sun has
buggered off completely. I can hear laughter, screams, conver-
sations about who did what to whom and when, but most of all
I can hear the voices of the two worst people ever. And they
sound like they're standing on top of me.

The first voice is the unmistakable twang of Ava Devar, Queen Bitch. "Where *is* Mark? He told me he'd be here straight after class."

"Ew, she drooled." And that, with its breathless splutter, is the voice of Elizabeth Something. Her surname isn't Something; it's just that I have no idea what it is. She's a sidekick—like anyone needs to know that level of detail about her.

"I can't believe she'd show her face here," says Ava, and I can visualize her signature hair-flick as she says it.

"I kind of feel sorry for her," says Elizabeth. "Her mum's a total deadbeat."

It's funny how you hear things better when your eyes are closed. Like the nervous shiver in Elizabeth's voice, as if every sentence is a question waiting to be approved.

Ava clicks her tongue. "Please. My dad's got shingles but you don't see me using that as an excuse to beat people up."

"Screw this." I open my eyes and scurry to standing.

Elizabeth slams against the bike shed with a squeal. Ava flicks her hair over her shoulder and scowls at me.

"I tried to sit it out but your lack of imagination is making me want to slit my wrists. I mean, come on, Satanic rituals? Can't you come up with anything new? You've been running with that since Year Seven."

"What are you even doing here, Freakie?" says Ava. "Didn't they kick you out?"

"I'd love to stop and chat but I—"

"Frankie!" Cara comes running to my side. She swings me round, hanging off my arm. "Sorry, babe, I got held back for talking in class. I didn't even say anything. Oh." She spots Ava and Elizabeth and looks down her nose at them, which is an impressive thing for a girl her height to do. "Hope we're not interrupting your trade here, ladies."

Ava smiles. "It's totally cool. Freakie was just about to give us some tips. She picked up a lot from her mum, you know."

Cara pushes in front of me before I can even open my mouth. "Please," she says. "What you don't know about being a slut could be written on Mark's puny cock." She wiggles her pinkie for emphasis.

Ava looks about ready to tear Cara's face off but then her gaze shifts over our shoulders and she smiles wickedly. Whatever she sees there has to be bad. Like, Vukovic bad.

Cara and I slowly turn around.

Shit. It's worse.

"Frankie?" Mark's step falters and his eyes grow wide with panic. Maybe it's because he's stumbled upon his ex-girlfriend talking to his current girlfriend.

"She was just leaving." Ava pushes past me to grab Mark. Her hand clamps around his forearm in the international sign for *Back off, bitch, he's mine.*

Mark frowns at the claw. "Did Vukovic let you back, Frankie?"

"I'm not even here." I grab Cara and yank her toward the computer block. "Got a Satanic orgy to plan. You still up for it, Mark?"

Mark's caught between a smile and some serious blushing. I'm surprised he isn't grimacing; Ava's nails are digging in. "Maybe next time," he says, but the corner of his mouth lifts.

"Pity," I say. "Satan loves meeting new people." He watches me pass, a full head turn.

Cara wiggles her pinkie under his nose.

"That supposed to mean something?" says Mark.

"Bye, Freakie," says Ava. She's got both claws attached to his arm now. "Thanks for the tips."

I give Ava my best weather-girl smile. "No probs. Only don't bother trying them out on Mark. I've been there, done that."

The look on her face is a small victory.

Course, the joke's really on me since my allegedly loving boyfriend cheated on me with the biggest bitch in the entire school behind the science block in Year Eleven.

Cara drags me toward the computer labs. "Weren't we supposed to be sneaking you in? Keeping a low profile?"

I throw a glance over my shoulder at Mark; he's still grinning at me. I ignore the heat that brings to my cheeks and link an arm through Cara's. "You can't expect me to go anywhere without causing a riot, can you?"

For the entire first day of Year Seven, Ava Devar and I were best friends. Neither of us had been to primary school with any of the other girls in the grade, so we sat next to each other in the first class because all the other chairs were taken. The other girls whispered and giggled and turned their backs on us.

At recess she cried behind the bike shed.

"I hate this place," she said. "I want to go back to my old school. My old friends. I was popular."

I put my arm around her because I didn't know what else to do. She left wet patches on my shirt from her tears—a little mask of dripping-wet despair. She clung to my side for the rest of the day.

The next morning in homeroom, Ava was huddled in the

corner with Elizabeth What's Her Face. I walked in and the two girls looked at me and then caved into each other, laughing.

That's all it took.

I sat on the other side of the room and stared at the board so I didn't have to see them whispering and pointing and laughing.

"She doesn't even have any friends," said Ava.

"What a loser," said Elizabeth.

A couple of days later I met Cara in the office and she saved me from five years of hell. But Ava never stopped trying to destroy me. Spreading rumors, riling up Steve to say things in class, stealing my boyfriend, tagging my locker with *freak*, *slut*, and *witch*, orchestrating an online hate campaign to outdo them all. I guess she hates me because I'm the only one who knows she's as fucked-up and lonely as the rest of us.

So what I'm asking myself is: Is it worth it? Fighting to stay at this school? This school where Ava Devar reigns supreme and Steve Sparrow is the comic relief? I used to lie in bed at night and make believe I had to move schools. Like Vinnie and I suddenly had to up and leave—to Queensland, maybe—and I could start over again. I'd walk into that new classroom for the first time like a Victoria's Secret model. Confidence, grace, the hint of a smile—but aloof, like I didn't care whether anybody liked me. And no one would know a thing about me.

Nothing.

Before Cara and I put my awesome brain wave into action, we google. Which is a good idea in principle but turns out to be a total waste of time. The problem is we just don't have any information to begin with. Turns out googling "half brothers called Xavier who show up out of the blue and then vanish" gives up nothing but useless blogs and, strangely enough, a Korean porn site.

"Give me his dad's address again." Cara holds out her hand, her fingernails chewed to the quick. She flicks her fingers. "Gimme, gimme, gimme."

I hand her Bill Green's address. "I think he's a mechanic," I say, and she enters "Bill Green" and "mechanic," but nothing helpful pops up. "Maybe he's an electrician."

"It's too generic," says Cara. "There's hundreds of Bill Greens. That guy there is a professor of basket weaving." She points to a photo of a small, rat-faced man with John Lennon glasses; so not the Bill Green I met.

"There's no such thing as a professor of basket weaving."

"Tell that to Professor Bill Green of New Mexico."

"So why don't we google Nate?"

Cara looks at me. For a second I think I must have farted.

"*You* google your boyfriend," she says. She puckers her lips and makes kissing noises at me. "And then tell me again how blue his eyes were."

"Gross," I say. "I wouldn't touch that with a disinfected barge pole."

There's no way I'm telling her about the other night outside the house now. Besides, there's no point. I probably won't ever see Nate again.

"I only told you about his eyes because they're freakishly blue. Other than that, he's a lying arsehole."

"Just your type."

"Not my boyfriend."

"Mark will be devastated."

"Not my boyfriend either. I'm just saying, finding out stuff about him might . . . oh, forget it."

She laughs. Maniacally. But then Cara doesn't know how to laugh any other way.

I fold my arms across my chest. "Are we making Missing posters or what?"

That's my genius idea: "Have You Seen My Missing Brother?" posters.

As much as I hate to admit it, the police probably know a thing or two about finding a missing person, so why don't I do what they're doing for Harrison Finnik-Hyde?

I don't have a spare dummy lying around or a caravan, but how hard can a Missing Person poster be?

"I'm not saying we shouldn't, but remind me why we're going to all this trouble for your drop-kick brother?" asks Cara.

She watches me while I think about it. I'm not exactly sure what the answer is but I think it might have something to do with a grinning angel.

"You know how you look at Pete Doherty and it's like, 'Ew, gross, take a bath and quit smoking crack, you crusty punk,' but then you listen to his music and you're all, 'Oh my god, this man is a lyrical genius, I'm all melted joy right now and I totally love him and forgive him for being so icky'? It's like that."

Cara gives a less than perfect brow raise. "If I knew who Pete Doherty was I'm sure I'd understand you perfectly."

"How are we even friends?"

Some little shit in oversize shorts taps on the clear paneling in the classroom door. When I look up he's cupping his testicles and licking the glass.

Yet another reason to fight tooth and nail to come back to this glorious place.

Cara doesn't even look. She's completely immune to the grossness of Year Seven boys because she lives with two of them—twins. She enters "burglar" and "Nate" into the search engine.

I push her hands out of the way and type "Wishaw" for his surname. She side-eyes me and my damn stupid face decides to betray me by blushing.

"You didn't really tell me what happened between you two last night," she says as I scan the results—random news stories, crime stats, and "hilarious" videos of "the world's dumbest criminals," but no Nate Wishaw.

She pokes my knee. "You were alone with him. On a dark street, late at night . . ." She lets her sentence hang. For all I care she can let it hang until its neck is broken. "Well?"

The kid at the door has a few mates with him now, all pushing each other out of the way to press themselves up against the glass. I'd forgotten just how annoying boys are. Like Nate. He's annoying. And confusing. Contradictory. Impossible to work out.

I glance at the clock above the teacher's desk. I've got fifteen minutes before I need to get my arse out of here. If a teacher catches me on school property when I'm suspended, I'm toast.

I bump her knee. "Missing posters?"

She leans back with a sigh. "You're so lame."

"Posters are a good idea."

"Not that. What's lame is you not giving me any goss." A loud tap on the glass gets Cara's attention and I can see one of the Year Sevens actually is her brother. She gives him the finger. "Whatever. You have the picture?"

I grab my phone and scroll through the gallery until I find my one and only picture of Xavier.

I let Cara take charge. I just point at the screen and give orders. She hogs the mouse and glares at me. A lot.

When we're done and the posters are printing, I stretch out the cricks in my neck. The bell is obviously about to go because more and more giggling Year Sevens are gathering outside the door.

"I'll perform a 'print faster' dance," says Cara.

She gets up and starts wiggling her hips and waving her arms in the air. "Oh, print gods," she says, "please make this brick of a machine go faster."

She makes me laugh so hard I don't even notice Mr. Tran has entered the room until he switches on the lights.

"Ms. Lam? You're not in my Year Seven class, are you?" He drops his books on the desk. "I know I only gave you a B-plus last year, but surely things aren't so bad that you have to repeat Year Seven English." His smirk falters when he spots me skulking in the corner I'd jumped into the second he'd walked in. He does an actual double-take. "Francesca?"

I stare at him; I can't even open my mouth.

"No," says Cara. "It's Frankie's twin." Her voice is so sweet and innocent I almost believe her myself. If I have a long-lost half brother there's no telling how many sisters I have. "They look so much alike, don't they?"

As much as Mr. Tran is a pompous old fart who loves the sound of his own voice, he's also pretty good at communicating his feelings with a single sardonic look. Like the one he gives Cara this second.

Cara shrugs. "Worth a try."

"If I leave now we can just forget this ever happened, right?" I say.

I can see him weighing up his options. Along with his regular teaching job he's also the Year Nine coordinator and was witness to one of the very few times I've ever let anyone see me cry. Steve Sparrow had stuck his hand up in Sex Ed and suggested to the stuttering, blushing Mr. Drysdale that Frankie Vega could take over the class since her mother was a—

Steve didn't get to finish because my pencil case found its way across the room and into his face.

I got two days' suspension and Vinnie marched down to the school with steam coming out of her ears. She stormed into the office and I could hear her going toe-to-toe with Vukovic while Mr. Tran sat with me in the corridor. He didn't say a word, he just sat there, arm around me while I cried. Not because of Steve. Because Vinnie was still going in to bat for me even after everything I'd put her through. Because she was still on my side.

Mr. Tran nods his head in the direction of the back door without a word and Cara and I grab our stuff and run.

"You're heading straight to fifth period, aren't you, Cara?" he says.

"*Absolument*," Cara calls over her shoulder as I push her out the door.

We're a tangle of giggling, wide-eyed, disbelieving girls as we tumble into fresh air and land with a clang against the bike-shed wall.

"Holy shit that was close," says Cara. The second bell sounds.

"You're going to be late," I tell her.

A wicked smile crosses her lips. "So why don't I just not turn up at all?"

"No way. I'm not here to get you expelled too."

She waves the posters under my nose. "But these aren't going to get stuck up on their own, now, are they?" She grabs my arm. "We're in this together, Frankie babe," she says. "Besides, you can't stop me."

Ain't that the truth.

Eighteen

"Do you think it's smart to post your number all over town?" asks Cara. She holds a poster to the telephone pole. I wrap the sticky tape around it several times.

"I told you, you don't have to help." I break off the tape with my teeth.

"I'm just worried about all the phone calls you're going to get. Middle of the night, heavy breathing. 'I've found your brother. Come and get him—he's in my pants.'"

"We'll be lucky if anyone even notices these."

It's been next to impossible to find a wall, a pole, a shopfront, or a fence that isn't already wallpapered with flyers for yoga, sex lines, shitty bands playing in shitty pubs, and rooms for rent. There's a constant visual noise in this place. Everything shouts to be heard—the people, the posters, the traffic, the sirens.

I shove the posters under my coat to keep them from getting wet as we walk through the drizzle.

"Do you think it'll work?" Cara has already asked me this. Three times.

"Better than doing nothing." I grab her arm to stop her. "Here."

There's a large fence cordoning off a construction site. Under the tagline *Your dream starts here* is an image. It's a dreamy landscape of children playing in a garden, a four-story apartment block in the background—it's got that eco-friendly Scandinavian look. The kids are perfect and their parents are too. They're talking and smiling and they've got white skin and are wearing pastels. Idyllic. The drug dealers are just out of frame.

Cara and I peek between the cracks in the boards; they've dug way down so I guess the place is getting underground parking. Maybe a gym.

Someone's sprayed *Open season on yuppies* right above the tagline, but there aren't many posters on the fence yet so I vote it's a good spot. I unzip my coat and hand Cara a poster. I put the rest between my knees to free my hands while I pick at the sticky tape, trying to find the end of the roll.

"Why did we cut you out of this photo?" asks Cara.

"I'm not the one who's missing."

Cara holds the poster to the fence while I pull off long strips of tape and paste it down.

Have you seen Xavier Green? Cara and I couldn't think what else to write; it annoyed me that it rhymed.

"Done."

I stand back to admire my work. Maybe putting up posters

could be my future career. It's probably not what Vinnie had in mind for me, but I think I'm pretty damn good at it.

Cara links her arm through my mine and we keep walking.

"So here's the question," she says. "Do I go back for sixth period or just hang out—"

"Holy shit." I dive behind a bin, dragging Cara with me.

"What the hell?" Cara shakes out of my grip. "I won't skip sixth, then."

I grab both her hands. "Don't make a big deal, okay?"

Her eyes grow wide. "What?"

I peek round the side of the bin to check that he's still there.

And when I say peek, I mean turn my head, because I'm pretty much already completely exposed—this bin's not wide enough to camouflage us both.

"Nate's across the street."

Cara's eyes are so wide they're about to pop out of her head. She's grinning like a madwoman. "Where?"

I pull her to my side. "See the punk poseur walking like he owns the universe?"

Cara breathes in my ear. "I see a bag lady, a hipster, a dude eating a pie, another hipster, and, oh—is that him? The tall guy in the skinny jeans who just got off the catwalk? He's hot."

I screw up my nose. "Are you looking at the right guy?"

Cara laughs. She's definitely got her hot-guy face on—big eyes, flushed cheeks, biting her bottom lip.

I try looking at Nate like I don't already know who he is. Like if I had the pleasure of just looking at him from afar, where he can't open his mouth and ruin the illusion.

He's wearing the Jacket again today and a dark maroon shirt, buttoned all the way up. He walks down the opposite side of the street, moving pretty fast, weaving between people. Bumping lots of shoulders and earning glares and "oi"s.

Cara squeezes my hand. "We're following him, right?"

My heart's beating fast. Adrenaline. "I don't know . . ."

"For research purposes."

I chew my lip. "For Xavier."

Cara nods sagely. "Of course."

We're lucky Nate is focused on wherever he's going because Cara and I are shit at spying. We keep getting too close, then too far away, then tripping over each other. Cara giggles and I shush her. Loudly.

"This is way better than Biology," says Cara. We hang behind a mailbox and watch Nate hurrying down the street.

I catch my breath. "Where's he going?"

"Ten bucks he's going to a drug deal," says Cara.

"Ten bucks he's going to rob someone."

Cara shakes my hand. "You're on. Now keep walking. We're going to lose him."

At the next corner we pause and peek around.

He's crossed the road, hurrying toward large wrought-iron gates. They're really ornate, flowers and vines weaving through each other.

We're on a kind of industrial street so I'm starting to worry that Cara was right. And I don't have ten bucks to lose.

When he disappears through the gates, Cara and I grab hands and hurry across the road. We duck behind the brick gateposts and wait. Cara's crouched behind me; I can feel her holding on to the back of my jacket.

"Where is he?" she whispers.

I haven't had the courage to look yet, just in case he's right on the other side of the gate.

Now *that* would be embarrassing. Not sure even Frankie Vega could talk her way out of that. *Oh, hi, Nate! Fancy seeing you here. What, me? No, I'm not following you. I have an interest in local history and this building is actually the site of a particularly fascinating—no, I'm not buying it either.*

I shuffle—which is really hard to do when you're crouched—until I get to the edge of the gatepost and then it hits me: What if he's meeting Xavier?

If I thought my heart was racing before, I had *no* idea. There's a rave going on in my chest now: *doof, doof, doof, doof.* A million beats per second.

If he *is* meeting Xavier, what the hell am I going to do? Hug the little prick or slap him? No time to debate—just look.

I peek round the corner. "Holy shit."

"What is it?"

"Well, it's not Xavier."

Nate disappears through the glass front doors of what's actually a pretty modern building, despite the ancient-looking gates. It's all aqua glass, white rendering, and lots of curves.

Cara peers over the top of my head, like she's frozen mid-leapfrog. "The Tate McClelland Hospice? They put my granddad in one when he had cancer. The only way you come out again is feetfirst."

Well, that sucked all the fun out of our little adventure. No one told my heart, though—the *doof, doof* in my chest is still pounding.

We stay crouched.

"Do you think he's visiting someone?" I ask.

"I'm sure he volunteers," says Cara. "He gives the old biddies sponge baths and reads erotic novels to them."

"Not funny."

"Please," she says. "You know he's there to steal drugs. Or buy them. My cousin got sacked from an old folks' home because she was stealing the dementia patients' meds and selling them to ravers."

She stands, pulling me to my feet. I look over my shoulder but the glass doors stay shut.

"Let's just go eat churros," says Cara. She's trying to pull me away from the gate, but I'm not budging. "Spying is really hungry work."

"But shouldn't we wait and see what happens when he comes out?"

She rolls her eyes. "I can tell you that without waiting. He'll have a pocket full of drugs. Which means two things. One: he's a dickhead, and two: you owe me ten bucks' worth of churros."

I whack her arm.

"I skipped school for you," she says. "Don't be a Bitchy McBitch."

A car zooms past, splashing water on us. We both stick up our fingers.

"C'mon," she says. "Xavier's not here, so what are we hanging around for?"

Good question.

She tugs me along the street. I'm a deadweight, looking back at the hospice while she drags me toward doughnuts.

I wonder if the Tate McClelland Hospice is anything like Peaceful Pines, where Nonna Sofia is. I hate that place. It stinks of pee, and the people there scare me. I know it's not their fault and one day it'll be me sitting there wondering what day it is, but it freaks me out. There's this guy who's always in the shared lounge. It's like his skin is melting—it droops, as if it's already on its way out, detaching from the rest of his body because it knows death is so close. Nonna's not so bad. She asks us every time when we're going to take her home and it always makes Vinnie cry. "Why do you go there if it makes you cry?" I ask her. She never answers.

Cara and I are arguing about whose shout it is when it starts raining. We run, Cara squealing about her hair getting wet.

At the corner of Johnston Street I stop.

"Come on," she shouts. She's got her jacket lifted over her head.

On the traffic light is the first poster we stuck up. It's been maybe an hour. Maybe two. Someone has drawn all over it in black marker. Xavier's got a cock and balls on his face, devil horns, and a Hitler moustache. The rain is making the ink run. You can't read my phone number anymore.

Cara grabs my arm. "Hurry up."

I let her drag me away but I've lost my appetite.

Nineteen

I sort my clothes into piles: keep, donate, burn.

Most things end up in the keep pile even though it's all stuff I'd forgotten I owned. I try on pretty much everything, struggling to remember why I bought it and convincing myself it really does look good. Who wouldn't want an oversize sweater with a giant middle finger on the front? And those acid-wash boyfriend jeans are so going to come back in style. In the background, Elliott Smith sings about love and misery in his whispery, broken-hearted voice: a mournful soundtrack for a mournful mood.

"How's it going?" asks Vinnie, pushing the door open and peeking in. Her curls are kind of messy today.

My stack of "keep" clothes has tumbled and is blocking the door. I scoop the pile out of the way.

"What the hell are you wearing?" she says. She pushes in farther and blinks at me. "You're wearing a dress."

I look down at myself: it's blue, floral, kind of tight, and with a sweetheart neckline. "Yeah. It's going into the donate pile."

"Looks pretty on you."

"Then it's definitely going."

I catch a T-shirt I want to ditch trying to sneak back into the keep pile, so I separate the stacks.

"Not that I'm complaining," says Vinnie, "but what brought on this little cleaning spree?"

I unzip the dress and pull it over my head, dropping it on top of the donate pile. "Just thought it was time."

Vinnie raps her long nails against the door frame. "It's Friday," she says.

I hold up a pair of black jeans. There's a rip in the knee of one leg that almost goes the whole way round. I drop it in the keep pile.

She's trying to look casual. Failing. "Guessing you've caught up on all your schoolwork?"

"Yep."

"So what are you doing tonight?"

"Working."

"After work?"

"Grounded."

"So you're actually planning on sticking to the rules?"

"Of course."

"Cara not doing anything?"

"She's grounded too."

"Ha! What she do? Get an A-minus?"

"Talking in class. Her third detention this month. I want to ask her mum if she still thinks *I'm* the bad influence."

Vinnie eases onto her knees and starts sorting through the donate pile. "This is so pretty." She's holding a pink skirt Nonna bought me a few Christmases ago. 'Nuff said. "You're keeping this, aren't you?"

I grab it out of her hands and dump it on the burn pile.

She sighs. She's not wearing makeup for once. "How about What's His Face? I'm guessing you plan on seeing him again?"

Hey, Xavier has graduated from God Knows Who to What's His Face. That's a big step up.

"I haven't heard from him." All too true. And all I can do right now is wait for my genius poster idea to take effect. I expected the phone to ring straightaway—even if it was just the crazies. But nothing. Not for two whole days. Which has given me plenty of time to go searching for more pieces signed by X Marks. Nothing better to do with my time. I've found five, including the purple-skinned girl and bird-flipping angel. The angel piece was even cooler in the daylight, with a multicolored geometric background and a creepy all-seeing eye just above her head.

Vinnie's folding the clothes in my donate pile but she's watching me.

I grip a T-shirt in my hand. It's faded black, holes all through it, but it's one of my favorites. "What if . . ."

I drop the tee into the keep pile and grab another black one and pull it on. I guess I have a style.

"What if what?" asks Vinnie.

I try sorting through my words in my head—keep, donate, burn. It takes me a while but Vinnie just waits.

"What if someone you knew might have done something bad," I say. "And maybe they weren't answering their phone and no one knew where they were. Would you worry about that?"

Vinnie watches me with her forehead all crinkled. "Maybe," she says, speaking slow and careful. "Maybe they don't want to be found. Maybe someone like that—someone who does bad things—is better out of your life."

"I'm speaking hypothetically," I say.

She nods. "Of course."

"And I don't mean bad like murder or anything. I mean maybe he's a bit misguided. Like, he doesn't have a clear sense of right and wrong. Because no one taught him." I think about Bill Green. What kind of dad would he be? Would he have marched Xavier all the way to school and made him apologize to the girl whose lunch he buried in the sandbox because she used his pencil without asking first? I look at Vinnie. "What if part of the problem is the guy just wanted to do something nice so that I—so that people would think he was good?"

Vinnie grips my hand and squeezes. "Whoever he is, I'm sure he'll show up eventually. And if he doesn't? His loss."

She smiles and I think about asking her the biggest what-if in my head. What if he can't show up? What if . . .

I reach for the sweetheart dress, saving it from certain death by plopping it on top of the keep pile. "Don't say I never listen to you."

She gives me a lopsided grin and pats my cheek, hoisting herself to standing. "That's my girl. You just focus on what you're going to say at that meeting and everything else will sort itself out."

I nod. I own a blue, floral, too-tight dress with a sweetheart neckline—what can go wrong?

———

Vinnie heads downstairs to open the shop and I grab my cell, scrolling through the list of numbers until I hit the one I think is Marzoli's. So much for burying his business card in bin juice.

I stare out the window while I wait for him to answer: rooftops are my rolling hills and chimneys are my towering trees. What if, what if, what if.

Marzoli answers on the fifth ring by barking his name.

"It's Frankie Vega." My words are all hacked up with uncertainty—I am, after all, calling a cop for help. Again.

Wherever Marzoli is, there's a lot of traffic. "Speak up," he says, voice crackling.

I shout-whisper my name, conscious of Vinnie downstairs. Conscious of my shift starting five minutes ago.

There's a long pause and I wonder if he's dropped out. I can hear him breathing, though.

"Can you hear me?"

"Just wait," he says. In a couple of seconds the traffic noises stop and Marzoli's heavy breathing subsides. "All right. Talk."

"My brother. Do you have any news?"

"I'll be there in a second, Peters," shouts Marzoli, not holding the phone far enough away from his face when he does. "Look, I'm busy here," he says, talking to me again.

"Any news?"

"No. Do you have any information for me?"

"I haven't seen anything about Xavier in the papers. Harrison Finnik-Hyde was booted to page six today, but it was still an entire page more than my brother had."

Marzoli holds the phone too close to his mouth, muffling his voice. "Do you know how many people go missing each day? They can't all get a front page."

"Just the pretty ones. And the rich ones. Are you even looking into it?"

"Of course I am but I've got another burglary here, Frankie. I'm up to my neck in this."

It sounds like a door opens—the traffic noise increases, then stops. Some guy starts yapping away to Marzoli.

"I've got to go," he says. "I'll call you if anything comes up, all right?"

I don't get a chance to tell him I don't believe him. I don't get to tell him to go to hell because he hangs up.

Buttons meows from down the corridor, high-pitched and accusing, and for once I agree with him. *You're an idiot, Frankie Vega.*

I go through my call log and delete the whole conversation. Like it never happened.

If only my brain was more like my phone. It would be nice to be able to touch a screen and have all my unwanted memories dragged to the trash, deleted forever. Xavier's disappearance? Straight to the garbage. Steve Sparrow? A three-point shot for the bin. Juliet? "Are you sure you want to permanently erase items in Trash (you can't undo this action)?" Yep.

Buttons meows again. He probably wants to be fed but that's not my job.

My job is downstairs, making kebabs.

My job is forgetting about Xavier, focusing on The Meeting, getting into uni, and marrying a fat, bald rich guy who'll never cheat on me.

My job sucks.

Twenty

The third time I break a glass, Vinnie points to the back stairs. "Get out of here, you clumsy clod. You'll do me out of business. It's late anyway. You may as well."

It's a wonder Vinnie didn't chuck me out ages ago. Along with murdering three glasses, I've stuffed up five orders and sworn at four dickhead uni students.

Vinnie *tsks* me. "Just go to bed. You look like Marianne Faithfull after she's been dragged backward through a wood chipper."

"Insults don't work if you have to google them."

Vinnie's Propane Passion lips curl into a snarl as she thumbs at the back door. "Get."

If I had a death wish I'd poke out my tongue, but I don't, so I nod obediently and scoop up the broken shards with the brush and spade conveniently stashed under the counter from the past two incidents. I'm happy to have scored early release—I just wish it was for good behavior.

As I head out back, some old guy gives me a garlicky salute as I pass. Guess I didn't stuff up his order.

When I'm through the back door it bashes into my arse as I pause in the space between the Emporium and the staircase: I'm one set of stairs, fifteen steps, two corridors, and three doors away from sleep. And the closer I get to bed, the more like a sloth zombie I feel. Can't. Wait. For. Sleeeeeeeep.

When I let myself into the flat, Buttons trots up and meows at me for the whole three seconds it takes him to realize I'm not Vinnie. I glare at him until I realize he's pillow shaped and fluffy and could come in handy if I decide to collapse right here, right now. He trots away, tail lifted so I get the full arse view.

It's like you *want* me to hate you, you fuzzy little turd.

I drag my feet to my room and go through the whole getting-ready-for-bed routine in a sloppy fashion. I crawl under my comforter, excited about all the awesome sleep I'm about to score.

And then . . .

Bam!

I'm toothpicks-propping-my-eyes-open awake. Long-haul-truck-drivers-high-on-speed awake.

It's like someone force-fed a chipmunk a shitload of speed and said, "Hey, want to be in charge of this girl's brain?" And the chipmunk was all like, "Hells yeah," and started cranking out all my worries in one big chaotic mess.

Where the hell is Xavier?

Is Vinnie going to hate me if I get expelled?

How come no one's phoned up about my awesome Missing posters?

Did Xavier get sick of me? Is that why he skipped out? Or has something happened to him?

What the hell was Nate doing at the Tate McClelland Hospice?

How has Marzoli kept his job this long?

What is the actual point of guinea pigs?

I punch my pillow into shape and try about fifty different positions. I scrunch my eyes shut and let Jeff Buckley serenade me through my earphones. But now that chipmunk is speeding down memory lane and panic floods through me in hot, shivery waves.

I get up and furiously pace the apartment, freaking out Buttons.

When will Vinnie be done? Was that a noise in my room?

Is Xavier throwing rocks again?

Shit—was that English essay due today?

I flip on the TV and for the five minutes I get to watch an eighties cop show I feel slightly better, but then it ends and there's a newsbreak—wars, bushfires, politicians in bitch-fights, and Harrison "I like to hog all the news" Finnik-Hyde. Still missing. Still rich and brilliant at violin. His friends have been called back in for "questioning." They shuffle past the cameras with their pressed shirts, combed hair, and furtive glances. They look so guilty I want to throw the remote at the telly. I throw a cushion at Buttons instead.

After a few minutes of Zen-breathing I grab my phone and call Cara.

She answers, mouth full. "Yup."

"What do you do when you can't sleep?"

"Get shit-faced and throw marshmallows at the neighbor's cat."

I look at Buttons—well, I look at his tail because it's the only part I can see on account of his having sought refuge behind the armchair. We have vodka, but do we have marshmallows?

"What's up?" she says. I think she's eating chips—whatever it is, it sounds crinkly and crackly. "Can't decide which non-boyfriend to have a sex dream about?"

I don't even have a comeback—just a sigh—so Cara flips straight into business mode. "Right. You're coming over here. Now."

"Faye's going to love me fronting up at this hour."

"Then I'm sneaking out—we're *both* sneaking out—and we'll go to Dights Falls and we can throw marshmallows at the ducks."

I pick at the hem of my top, a New Order T-shirt that I've had since it was more like a dress. "Don't know. Seems like a waste of marshmallow."

In truth, I'm not really worried about the marshmallows—they taste like fairy poo.

It's Vinnie.

It's always Vinnie.

It's always me disappointing Vinnie.

And when I think about Xavier and his epic slide from "Hey, awesome, I got a cool new brother" to "Shit, my brother is a thieving arsehat," I realize we've got another thing in common: we were both born to disappoint. The only difference is, Vinnie didn't want anything to do with Xavier. She knew he was trouble just like she knew the same about me. But she took me in. I was the *only* one she let in and here I am about to . . .

Great. Something else to keep me awake at night.

"Do you think people are born bad?" I ask.

"Jeez, you really are in the shit."

"You study bio, right? Is there a bad gene? If you put Xavier's and Juliet's blood under a microscope, would you find a teensy little black-clad gene smoking a cigar, stroking a cat, and talking in a German accent?"

"First: Why are movie villains always German? Either German or Korean. That's legit racist. Second: Meet. Me. At. Dights. Falls. Now. We'll swear at the ducks. We'll call them fat-lips and beady-eyed mermaid rats and give them a complex about their fat duck arses."

I splutter a laugh but I'm grimacing too because I really should say no. I should hang up, count sheep, and just get over myself. Sneaking out and getting drunk is the Wrong Thing. I *know* this.

I know it in the same way I know churros are 99 percent fat and will go straight to my thighs via my arteries.

And yet . . .

"You win," I say, and Cara squeals. I imagine chip crumbs flying out her mouth.

"This is so awesome. We haven't done this in forever. I'll get the marshmallows, you bring the booze, and we'll—"

"Wait. How is that my job?"

"Because your place is practically a bottle shop. Don't think I don't know about Vinnie's stash."

Shit.

I mean, really.

I mean, for flip's sake.

I've got to feel guilty about sneaking out *and* stealing from Vinnie?

"She'll *know* if something's missing. She'll sense a distur- bance in the force."

"She'll get over it. She'll be like, 'Whatever, at least it's not another broken nose I've got to pay for.'"

"Have you met Vinnie?"

"Point is, my mum's going through this green-juice-yoga-quinoa phase so she even poured the cooking sherry down the sink and I don't have money and I don't have a fake ID so we're, like, actually being forced to do this."

My head rolls back, eyes locking on the cobwebs clinging to the ceiling, and the whole thing—the enormity of it all—whooshes through me. I can't sleep. I can't quiet my head. I can't not *be* me. I can't shift that speed-freak chipmunk out of my brain—he likes it there. He's talking about moving in. I can't find my brother. I can't. Can't. Can't. Can't.

"Fine. I'll score us booze. But I'm not happy about it."

There's another chip-spitting squeal as Cara celebrates down the end of the line.

"Meet you at the falls in thirty minutes," I tell her.

When I hang up I catch Buttons giving me dirty looks. He has no idea how close he came to being a marshmallow bull's-eye so what's he being all pissy about?

"I can't tell the difference between your arse and your face," I tell him, but he just flicks his tail at me.

I sneak into Vinnie's room, looking over my shoulder the whole time. There's no telling what time she'll close up—it depends on how many drunks are craving kebabs.

Under Vinnie's bed is a pirate's treasure cave. If that pirate's idea of treasure is booze, bad romance fiction, and chocolate. I grab a little of each; the romance novel is so we can read passages out loud and play the euphemism drinking game—one shot for every throbbing member. That ought to keep that little chipmunk bastard at bay.

Before I leave the flat I shove a couple of pillows under my comforter in a humanoid shape—Vinnie hasn't checked in on me since I was ten but with my luck this will be the night. Plus, it's what they do in the movies, isn't it?

When I'm down at the bottom of the stairs I peek through the little window. Vinnie's chatting with a drunk and carving the meat. She's throwing her head back as she laughs, bottle-blond curls doing the happy dance. Good.

It takes maximum effort to shrug off the guilt as I push through the gate and into the alley.

Where it's cold.

The kind of cold that I really *could* write a book about.

I cut through side streets and alleys, power walking in an effort to stay warm.

There's a heap of people about. It's Friday, after all. Or Saturday now. My little pocket of Collingwood is bursting with late-night activity—some legitimate and some way south of legitimate. Up the other end of Smith Street, I'd be walking past organic cafés, tapas bars, and designer stores that charge my entire life savings for a shirt that looks like Buttons got to it first. Down this end, two-dollar shops, tattoo parlors, and an overflowing Salvos donation bin dominate the landscape.

The cold wind slaps me about—apparently it has views on me sneaking out too. Pity it can't do anything about the Xavier-shaped tumor forming in my head.

Sure, he has dimples, bought me dumplings, and went to shitloads of trouble trying to impress me. Sure, he's maybe the best graf artist in town. But he stole, lied, and vanished. A certain other blood relative did that to me fourteen years ago and I couldn't give a shit what's happened to her.

A group of boys whoop at me from across the street, offering to do things to me that boys like them don't know the first thing about. I'm tempted to tell them that. But rule number one when walking the streets at night is don't talk back to crazy. Or anything wearing a hoodie. I just walk away, leaving a chorus of laughter in my wake. I wonder if that's what Xavier's like. When he's with his mates.

When I reach the track that runs along the river, I'm not surprised to find actual fog settling over the water. The kind of fog that's besties with Jack the Ripper. There are lights along the path, tall silver posts that look like giant dentist drills and glow orange. The creepiest shade of orange you can imagine. My breath shoots out in little gray puffs as I hurry along the rambling path, a wide curve beside the Yarra, stretching all the way to Dights Falls.

A Cara-shaped shadow starts dancing about on top of the Old Turbine Mill when I get close.

"I've got M&Ms! Fucking ducks won't know what hit 'em!" The packet crackles as she waves it over her head.

I exhale. A tiny piece of awesome settles into place and I feel like I maybe have enough strength to get through whatever tonight's freak-out is.

I wave the bottle as I reach the top of the path, and she cheers.

This is the best idea ever.

Twenty-one

Drinking was a bad idea. Not like robbing a bank or unprotected sex, but it's up there.

My head aches. Not because of the chipmunk kung-fu-ing his way through my head—a few hefty swigs of vodka and excerpts from *Her Wildest Dreams* sorted that furry little bastard out. And it's not because I'm wasted. It's because Cara is. And getting her home when she can barely walk and when I'm not exactly at the top of my game is the opposite of fun.

I push Cara toward her front garden. Drag. Shove. Hold up.

"Never have I never," she slurs.

"Ever."

"What?"

"The game is Never Have I Ever."

She dongs my arm with the half-empty bottle. "That's what I said, dummy."

I tell her to keep her voice down, but she just cackles.

"Never have I never gone a week without showering." She takes a swig and drapes the bottle over her shoulder for me. If it's true, I should drink, but I wave it away and keep shoving her toward her house.

"Never have I ever used a wad of toilet paper as a pad when I've been caught short," I whisper.

"Amen to that." Cara takes another swig.

The side gate creaks—practically screams—as we stumble through. A prickly hedge hugs the fence and spills over half the path—you've got to walk at an angle to avoid losing an eye. There aren't any lights on but that doesn't mean Cara's mum isn't hiding in the shadows, waiting to jump out and lecture me about being a bad influence. Yeah, that's right, the one who's a teensy bit tipsy is the bad influence.

I dig my hands into her back and keep her moving. "Back door, okay?" She nods so vigorously I'm worried her head's going to fly off. It doesn't but it does bash into my chin.

"Oof."

"Never have I never had a sex dream about Mr. Tran." She waves the bottle at me.

"Do not drink to that."

Cara giggles as I push her to the back door. Thank god her older brother is allergic to dogs and there isn't a Doberman waiting to bark/bite/kill me. We stumble up the back step and then she spins to face me, overshoots, and almost falls backward.

"Whoa!" I steady her and then grab the bottle out of her hand. She grins.

"You know who's sexy? Mark. He *wuvs* you."

"He cheats. And I don't forgive, remember?"

"You're still looking for your brother and he's a burger."

I wave down her voice. "Burglar."

"What I said, dummy."

I dig through her pockets for her keys. "I have to find Xavier because . . ." Shit. Why do I need to find him? "I need to know the truth—"

"You can't handle the truth!"

"Shhhh! You'll wake your mum. And if you do, could you at least pin this one on Ava Devar?" I fish the keys out and unlock the door. Slowly. Quietly. Cara holds a finger to her lips and giggles.

Right before I shove her inside, she props herself up against me. For a minute I think she's trying to hug me but then I realize she's making a grab for the bottle. Sneaky wench.

I hold it out of her reach.

She frowns. "Did you say you had a burger? I'm starved."

I *can* handle the truth. I heart the truth.

I have to find Xavier because . . .

"Never have I ever trusted the wrong person," I say. I take a swig of vodka, then I shove Cara inside.

"Amen to that," she says.

Smith Street at night is straight out of the nightmares of every suburban housewife. I dump the vodka bottle/evidence in a bin and clomp past the blacked-out windows of an outlet shop where I have to dodge a scraggy-looking dude in an army jacket sliding a baggie into the hand of a bearded dude in mum jeans. Being tipsy, I'm not dexterous enough to dodge a puddle of vomit splattered on the pavement. As I hurry past pub after pub I accumulate drunken catcalls like a Hollywood starlet accumulates rehab stints.

Collingwood—it's a paradise.

I'm already in a mood. I've drowned the chipmunk in vodka but he's left behind a dead-rat kind of smell. And there's no more Cara to distract me.

So many questions, no freaking answers.

But what really pisses me off is that there are people who *know* things. People who are hiding important information from me.

Nate people, for instance.

Friends *always* know, and that punk poseur definitely knows more than he's letting on. I should get all black belt on his arse.

As I'm skirting around two guys punching on, a lightbulb pings in my head. I stop dead—a glass smashes on the pavement behind me.

I'm a freaking genius. I'm Sherlock Holmes meets Stephen Hawking.

Best. Idea. Ever.

I pirouette 180 degrees, skip over the glass, duck under the flailing dude's arms, and head back the way I came. I take the same path Nate led us down the other night, past the police station and past my brother's angel graffiti. I stop to ask the angel where Xavier is, but she's got nothing but that all-knowing grin. I wonder if she knows how much trouble I'll get in for defying my curfew again. I grip my stomach at the thought: Vinnie's *really* going to kill me this time. But there's something driving me on, something that even dark streets and unfamiliar sounds and thoughts of Vinnie's anger can't stop. So I keep going. And when

I find the creepy house, it's as dark and as crumbling and as cane-toad-like as I remember.

This is such a good idea that I laugh maniacally to myself for a whole minute.

Things I know: vodka is good for you, and Nate won't want to help. But I'm fairly certain he knows what the hell happened to Xavier.

Things I don't know: If Nate even lives here. How I'm going to find him. Why I'm not in bed dreaming of Ian Curtis. How I'm going to explain the missing vodka to Vinnie.

I stand on the opposite side of the street and watch. The house watches me back.

A shitload of bats screech overhead. Bats aren't always prophets of doom, right?

Screw that.

I cross the road and pretty soon the gravel driveway is crunching underfoot as I approach the rotting bungalow. I ignore the slight tilt to my gait and the fact that there could be someone inside waiting to kill me with a chain saw.

I take deep breaths before knocking on the front door.

Nothing happens. And I mean *nothing*. Even a chain saw revving would have been something.

I knock harder. Then I bash the stupid thing.

"Ouch."

Door: 1, Frankie: 0.

There's no movement inside, no lights, and no sign that anyone lives here. Maybe Nate was telling the truth when he said this wasn't his house. Maybe it's just a revolting crack den. My options are: bash the door again, stand here shouting Nate's name until he shows up, create some kind of bat-signal with my phone flashlight and hand puppets or . . .

I'll break into the creepy house.

I walk round the side where there's a path heading to the back garden. I say "walk" but "stumble" is a better word. "Hike," maybe. "Climb," definitely.

A little bit of moonlight kindly lights the way as I walk/hike/climb the side path. This is *such* a good idea.

I wade through thickets of grass, straddle fallen posts, and stub my toe on piles of unexplained bricks. I make a fair bit of noise and swear a lot too.

Which I guess explains why I'm so damn easy for the guy to find.

Out of the shadows comes an unexpected voice. "Who the fuck are you?"

I bash against the wall as I jump back, holding a hand over my heart so it can't break out of my rib cage. I see the shape of him approaching from the back end of the house. When he gets closer I see he's got a shock of white hair and blemished, scarred skin. He's wearing a large puffer jacket, one that goes all the way to the knees, and it swooshes as he moves.

"Holy crap, you scared me." My heart beats frantically to the tune of *bad idea, bad idea, bad idea* . . .

He taps his knuckles against his bottom lip. "You shouldn't be here. Who sent you?"

"I sent myself."

"Was it Lethal?"

I shake my head. Think I'm going to throw up.

He bangs his fist against the weatherboards. "I told him I'd sort it!"

I back away but he presses his hand against the house. His arm is beside my head like a boom gate locking me in. I get a faceful of his sewage-stench breath. "Give me your money, phone, rings, whatever." He presses in closer, eyes darting. "It's not personal, yeah? I just need the cash."

Holy shit. How do I tell *this* guy that I have zero money? The subtle vodka haze clouding my decision-making skills is clearing and I'm freaking out.

When I don't immediately pull thousands of dollars out of my pockets, he reaches into his jacket. Now there's a knife at my throat. I go very, very still.

Oh god, I don't want to die.

I hold out my phone. "Please let me go."

I'm weighing my options—cry, scream, or faint—when a set of heavy boots thumps toward us, coming in fast from the left.

I can't turn my head because of the knife, but the guy turns, eyes bulging. He presses in tight against me. "Back off!"

"Take it easy, Dave," says the voice of a burglarizing, arrogant arsehat. An arsehat who might be about to save my life.

I'm too scared to breathe.

"I don't have a choice," says Dave. "Point that thing someplace else."

Oh god. Has Nate got a gun?

"Either you step away or I start swinging."

Swinging?

Dave curses but he lowers the knife and there's air—glorious, fresh, open air—between us. I jump as far from him as I can, bashing into the side of the house as I do. I suck in a stream of swearwords, grabbing at my not-remotely-funny funny bone as it throbs.

Dave backs away, puffer jacket swooshing. He's still got the knife. "Shit, Nate. Why'd you stop me, man?"

Nate is holding a cricket bat. I don't know anything about

cricket but I'm pretty sure you don't step up to bat holding it like that.

Nate points to his face, to his black eye. "Why'd you punch me? Man."

"You kicked me out!"

"Yeah. And I remember telling you to stay the hell away."

"Do you know what they're going to do to me?" There's anguish in Dave's voice. Honest-to-god anguish. If he keeps tugging at his hair, he's going to rip out a whole chunk. "It's not my fault!"

Nate looks at me, then back at Dave. He lowers the bat. "Just get out of here, okay? Split."

I turn an open-mouthed stare Nate's way. I believe in aliens, Bigfoot, and Lindsay Lohan's acting talents fifty gazillion times *more* than I believe what Nate's doing—letting a knife-wielding crackhead go free.

Dave is clearly smarter than he looks, because he doesn't wait to be told twice. He bolts.

Seeing him run is a slap to my face. My shock vaporizes, leaving nothing but heat, rage, red . . .

This guy was going to rob me. *This* guy just held a knife to my throat. *This* guy pressed his filthy, grimy body against mine. *This* guy is going to get it.

I lunge after him, red spots blurring my vision, but Nate grabs my arm.

"Let me go!"

"No."

"Arsehole!"

"Likewise."

There's a loud crash. Dave's taken a tumble over a pile of bricks. He scrambles to his feet. I yank hard but Nate's not letting go. I yank again and overbalance, falling on my arse with a serious thud. Nate falls on top of me, our limbs tangling and heads butting.

I try twisting round to see where Dave runs off to but I've got a six-foot-something burglar on top of me and my head is spinning. I hear Dave's boots clomping against the earth as he bolts, listen to them fade to nothing.

I dig the heels of my palms into Nate's chest and push. "Look what you did! He got away."

"What I just did was save you, Vega. What do you think you were going to do? He had a knife."

"I was dealing with it."

He struggles onto his knees and I scoot out from under him, pain shooting up through my back. Shit! I've broken my coccyx.

He offers me a hand but I knock it away. He scowls. "Whatever. You realize you stink of booze, right?"

"I'm *inferring* hostility from you, Nate."

"Maybe because Druggie Dave was *implying* he was going to fuck you up. What the hell are you doing here?"

I get to my feet. Okay, so maybe I haven't broken my coccyx but I'm sore as hell. "You *owe* me."

"Are you serious?" He tucks the cricket bat under his arm. "Even if I did owe you, I've got news for you: you just called in that favor. Do you even get what a creep like Druggie Dave could have done to you?"

I can practically taste Dave's filth. "Yeah," I say. "I get it. What the hell is that guy's problem?"

"He samples more than he sells. I guess he owes shitloads to some scary people. He's an addict. He's . . . messed up."

My body is starting to shiver; it's the adrenaline, I guess. The almost-got-robbed/raped/killed shakes. It's one hell of a way to sober up.

The only noise comes from the bats flapping overhead as Nate and I stare daggers at each other. Now there's a super-power you don't see enough: someone who can shoot actual daggers out of their eyes. I could have used that power about a minute ago.

We try to outstare each other. There's a crease between his brows as he looks at me. I figure I've got dirt all over my face or maybe I'm actually asleep and this is one of those late-for-an-exam/walking-down-the-street-naked kind of dreams. I look down to check.

"Are you waiting for another psycho to come along and kill me?" I fold my arms across my chest.

He leans against the side of the house. "Would it get you off my case or would you just come back and haunt me?"

"Nothing," I say, "will stop me from annoying you until I get what I want. When I was ten I really wanted a My Little Pony. I followed Vinnie everywhere: 'Can I have a My Little Pony? Can I have a My Little Pony? Can I have a My Little Pony?' I sang 'Horses' by Daryl Braithwaite for two hours straight. And I only know one line of the chorus."

"*You* wanted a My Little Pony?"

"I was ten."

He laughs. It only pisses me off more—which is probably the point.

"I know you have information about Xavier."

He groans. "How drunk are you?"

"Not drunk enough."

I can't stop looking over my shoulder, half expecting Dave

to come running at me out of the shadows. Why can't I stop shaking?

Nate sighs. "If I answer your stupid questions what's in it for me?"

Ha! I win.

"They won't be stupid and I promise never to bother you again. How does that sound?"

"Perfect." He frowns, dusting some paint flakes off his jacket. "Follow me."

Twenty-two

Nate leads me into an overgrown back garden—the ideal place to bury a dead body.

Shit. Why'd I have to think that?

Jogging up the back steps of the house, he approaches a door that is actually just a bit of plywood half nailed to the frame.

He pulls back the board and lights the way with the flashlight on his phone.

As soon as I squeeze through, I'm hit by the stench of dust, grime, smoke, and rotting food. Eau de Filth. I think about saying something, but one look at Nate's scowl and I think better of it. Nate pushes a hand into the center of my back to keep me moving. I shiver from the cold.

We're in the laundry. It's slowly being reclaimed by nature through the cracks in the floorboards. The walls are moldy, covered with cracks and holes (probably filled with rats), and tagged by someone called "Killer Bob." Deeper inside the house, some guy starts singing the blues. He actually has a nice voice, but I want to know why the hell he didn't answer the front door when I knocked. I've got the left-outside-in-the-cold-with-Druggie-Dave blues.

Nate leads us up a corridor that could have come from a postapocalyptic film. One where major landmarks like the Opera House or Federation Square are totally overgrown, with monkeys hanging off the chandeliers and sharks in swimming pools.

"Watch for holes," says Nate. "I don't want to have to deal with you when you're injured."

"And rats."

"Huh?"

"I'm pretty sure I should be watching for rats. And spiders and snakes and Killer Bobs and, in the long term, some serious lung complaints—have you noticed the mold?"

"You were expecting the Ritz? No such luck. Welcome to the Shitz."

The corridor opens into a wide space, all the windows boarded up. It might have been a living room when the house was functioning as a house but right now it looks like a squat. Which it is. There are sleeping bags, clothes, shoes, and junk scattered all over the floor. Most of the sleeping bags are full.

I can't hear the blues anymore.

"You live here?" My voice echoes through the crumbling space, returning to my ears with more disgust than I'd intended. I look apologetically at Nate but he's got his eyes on his boots. "I didn't mean—"

The sleeping bag next to my foot rustles and a groggy voice tells me to shut the fuck up.

Nate yanks me to him before I can kick Mr. Rude in the sleeping bag.

He leans close and I realize that, weirdly, he smells like chlorine. Same as Mark. Is there some male cologne—Eau de Swimming Pool—that I don't know about? More important, why do I find it so appealing?

"Your housemates are arseholes," I say, but I'm not sure if "housemate" is the right word.

"Just whisper, okay? People are trying to sleep."

"Then what are we doing here?"

"You practically begged me to invite you in and now you're complaining?"

We get shushed again.

"No," I say with as much anger as a whisper will allow. "I mean, how are we going to have a conversation with all the shushing and the rude people?" My voice gets a little loud on the "rude people" part so something small, white, and pillow-shaped flies past me, just clipping my shoulder.

"That's it." I go to leave, but Nate grabs my hand and yanks me in the opposite direction.

"This way," he says.

We pick through the tangle of sleeping bodies and junk. Nate grips my arm; his hands are calloused and rough, strong, too, which I guess they'd need to be to do all that breaking and entering.

We head into another corridor, holes in the floor and a giant mural on the right. I don't even need to find the little red X to know it's my brother's work.

This time, she's a zombie. She looks a lot like the angel but an angel on ice, with teeth decaying and dull eyes, her pale skin rotting, covered in weeping sores. She holds both arms out in front of her body. *Brains* is written in large, melting green letters above her. She looks how I currently feel.

Which is ironic considering I'm pretty sure it is me. Same long dark hair, same so-brown-they're-black eyes, same slightly hooked nose. And on one hand I'm flipping out over how good he is—how he only met me a few times and yet here I am in extraordinary detail—but on the other hand . . .

"The little prick." After all the whispering, my normal voice is a shock. I fling a hand at zombie-me. "What's this supposed to be?"

Nate is leaning in an open doorway. Whatever's in the room behind him glows amber. He looks over my shoulder. "You mean the frighteningly realistic portrait of you? I like it. Anyway. Talk."

"So we're going to talk in the corridor? With the zombie?"

He glances at his feet. Combat boots. Like mine. "Sure," he says.

I try peeking over his shoulder into the room behind him, but he's too tall.

"What's in there? That looks cozy."

"No one goes in there."

I stand on tiptoe. "Are those candles?"

"No."

"They look like candles."

"They're not."

"Have you brought me to a day spa?"

He groans, rubbing his face with his hands.

"I'm just asking."

"Fine." He moves aside, all of five centimeters. The amber glow intensifies. "But I'm not happy about this."

"Gee, really? I couldn't tell."

He doesn't budge. I try squeezing past, but he's still in the way. "You say anything smart-arsed," he says, "and I kick you out."

The amber flickers across his face, lighting up his eyes. The bruise around his right eye is turning yellow, or maybe that's just the candlelight. There's a small cut on his bottom lip I didn't notice before. Guess I don't spend a whole lot of time staring at his lips. Why am I staring at his lips?

"I promise I won't be a cow," I say, gripping the door frame behind me.

He leans back. "We'll see."

I scramble the rest of the way in, almost falling face-first into an acoustic guitar.

There are candles everywhere, flickering and smoking, some propped up in empty coffee cups, some in what I'm assuming are stolen vases—the spoils of Nate's day job. They're all shapes and colors, casting a warm glow over the room.

I'm guessing there's no electricity.

I look over my shoulder and Nate's watching me, eyes dark, arms folded across his chest.

"It's nice," I tell him. "Very . . . dystopian chic."

I quickly look away again as his eyes narrow. I'll give him a moment to process that.

He doesn't have much stuff but there's a single-bed mattress on the floor, a comforter flung halfway across it, and a pillow, a decorative one meant for a couch. A milk crate/seat, which doesn't have my name on it, and there's even a lamp. No light-bulb in it and it's not plugged into anything, but it does make a handy clotheshorse.

There's a dictionary on the floor next to the bed.

He shoves past me and sits on the crate, shifting the guitar that had been leaning against it. "It's nothing," he says. "Just somewhere to crash." He points to the bed. "Sit."

I shake my head. "I'm not going anywhere near your bed—I'm not that drunk."

I look around, imagining zombie rats swarming up through the holes in the floor.

He grins and leans back, arms behind his head, a tiny strip of white skin showing between the top of his jeans and the end of his T-shirt. *The Velvet Underground* is written across his chest. "You have questions? Shoot."

"How do you take a shower? Does this place have plumbing?"

His arrogant smirk wavers. "I mean questions about your brother."

"Why did Dave hit you?"

"See previous statement. Add a little more menace to the tone."

"How come you have your own room? Are you King of the Squat People?"

He doesn't bother saying anything, because looks really can kill.

I chew my lip and wonder what it would be like to sleep here. To breathe in this chill, this stench, this hopelessness every single night. Note to self: be less of a judgmental bitch.

I lean against the wall and pray it doesn't give way. "Did my brother stay here?"

"Sometimes."

"And you're his friend?"

"Couldn't stand the little shit."

My look is colder than the room. "While I appreciate your honesty, go fuck yourself."

He smirks. "Go fuck yourself. I didn't ask you to come here."

I fold my arms and stare at the holes in the floor. Come on, zombies, rise and feed off Nate's brain. Your queen commands it.

"Why did you call my brother a little shit?"

"Because he was. He stole anything that wasn't nailed down."

"You're saying that's a bad thing?"

"X steals to buy shitty overpriced material possessions. And he'll rip off his friends, too. I don't do that. Someone like Dave steals to feed his drug habit. And I don't have one of those."

"So when you steal it's like a political statement?"

Nate needs to be careful he doesn't choke on his own self-satisfied grin. "Yeah," he says. "That's exactly it."

"You're telling me that those skinny jeans you're wearing are the twenty-first century's answer to tights and you're a modern-day Robin Hood?"

He scowls as he picks up the guitar and starts picking out a tune. Nothing I know but it's kind of nice. A little bit Nick Drake. I listen for a bit before I realize this means he's now ignoring me.

Okay. So I'm not sure this is how the cops would have interviewed Harrison's friends. I've got to start asking the right questions.

"Do you know where my brother hangs out?"

"Nope." He doesn't take his eyes off his fingers. I need to get him a name badge: *Hello, my name is Petulant Nate and I'm a snarky little bitch*.

"Did he at least say where he was going after you saw him last?"

"He said he owed his dad money. And a few others, too.

I guess he was going to pawn the stuff we stole and divvy out the cash. Maybe. I don't know."

"His dad hasn't seen him. How much would he have gotten? Four and a half grand?"

"A couple hundred at most. Your neighbors have shit taste. Wait, four and a half grand?"

"He stole his dad's credit card. Maxed it out to buy me a Joy Division record. No telling who else he ripped off and how much he actually owed."

The music stops. "Four and a half grand? For a CD?"

I narrow my eyes. "Vinyl. Rare. Joy Division."

He snorts and starts playing again.

I walk to the side of the bed and squat. There's something under the dictionary. A few somethings: records? "He called me Thursday," I say. "Said he'd got the cash. More than enough. Where's he going to get that kind of money?" I reach out to shift the dictionary so I can see the records underneath. "I mean, if you—and I'm giving you a compliment here—if you couldn't steal four and a half grand worth of stuff in one go, then where's he going—"

My fingertips have only just connected with the top record when Nate dumps his guitar and grabs my wrist. "Hey, didn't anybody teach you it's rude to poke around in other people's stuff?"

He pulls me to standing and I overbalance.

"Careful," he says, holding me upright.

I open my mouth to give him a serve, but he's not just gripping my wrist; his other hand is pressed into my back. Is it 1950? Are we about to waltz?

I find myself looking into a deep blue stare. The kind you could get lost in.

But not me. I'm focused. One hundred percent.

Maybe ninety.

He shifts closer. I don't move; my eyes flick to the cut on his lip. Eighty percent. "At least tell me where Xavier would go to pawn the stuff," I say.

He watches me. Silent.

Seventy percent. I'm seventy percent focused. So focused on his lips I don't notice how close we are until . . .

"Shit." I bump against the wall as I pull away. "I mean . . ."

He jumps back, tucks both hands under his armpits, giving the floorboards exclusive access to his blue-eyed stare. "Whatever." The amber glow flickers across his cheeks. He clears his throat. Loudly. "If I give you the pawn guy's details, will you quit bugging me and stay the hell away?"

I nod. Vigorously. The room doesn't spin. Excellent.

He walks back to the bed and drops to his knees, yanking up one of the floorboards. There isn't, surprisingly, a swarming mass of zombie rats underneath, just a black backpack.

I peer over his shoulder. "Got any corn chips buried in there? I'm starved."

He pulls out the backpack and rifles through, pulling out a black leather-bound notebook. Those expensive ones that Hemingway used. There are pages and pages filled with scrawl—words scribbled out here and there; mostly the writing is set out in long, uneven columns. Nate writes poetry? No way.

"Is that your manifesto for world domination?"

He scribbles something on the corner of a blank page and tears it out. "The guy's name is Ted." He stands, holding out the piece of paper. "I'm pretty sure you owe me. Again."

"Tell you what." I grab the address and shove it into my pocket. "I don't kick you in the nuts and we call it quits."

For a second he frowns at me, but it doesn't last. He laughs. "Deal. And now I'll help you one last time. I'll show you how to get out of this place."

I spin around and out the door.

"Left," he says. "Other left."

I give him a scowl over my shoulder and turn left. The other left. I stumble my way down the corridor with Nate behind me.

But only until I see her.

There's another painting on the wall, about ten meters down from zombie-me. I don't need to look for the little X to know it's one of Xavier's.

"What the hell, Vega," says Nate. "Keep moving."

But I pull out my phone and hold the lit screen up to the wall.

It's all wrong. Like when I rewatched *The Dark Crystal* last year and I could see that the creatures were puppets and the movement was all jerky and the magic had gone.

There's an iron fist around my heart. Closing fast.

It's a portrait of Juliet Vega.

There's the manic glint in her eye, the pointed chin, the bleached-blond hair; god knows what color it really was but the roots were always dark.

She's got bigger eyes than I remember. Or maybe that's what they call "artistic license." Like the way her skin is scab-free and she's smiling.

But it's wrong because she's so much older than I remember. Crow's feet around her eyes, lips ringed with lines from years of smoking.

"When did Xavier paint this?" The light from my mobile falls softly across her face. The plaster peeks through where the paint is thinnest.

"I don't know. A year? Around the time he first moved to Melbourne."

"A year ago? From Townsville?"

He nods.

"Queensland?" I say, barely audible.

I reach out my hand, fingertips grazing the bridge of her nose. Long and thin. Just like Xavier's.

This is not the truth I came here to find.

"Frankie, are you—?"

I run.

Twenty-three

And then I sleep.
   Saturday's canceled.

Twenty-four

And Sunday.

Twenty-five

Dear Dickhead Arsehole Pus-face half brother Xavier,
You suck.

    I handed this to Daniel but he says I have to write more.
He sucks too.

    How many times can I write "fuck you"?

    So I guess you're wondering why I'm writing you a letter.
Or not, seeing as I'm not going to send this. That's the point,
isn't it? You write the letter, get all the angry stuff out of your
system, and then you throw it in the bin.

    It's another one of Daniel's "therapeutic exercises." Like the
time capsule. And the shouting-at-the-empty-chair-pretending-
the-person-you're-angry-at-is-sitting-in-it thing.

    I shouldn't have told him about you. He got all excited and
started taking notes.

    "How does that make you feel?" he asked.

Why is he so damn excited about my pain?

Whatever. I don't care.

What I really want to know is who's been using the other desk. I don't care about anything else. Last time I was in this office, the spare desk in the corner was clear; now it has a stack of papers, used cups, and a photo frame—I can't see what's in the frame because it's angled away from me.

I asked Daniel who sits there but he told me to quit deflecting.

Deflecting?

I deflected his stupid chicken timer right across its beak and told him it's warped having a chicken for an eggtimer. I mean, he's asking a chicken to help him boil and eat its babies.

You have no idea how excruciating this is. Locked in a small gray office with someone who's excited because my brother turned out to be an arsehole. It's worse than school because it's just me and Daniel. The second I stop writing his chin jerks up and he glares.

Oh, gods of novelty eggtimers, please make the chicken cluck sooner.

Now Daniel's taking notes. I'm on one side of the desk and he's on the other. Maybe he's doing his shopping list. I bet he's gluten-free or sugar-free and he probably eats kale. And likes it.

You wouldn't like kale; it's green.

He's doing the full-stop thing again. Twisting the pen hard into the paper at the end of each sentence. It doesn't fit with who he is. He's the master of the serene—like he OD'd on Zen—but the full-stop thing is passive-aggressive, don't you think?

Or maybe that's really him. Maybe the sleepy smile, the

quiet manner, and the laughing eyes are an act, and underneath he's an aggro prick. Like me. Like you.

Hey. I could be a psychologist. Then I could figure this all out. Like, why did Juliet stick it out with you? What's so special about you?

You could have told me, you know. I would have punched you, but siblings beat up on each other all the time, don't they?

I get it. I get why you left that all-important tidbit out of our first meeting. Things would have gone down a totally different path if you'd told me the truth from the start, if you hadn't let me make the world's stupidest assumption.

"Hi, I'm Xavier. I'm your brother."

"Hi, I'm Frankie, I didn't know you existed. Sorry."

"It's okay. Mum never mentioned you, either."

"Well, she wouldn't, would she? She dumped me in a barn with a bunch of guinea pigs when I was four."

"Oh. She stuck it out with me until I was thirteen, so I guess I did better than I thought."

"Great to know. I've been feeling way too positive about myself lately. It's a real relief to find out it wasn't her inability to be a mother that forced her to dump me in a barn. Here was me thinking it wasn't personal when really it was. Thanks for clarifying that."

But I guess Marzoli was right. You're just so shitty at facing up to consequences that you'd rather run away than fix things. I shouldn't be surprised. Juliet moved all the way to Queensland so she didn't have to face the consequences of having me.

And you should know that I blame you completely. Not just because Juliet dumped me to be with your father. I blame you for pretty much everything. Wars, natural disasters, the lack of milk in our fridge.

I blame you because you were rubbing my face in it. Patronizing me. Like, don't tell Frankie that Mum kept me or else the poor little thing will go on a nose-breaking spree. Is that why you bought me that ridiculous gift? Did you steal four and a half grand just to buy a sister? A sister who might have liked you anyway?

Fuck you.

Did you know that it was a whole month after she dumped me before I found out where she'd pissed off to?

I guess Vinnie got sick of me asking because she sat me down and gave me the your-mum's-moved-to-Queensland-so-you-can't-ever-see-her-again talk. I was four, so Queensland was just a word. It didn't become a place until I was older, and even then I wasn't sure why Juliet was there and why it meant I couldn't see her. It doesn't matter how shitty your mother is, how much better off you'll be with someone else. Just drop a kid in the middle of a shopping center and watch their face when they lose sight of their mum. The confusion, the panic, the heartbreak. Every one of them.

Even me.

So Juliet wasn't completely incapable of being a parent. Or maybe you were just so perfect that she couldn't help but keep you. Well done, you. Gold stars. Child of the Year Award.

She gave you up in the end, though, didn't she? What did you do to fall out of favor? Do you know where she is? Did she dump you with Bill Green and the phone number of her first-born?

But you don't even have the decency to be here so I can ask you. So I can yell at you and not an empty chair. I'm sick of people not being here when they're supposed to be.

You're a dickhead, Xavier. At least let me say it to your face.

I put down my pen and reach into my pocket, pulling out the scrap of paper Nate gave me: *38 hudson st—talk to ted.* Nate has messy, almost unreadable handwriting. Like a child who needs those dotted blue lines to help him write straight. He didn't even put a full stop at the end of it.

Why do I still have this? I'm done looking for Xavier. Aren't I?

Daniel lays down his pen, firmly enough to make a noise.

"Done?"

I look at my letter. It's scrawl, harder to read than Nate's. And I don't even feel any better.

"Done," I say.

Daniel smiles. He's already chalking me up as a success.

"I've been asked to write a report," he says, stretching back in his chair. "For your school."

I curl my fingers around Nate's scrap of paper, watching it disappear inside my fist.

"What do you think I should write?" Daniel asks. "Do you know why you react the way you do? Why you lashed out at your classmate? Your principal thinks the boy said something to you. She doesn't think you'd do it without a reason. Last week you started—"

"Why do you think I did it?"

His brow crinkles. I imagine the desert. Waves of sand.

"Because you think you deserve to fail," he says. Doesn't even stop to think about it. "Because 'being wrong' was the only way you ever gained your mother's attention. And even then she still left you. And you blame yourself for that. You think she abandoned you because you weren't good enough. So you push away people who love you to prove that you're a bad person who repels people. Your whole identity is based on feeling that way. And if it turns out not to be true—that you're actually a good person and your mother abandoning you had nothing to do with you—who are you, then?"

I stand, heart in my throat and red ink blots pooling around the edge of my vision. The timer hasn't clucked but fuck the chicken. There's no way I'm letting poultry dictate my life. "Write whatever you like."

"We have ten minutes left," says Daniel. He points at the chicken.

"But I have somewhere I need to be." I wave Nate's little scrap of paper at him. "It's important."

"What's more important than your future, Frankie?" He stands as I yank open the office door.

"Bees."

His forehead crinkles. "Bees?"

"They're dying out. And they pollinate most of the world's grains and vegetables and shit so, yeah, saving the bees is far more important than worrying about my future."

I think this is the first time Daniel has been genuinely worried about my sanity. He clicks his pen, switching from blue ink to green. So that's what the green ink is for. "Do you want to stay and talk about the bees, Frankie?"

"Nope." I wave the little scrap of paper again. "I have more than bees on my mind."

He moves to take a seat again but stops halfway. "Okay," he says. He smiles. "Bees," he says and finally sits.

The last thing I hear as I shut the door behind me is laughter. I guess I'm not done.

Twenty-six

Thirty-eight Hudson Street isn't a pawnshop. It's not even a *shop* shop. I check the address. It could be 83 or 33 or 88 or nothing to do with an 8 or a 3. It might not even be Hudson Street. Nate needs to go back to school.

While it may not be a pawnshop, 38 Hudson Street is most definitely a brick box. The roof is flat, the front window is small and blacked out—the whole place is narrow, decaying, and sad.

I walk across the concrete front yard, past two sedans and an SUV. There are stickers on the front door: *Fuck off, we're full* and *Fish fear me, women love me*.

I press the doorbell. I can't hear it ring inside but I wait just in case. Nothing happens, so I knock. While I'm waiting I text Cara: *If I go missing, tell the police I was last at 38 Hudson Street, the home of a racist fisherman.*

The door opens a crack. At some point this house has sunk,

because the bottom of the door drags along the carpet. The guy has to yank it, cursing the whole time.

"Why didn't you use the back door like everybody else?" he says.

I peek round the corner of the door as he struggles with it. "I'm looking for Ted."

He makes one final push and then we're kind of looking at each other, as best we can with the door only about 40 percent open.

"Who's looking?" The guy scratches his chest through his singlet, right over the "nt" in "Bintang." He's about a head shorter than me, which isn't hard because I'm pretty tall. He's bald on his crown with a round tuft at the front like a little hair island.

"I'm a friend of Nate Wishaw." "Friend" is a stretch but it's safer if he thinks he's got Nate to contend with if he tries to screw me around. I don't think this guy's heard what I can do with Shakespeare.

He gives me the once-over. "You look his type," he says. "Come in."

Ted stands aside and waves me into his domain. "But don't touch anything," he says.

When I squeeze all the way inside, I immediately realize how hard it's going to be to stick to Ted's don't-touch-anything rule.

Ted is a hoarder. A TV-show-worthy hoarder. The room is overflowing with boxes, rubbish, clothes, and . . . stuff. There's a gray dog asleep on the sofa and I'm betting there are a few cats lurking about the place; every bit of furniture is sprinkled with animal hair and the whole place smells like a giant kitty litter tray.

With my first step, my boot knocks against an old Chinese takeaway box. I wait for Ted to go mental at me for touching something but apparently he doesn't rate Chinese takeaway highly. Breathing only through my mouth, I say, "So this place is nice."

"Mum's in Bali," says Ted.

I want to tell him he's a man in his forties who could pick up a piece of rubbish even while his mother's getting drunk in Kuta.

He pulls out a tissue and blows his nose. "You got a name?"

"Ava. Ava Devar." Teach you to steal my boyfriend, bitch.

"And Nate sent you?" He pockets the tissue, but not before checking out whatever he deposited in there.

I walk farther into the living room. I can hear thrash metal blaring from the back of the house somewhere. When I knock over a tower of old computer parts I wake the dog. He pees himself with fright.

I look at Ted but he doesn't say anything.

"I sent myself, actually," I say.

Ted looks at my empty hands. "You got something to sell?"

"I just want to ask you about someone." I find a section of couch without too much cat hair and junk and sit on the very edge. "Xavier Green?"

He laughs. "He owe you, too?" He shoves his hands in his jeans pockets and leans against the wall. He's standing between me and the exit; an alarm bell goes off in my head. I probably could have asked him about Xavier while I was *outside* and free to run.

Oh dear.

"Yeah," I say. "He owes me big-time."

The dog pads over to me, sitting on top of my boots. I try

to pull my feet out from under him but he leans against my legs.

"Well, I haven't seen him since he stiffed me on some electronics," says Ted. "He knows not to come here again."

And the list of people my darling brother ripped off just got longer.

"When was that?"

Ted screws up his nose. "Dunno. Maybe a week."

"Was it a Thursday night? The fifteenth, maybe?"

There's a cat watching me from inside a cave of laundry. One eye closed, it's doing that soul-piercing assessment that only cats can do. Ted's got a bit of a cat-stare going on too.

"Could have been," he says. "Actually, nah. Took Mum to the airport that night and I stopped by my mate's on the way home. Didn't get back here till the next day. That little shit was waiting for me on the doorstep. Looked like he'd slept there all night."

"And he had stuff to sell?"

"Cheap shit mostly, but he said he was desperate. Prick sold me an MP3 player that didn't work. I should have checked it but I was dead on my feet."

I pull my boots out from under the dog and his arse plonks on the ground with a thud. He guilt-trips me with mournful eyes. I know, buddy; I'd be depressed too if I lived here.

"How much did he walk out of here with?"

"These are pretty specific questions, Ava," says Ted. He pulls out another tissue.

I wonder if he hoards the tissues, too.

"I know but I'm trying to get in touch with him and no one has seen him."

Ted eyeballs me, the tissue held in both hands. And then he grins. Not kindly and not in an amused way. It's an icky grin.

"Yeah?" he says.

Suddenly I'm having flashbacks to Druggie Dave and his knife and his breath and his fingers digging into my skin. Proper flashbacks that make me hold one hand to my racing heart. I think I'm going to be sick.

Get a grip, Frankie.

My phone rings. Oh thank god.

I check the caller ID as I shoot up to standing. "Sorry, but I need to take this."

Ted shakes his head, smirking. "Be my guest."

I look toward the door, but Ted's still blocking the exit. So I pick my way through the piles of junk until I find the kitchen. The music's louder here. The benches are covered with stacks of unwashed dishes, growing all sorts of crazy science experiments on them. I didn't know mold could come in so many different colors. I'm definitely not coming away from this place empty-handed—I'll have some kind of rare tropical disease for sure.

When I answer the phone, Cara screams into my ear and I can't even tell what's she saying at first.

I whisper "Calm down" as I peek through the kitchen door: there's no movement in the living room.

"Where are you, Frankie? What the hell are you doing?"

"I'm somewhere in Preston. Off Murray Road."

"With a racist fisherman? Did he kidnap you? Oh my god, he's drugged you, hasn't he?"

"Cara, listen. He's some guy who saw my brother before he disappeared. I just want to find out what he knows." I start opening and closing cupboards. They're full of junk—mostly newspapers and probably every edition of *Woman's Day* ever published.

"Are you an idiot, Frankie? Get the hell out of there. He could be a serial killer. Hang on"—her voice switches from terrified to pissed off in record time—"you mean you went investigating without me? What gives?"

"Sorry. I know. But you're right." I back up. "I was stupid coming here. I'm going now. Stay on the line while I—"

I back up into something warm and solid and Ted-shaped. I swear and almost drop the phone.

"Thought maybe you were lost," says Ted. There's that grin again.

I draw the phone to my ear again. "Oh, don't worry, Daddy," I say into the phone. "You know what I'm like." I hold my hand over the speaker and whisper to Ted: "It's my dad. He's a cop, so he's always worried about where I am and what I'm doing. If I'm not home soon he'll send the dog squad out looking for me." I roll my eyes, but all I get from Ted is a sneer.

"Frankie? What the hell is going on?" asks Cara down the line.

"I'll see you soon, Daddy," I say loudly. My one and only foray into acting was at St. Thomas Primary. I got to be the donkey in the nativity play, but I tripped over my hooves and smashed the baby Jesus.

"Don't be silly, Daddy. It's not far at all to travel back from thirty-eight Hudson Street in Preston."

The dog has joined us in the kitchen, his arthritic legs struggling to carry him.

"Bye, Daddy."

"Don't hang—"

I shove my phone in my pocket and smile like a weather girl. "Parents are so lame, right?"

"Your brother," says Ted. He's not smiling.

"No, that was my dad, Detective Inspector—"

"No," says Ted. "You said I was some guy who saw your *brother* before he disappeared."

My smile falters; storms are approaching. Lightning. Thunder. Volcanic eruptions. "Didn't I mention that?"

Ted shakes his head. "You said your name was Devar. I thought you were looking for Xavier Green because he owes you money."

"We have different fathers. So we've got different names."

I have never been stared at so intently in my life, not even by Buttons, spawn of Satan.

I start backing out of the room. Ted follows, arms folded across his chest.

"Good," he says. "Cos I buy stuff from that prick's dad. Don't want to find out he's a cop and he's setting me up."

"Bill?" I bump into a stack of boxes filled with wires and electronic entrails. I push against the wall to help myself climb over them. "Has he ever said anything to you about Xavier?"

"Just what a useless prick he is. I wouldn't be surprised if Bill was the one who gave him the beating."

I stop mid-climb. "What beating?"

"Friday. He was all messed up. Black eye. Cut lip. Bruised all over. Someone was mighty pissed at him. Might not have been Bill, I guess. Could have been any one of the nasty people he owed money to."

"Did he—"

"I'm done doing favors for Nate Wishaw," says Ted. "It's about time you pissed off."

I back up until I bash into the door, the handle digging into my back. I grimace but manage to keep my mouth shut.

"It's actually easier to take the back door," says Ted. Oh god, there's that grin again. "Down there." He nods back the way we came, toward the dark corridor, the thrash metal, and the rape dungeon (probably).

Down the other end of the house the thrash metal gets really loud and then quiet again as a door opens and closes.

Oh my god. This is it. It's going to be some giant, hairy biker and the pair of them will do unspeakable things to me. And when they're done I'll be just another piece of junk they refuse to throw out of this hellhole.

Ted looks over his shoulder as a scrawny kid appears around the corner. He's about nine, and I wouldn't even need a hardback to break him—a bookmark would do.

Ted growls at the kid. "What you looking at, Pus Face?"

The kid flips Ted the bird and stalks off into the kitchen. The fat dog does a surprisingly tight U-turn and follows him.

When I look back at Ted, he's sneering at me. "You still here?"

I shake my head. I'm a thousand miles from here.

He points at the door. "Twist, lift, and pull."

Twenty-seven

I get back to the Emporium with exactly zero seconds before my shift starts. My plan, once I've safely snuck in, is to switch onto autopilot so I can churn out kebabs while concentrating on figuring out who beat up Xavier.

What was it that poet dude said? Best-laid plans always get fucked up. Something like that.

I burst through the front door and I'm knocked over by the force of Vinnie's death stare.

"Don't give me that look." I'm breathing hard from all the running it took me to get here, running while yelling apologies over the phone to Cara. "I'm exactly on time."

I hurry behind the counter, dumping my bag and shrugging off my jacket. Other than a pissed-off aunt, there's no one else in the shop.

"Your session with Daniel ended hours ago." Vinnie's eyes

follow me everywhere I go like a furious Mona Lisa. I don't know what color her nails are today, but it looks like she's been finger painting in blood.

"Relax. I went—"

Vinnie grabs my chin. Not in the cutesy way she does when she's about to call me her princess, but in a way that makes me drop the knife I just picked up and gasp. She pulls me around until I'm facing her, eyes glinting like Buttons's right before he carves up my leg. Oh dear god, I forgot about the vodka. Busted.

"You seem to have forgotten that you are grounded, Francesca Vega. You seem to have forgotten the rules. You will keep up with your schoolwork. You will leave the house only when I say so and only for preapproved activities: counseling, grocery shopping, visiting your nonna. You will return home immediately after. You will keep your nose out of trouble and you will grovel your way back into that school. I've had it up to here with you, Frankie. And when I say 'here' I mean high up an astronaut's arse. Are you feeling me?"

I nod. She drops my chin.

"That's a contract of good behavior right there," she says. "Don't make me sign it in blood." She eyeballs me for a few more seconds and then sighs, her death stare replaced by tired, sad eyes. "You know I don't like getting heavy with you."

I pick up the knife and stab a tomato. "I know."

Plan B: In between churning out kebabs, I will write a practice essay on *Nineteen Eighty-Four*, recite Italian verbs, memorize the inner workings of a volcano, list five causes of the October Revolution, and compare thee to a summer's day. Oh, and think real hard about how to stop disappointing Vinnie.

Simple.

But, hey, at least I got away with the stolen booze.

Vinnie slings her handbag over her shoulder, her coat already on. "Unfortunately, I've got an appointment to get to. I don't like leaving you here on your own but . . ." Her coat rustles.

"Appointment? At five p.m.?" I look at her feet and gasp. She's wearing her red Special K heels. "Oh my god, you're going on a date?"

"It's not a date."

I wait for her to tell me what "it" is, but she just frowns at her shoes and then heads for the door.

"Make sure he's suitable. I don't want a cult leader for uncle number four."

"Just be good and don't burn the place down," she says. "We have a contract now." She's almost out the door but she stops, leans back in. "Oh, and you owe me a bottle of vodka and three more months of being grounded." She blows me a kiss and then slips out the door into the cold.

Shit.

Vinnie raps her fingers against the front window and then hurries up the street. Gone.

So I can't sneak out and visit a racist fisherman but she can go on secret dates with a cult leader?

I glower at the empty Emporium.

Is this my life? A humming fridge and a garlicky stench?

At least it's Monday. No one wants to buy a kebab on a Monday. It's like a law or something.

This is a good thing—I can't get into any trouble on my own at the Emporium and I can't disappoint Vinnie. I can just sit here, bring down my school catch-up work, and really get Plan B under way. Forget this whole Xavier thing because it's way too complicated.

But first: salad.

I cut the tomatoes and then the onions. It makes me cry.

My phone vibrates. I sniff and wipe my eyes. The back of my hand comes away with a large black smudge so I check my reflection in the stainless-steel flume. Stupid onions: now I look like a goth clown.

It's a text from Cara: *Don't hate me :)*

I text back: *Why would I hate you?* My phone buzzes again. *On way to you now . . .*

I frown. Why would I hate Cara for dropping by? Okay, so Plan B might need to take a backseat for a bit. Catching up with the BFF trumps homework. Sorry, Vinnie, but it does.

I text back: *Cara coming over equals happy Frankie (unless you're bringing more catch-up work from school—if so, screw you).*

But before I can press send another text comes through that changes *everything*.

Ran into some peeps. Bringing them too :)

Peeps? Peeps?! I don't like regular people, let alone peeps. I start dialing Cara to get a proper explanation but that bitch is way smarter than I give her credit for.

I get one measly ring in before Cara presses her nose to the front window of the Emporium and waves at me, phone in hand.

Technically she sent me a warning text but she didn't leave enough time for me to call and talk her out of it.

Sneaky.

Evil.

The door jangles.

"Heya, Frankie babe," she says. Is the flush in her cheeks from the cold or guilt? "Got room for three?"

Three?

Again, I'm not given a whole heap of time to lodge a complaint. Loping in straight after Cara is . . .

Poo, bum, crap, shit.

"Hey, Frankie," says Mark. He offers a sheepish smile and a small wave. One of his mates—PopAsia—trips in after him.

Cara smiles. "Isn't this great?"

Super.

Cara's got an ink forest growing along her hands and up her arm. Obviously she hasn't been home since school ended because she's still wearing her uniform, an oversize hoodie swamping most of her summer dress, sleeves pushed up to her elbows, and a little badge over her left breast that says *Joe's Rock 'n' Roll Diner.*

"You hate me, don't you?" she whispers.

I glance at Mark and his disciple sitting at a table by the window, pretending they don't know we're talking about them. That's cool, because I'm pretending they don't exist.

I know this is payback for me not bringing her with me to Ted's house but seriously. These things are not, in any way, equal.

"Whatever gave you that idea?" I say, piling onions, garlic sauce, and chili onto Cara's kebab.

She points at the kebab. "I'll never be able to kiss anyone ever again."

I go back for more onions. "Who are you hoping to snog? Scrawny boy-band dude with zits?"

She grins, leaning into me. "His name is Truc and he might

not be much to look at now but you haven't heard him play gui-tar. Trust me. This one's a long-term investment."

My fingers hover over the jalapeños. "But did you have to bring him here? With his *friend*?"

At least she has the decency to look guilty. "Sorry, but dick-head was standing there when I asked Truc out and he invited himself along. It's not my fault he's got a hard-on for you. Just grin and bear it. Please? For me?"

I leave the jalapeños be and start wrapping the kebabs. Mark is folding his napkin into a swan. He used to make them for me all the time, which led to the Great Paper Swan Fire a week after we broke up; maybe I should try origami with the kebabs. A giant middle finger?

"Eat and leave," I tell her. "I will not be pimped out for your benefit."

"Why? You got a racist fisherman you'd rather hang with?" She sticks out her tongue as she scoops up the kebabs, sashay-ing over to Truc and Mark. "Table service," she says. "How fancy is that?" She hands them each a kebab and takes a seat. The one closest to Truc.

"Kebabs are awesome," says Truc.

Kill me now.

I'm not being mean; Cara deserves to be in love, but this is only going to end badly. Like Winston the violinist who couldn't keep it in his pants. And Ollie the drummer who couldn't keep it in his pants. And Axel the trainee tattoo artist who—surprise surprise—couldn't keep it in his pants. If I can discourage her now, I'll save both of us a night in the rain painting *Truc is a lying scumbag with a small cock* on the art block wall, and all the tears and forced repeat watching of *The Notebook*.

I file this moment away as a down payment on a future serving of revenge and trudge out from behind the counter. I guess it's okay for me to leave my post when there's no one else in the shop. And if Vinnie comes back now it won't just be me she kills. Totally worth it.

I drag a chair close to Cara and sit. I do not care if I cockblock her; I will not sit within punching distance of Mark. For both our sakes.

I stare unsociably at the scuffed table, remembering the first time I met Mark. He was lanky, black fringe flopping across his eyes, with the cheekbones of my music idols. He walked right up to me with his hand thrust out. He asked me my name but I lost my voice. Not because he was so cute I couldn't talk— I'm not *that* pathetic—but I couldn't get over the balls it took to walk up to someone you didn't know and just start talking. "You're going to have to tell me your name," he said, grinning, "or I'm going to give you a nickname. And my best mate's called Stinko."

"So what's the plan?" asks Truc through a mouthful of the magpie special. I do not understand how Cara is giving him gooey eyes while he's massacring his food like that.

I reach for Mark's swan napkin when he's done making it. Even through all the meat and garlic and chip fat I can smell the chlorine wafting from his skin.

"What plan?"

"I know," says Cara, "when Vinnie gets here we'll all go to the movies."

"Cool," says Truc. "It's cheap night at Nova."

This guy's the best one yet.

"I'm working till closing," I say. "Oh, and I'm grounded for all eternity."

"Then we'll hang out here." Cara pinches my thigh under the table. I make the swan peck at her kebab. She slaps my hand.

"We better not," says Mark. He finally tears open his kebab. "If Frankie's working we should—"

"Poo-y," Cara says, sinking into her chair. "I never get to see her anymore. She's either working or running around with cute burglars."

The entire inside of Mark's kebab goes splat onto the floor.

Truc laughs so hard he spits lettuce across the table.

"Sorry." Mark looks between his legs at the mess.

"It's fine." I stand and give Cara my best attempt at the Nonna Sofia. "Cara has that effect on people."

She gnaws on her lip but not out of guilt—she's trying to contain a smile.

I head behind the counter and pull out the cleaning tray from under the sink. Vinnie only specified I wasn't to burn the place down while she was out, but I think she'd have fairly strong views on food spillage as well.

"Did you say burglar?" asks Mark, two red patches on his cheeks.

Cara wiggles her pinkie at him. "Sorry, Marky Mark, but you missed the boat. There's a new guy on the scene and he's hot. Hot in appearance *and* hot for Frankie."

I dump the cleaning tray on the table. "He is *not* interested in me. Friday night was just a—"

"Friday night?" Cara's jaw drops—and she hasn't even tasted my kiss-me-not kebab. "But you were with me on Friday! You never told me you saw him."

I wring out the sponge, drips splattering all over the table. "It was after and, anyway, I'm kind of busy here, C. Someone has to clean this mess up."

"I'll help," Mark says. He dumps the soggy pita onto the tray. He starts to get up, but I hold out a hand.

"Forget it. You guys go to the movies without me." I get down on hands and knees, armed with my sponge and a resolute scowl. I'm way too close to Mark's crotch for my liking.

"Seriously. Get out of here," I say.

I scoop kebab innards into a handful of paper towel. If I ever need a metaphor for my life . . . I don't look up, but I know they've heard me when chairs start squeaking, bags start rustling, and boots start clomping. I rub the floor in slow circles.

"Thanks for the kebab," says Truc.

I salute him but I guess he can't see me.

Mark's feet hover in my periphery. Expensive-looking sneakers. Brand-new. I've missed an opportunity here, haven't I? Could have tied his laces together under the table.

Turquoise hair falls across my shoulder as Cara leans over me, lips brushing my ear. "You *will* tell me about Friday night. Text me." She plants a kiss on my cheek and straightens. "C'mon, guys. We can probs catch the late showing if we hurry."

"I'm in," says Truc. He slings his arm around Cara.

"Bye, Frankie babe," says Cara, but her eyes say *He's got his arm around me! Squee!*

I sit back on my butt and watch them leave.

Mark's the last to go, giving me the old laser light show with his eyes as the door wobbles shut behind him.

My shoulders slump. I reek of garlic and I'm sitting on a sticky floor with a spongeful of mushy kebab. I'm an eighteen-year-old orphan with a missing brother. Talk about a hard-knock life.

But Plan B is still a goer. I really need to orchestrate it so that I'm nose deep in a schoolbook when Vinnie gets back. That would be some seriously good PR. I need—

The door opens with a *jingle-jangle*.

Shit. I need a Plan C.

I scrub the floor madly. "How was your 'appointment,' Vin? Should we be getting ready for the apocalypse?"

Except it's not Vinnie who walks in. It's not even a random customer.

It's a pair of ridiculously expensive sneakers. Brand-new.

"Sorry," says Mark. He holds the door ajar and hovers there like he can't decide if he wants to come in or not.

"Mark?"

He nods. Okay. Good. We've established that he's Mark and not some kind of pod person.

"Did you forget something?"

He opens his mouth but nothing comes out.

I fidget with the sponge. Well, this is going swimmingly.

His mouth gets another couple of test runs before he finally blurts out: "I forgot to tell you how much I miss you."

Plan C: Find a way to rewind time and play that back again. Because I mean, really. What. The. Fuck.

He looks down. "Sorry. Didn't mean to vomit that."

I slowly scoop the last of the lettuce and garlic sauce into my palm, dumping it onto the cleaning tray. I grip the edge of the table and pull myself to standing. I am so cool, calm, and collected I may need to check my pulse to make sure I'm still alive.

"I miss you," he says with a small shrug of his shoulders. "I wish I never . . . I wish none of that stuff happened and we could have just . . ."

I've never seen this Mark who doesn't know what to say,

what to do with his hands, how to look me in the eye without blushing.

I remind myself that this is the guy who cheated on me and broke my heart.

But he's also the guy who sent me a note a few weeks into Year Nine: *Do you want to be my girlfriend: circle yes or no.* He's the first-time guy. The first-love guy.

"There's nothing between me and Ava," he says, hovering by the door. "I'm done hooking up with her. She's just not into the same stuff as me, you know."

"Like you're into origami and she's more into baby-sacrificing?"

A shy grin sweeps across his face. "That was supposed to be your gig, wasn't it?"

I really want to smile, but then I remember what it was like—Year Eleven. I remember people whispering and laughing, catching the words "Mark," "Ava," "science block," "kissing." I remember walking up to him and cracking my palm across his face. Him saying: "What did you expect, Frankie? I've tried. You won't talk to me. And you're so angry all the time."

So I don't smile.

I just stand there watching him, remembering.

"Can I ask you out or are you going to break my nose for trying?" he says. He hasn't registered the change in my expression because he's still smiling, cheeks flushed red.

I swallow a few times, trying to get some moisture back in my mouth.

"Mark, I—"

He bounds over to the counter. "We can check out a band." He grabs the order pad and a pen. "I've got a new number. It's totally your decision. Call me. Or don't."

He rips off the corner with his number scrawled on it and holds it out for me. "I really want to see you again, Frankie," he says. The laser eyes switch on for an encore performance.

I can't decide what I want to remember: the note in Year Nine, or Year Eleven behind the science block.

He frowns when I don't say anything, when I don't reach out and take his number. But he forces a grin as he shoves the scrap of paper under the order spike and heads to the door.

"I hope you call," he says. "I really do."

The door closes behind him.

Do I have a Plan D?

Twenty-eight

Sometimes I think about Ian Curtis wandering into my room and it all gets a little X-rated from then on. What I don't usually daydream about is spending the last of my Saturday night reading one of Vinnie's crappy romance novels—*Once Bitten*—and stressing about a scrap of paper in my back pocket. But that's what I end up doing once my shift ends.

I crank up New Order—if I'm going to freak out, it may as well be to a kick-arse soundtrack.

It's just a scrap of paper. It's just a bit of mushed-up tree with some guy's number scribbled on it.

Yeah. Some guy. You keep telling yourself that, Frankie.

You never go back. It's a rule. Once bitten, twice shy (thank you, crappy romance). It doesn't matter how uncomplicated the guy is or how appealing it is to find something familiar.

Ava and Mark have broken up about fifty times this year.

And each time they do, Mark gives me moon eyes until he and Ava hook up again. So I'm not dumb, I know the chances of those two getting back together again are Snoop Dogg high. And I know Mark really regrets cheating on me. It's just, I'm not sure he remembers what we were really like together.

Sigh. I start skipping pages, looking for a sex scene.

There's some shuffling outside my door and then a knock. I look at the time—way past bedtime. Guess Vinnie's "appointment" went well.

I roll onto my side. "You can come in but I do not want to hear details about your date. No kissing, no tongues, no sweaty hands."

The door creaks open. "How do you feel about third base?" asks a *male* voice.

A *Nate* voice.

I bolt upright, knocking *Once Bitten* to the floor. My heart doesn't just leap out my chest, it applies for a visa and goes to live in Siberia.

He leans against the door frame—hair ruffled, ripped jeans, white shirt, the Jacket, and, for some reason, a black skinny tie. He's acting like materializing in my bedroom is all perfectly normal and natural and expected.

Oh my god, there's underwear on the floor.

"Cute socks," he says.

I look down at my furry bedsocks. My pink furry bedsocks. The kind with individual toes. "Nice jeans," I say. "Do they sell those at Punk Poseurs R Us?"

I throw my pillow at him. "Are you here to kill off the only witness to your burglary spree?" The pillow lands at his feet. His black combat boots are caked in mud. "Wait a minute . . . you *broke* into my house? What the actual fuck?"

He laughs. "You need to replace the locks. That was way too easy."

"So this is some kind of public service?"

"Sure." He holds out a blue wallet, dangling it between pinched fingers. "I come bearing gifts."

"Are you offering to pay for my silence?"

"Just take the damn wallet."

I crawl to the end of the bed. The springs sing out like I weigh a thousand tons.

He dangles the wallet just out of reach before dropping it into my waiting hand. I handle it like it's a bomb. It's one of those surfy-brand wallets, Velcro fastening, patterned like a Hawaiian shirt. I flick through. Zero money, a gym membership, a bank card, and a probationary license: the guy grinning in the photo is of the ex-boyfriend variety.

"You robbed Mark?"

"Actually, that's not the favor. I did that just for me." Nate's got his lopsided smile going on. He reaches into his pocket and pulls out a mobile. You'd swear it was Christmas. "This is the favor."

He holds the screen in front of my face, showing me a photo of two people. Two people I know all too well.

"See the time stamp?" he says. "Half an hour ago."

First thing I think is: Hey, that's a seriously nice phone for a guy who lives in a squat. The second thing I think is: Hey, my carpet needs a steam clean. I should tell Vinnie. And then I keep thinking about the carpet—keep my eyes on it too— because it's way better for my mental health than looking at "Exhibit A."

"Well?"

I scoot back along the bed, far, far away from the offending mobile. "What are you even doing here?"

He frowns. "You don't want to know the guy hitting on you likes to spread the love?"

I don't say anything. I don't need to: A picture says a thousand words. Especially a picture where the "completely single" guy who gave you his number and told you how much he misses you is whispering seductively into the ear of Ava Devar, probably telling her he wants her back, he'll do anything to make it up to her.

See? This is why I'm so angry. Because the second you consider opening yourself up to someone they tear your heart out.

It's not like I didn't know I was slotted to be Rebound Girl, something familiar to return to, something I'm sure Mark genuinely wanted—just not more than Ava. The second she wanted him back, he'd have been right behind that science block again, breaking my heart.

I swing my legs over the edge of the bed. Nate watches me but, bless him, doesn't say a word. I go back to looking at the carpet.

Why is Nate telling me this? Maybe he just wants to see me suffer.

I look up. No. His brow is majorly creased.

I didn't realize Nate gave enough of a shit to worry about who's hitting on me. It's surprising and weird. Like running into your teacher at the supermarket buying tampons.

Wait.

"How do you know Mark was hitting on me? Were you *watching* us?"

He shoves the phone in his pocket and flashes a half sneer,

half smile. A snile. "Don't flatter yourself. I was waiting to talk to you but wasn't game to interrupt you and your friends."

"Light-fingered *and* unsociable. You've got all the best qualities."

He gives me the finger.

"And a wordsmith. Hey there, Hemingway, I think I'm in love."

"My name," he says, taking a massive step forward. With his giraffe legs, one step means he's pretty much on top of me. "Isn't Hemingway. Whatever the hell a Hemingway is."

Man, those eyes are blue.

"I know it isn't." My voice—damn it—shakes. "But it suits you."

He studies me a little longer with those broken-love-song eyes. He's either going to laugh at me or . . .

He frowns deeper. Then he steps back.

Breathe.

He starts pacing. It's not a big room so it takes two steps before he's reached one end and has to turn around. Two steps, turn. Two steps, turn.

He stops at the far end of my room, pointing at my Ian Curtis poster. "See? I was right."

"Yeah. And?"

"If we're talking desert island and I have to choose between Morrissey and Curtis, Morrissey every day of the week. But I guess they're okay." He scratches his chin. "Where do you sit with Coldplay?"

That's easy. "I sit on a throne made out of the blood and sweat of genuine artists watching those arsehats being fed to lions. Zombie lions."

He smiles. Not a grin, not a snile—a smile. Actual teeth

showing. And when he's not scowling, he has a nice face. Lots
of angles and everything in proportion. Ian Curtis meets Jeff
Buckley meets Faris Badwan. Maybe he's not so bad. Maybe
he's just shy or awkward, or a little bit broken, like me.

"Xavier told me about your mum," he says. "The whole
children's farm thing."

"Did he."

It's not a question. It's a prelude to throwing up. Or kicking
out. Or both.

I wait for the follow-up—the punch line to whatever joke he
thinks he's making—but he just frowns, pressing the tip of his
finger against the poster, pushing down an air bubble. "How
come parents are allowed to be shitty but we're not?"

It's his tone of voice that stops me from shooting off something cutting. I mean, I want this guy knowing about my past
about as much as I want a punch in the face, but I'm pretty sure
he's not talking about me anymore.

"It's the number one perk of being an adult, isn't it?" I say.
"Do as I say, not as I do?"

He smiles. Wryly. His finger runs the length of the poster.
"But I'm nineteen," he says. "Where's my free pass to be a jerk?"

We grin at each other. "You probably used it up already,"
I say. "You're handing out IOU jerk passes like crazy."

He tries looking cut but can't stop the smile from spreading.

"Your notebook," I say. "The one in your cozy nuclear bomb
shelter of a room. Looked like poetry to me but now I'm thinking song lyrics."

Maybe he's noticed my carpet needs a steam clean too. "At
least my room doesn't look like a bomb already hit it," he says.

Truce over. Whatever.

I run my fingers through my hair, pushing my fringe out of my eyes. It always clumps together after a shift. It's the oil in the air. And there was extra oil tonight with Mark being around. "What did you want to talk to me about, then?"

"Huh?"

"You were waiting outside the shop to talk to me, remember?"

He goes back to pacing. "Right. We need to talk about Ted."

"You gave me the address so I could go see him."

"But not so you could piss him off. How come I had Ted on the phone banging on about you being the daughter of a cop?"

I snort. It isn't a very attractive thing to do but it shows the right amount of contempt. "So you break into my house to tell me off? What are you going to do, spank me?"

He pulls up short, eyes wide, and then—and this is the big surprise of the evening—blushes.

"Calm down. I didn't mean—"

He holds up his hands. "Hey. I'm not complaining. Let's just agree on a safe word first, okay?"

"Stop it. I'm trying to focus," I tell him. "Ted saw Xavier Friday morning. He said someone had beaten him up."

"He say who?"

I shake my head.

Welcome back, Detective Frankie.

There was a news report tonight. A shot of Harrison Finnik-Hyde's father being led into the station for "questioning." The neighbors told police they heard arguing the night before Harrison vanished. Raised voices. Why the hell didn't they speak up earlier?

The dad didn't look happy about the cameras shoved in his face, ducking his head as his lawyer hurried him into the station. It made me think about Bill Green sneering while

I asked him about his missing son. About the sting in his voice when he said Xavier owed him money. And Ted's words: "Black eye. Cut lip. Bruised all over. Someone was mighty pissed at him."

I sit forward, bed springs chorusing. "Why is Bill not looking for Xavier anymore? At first he wouldn't stop calling me. If Xavier stole stuff to pay Bill back, then he got some money off Ted, didn't he? So why did Bill tell me he hadn't seen Xavier for weeks? At first I thought something happened that stopped Xavier reaching his dad's but maybe . . ."

From my dresser, Nate picks up the statue of a girl holding a kitten, her yellow sundress frozen in a twirl. Vinnie gave it to me about a thousand Christmases ago, before she realized I was never going to share her love for the feline species.

"You know Bill was in prison for assault, right?" he says.

Damn the police. They're right again: always look into the dad.

He dumps the little girl back on the dresser with a thud. Hanging from a hook next to the mirror is something I'd rather he didn't touch—a ballet-shoe pendant swinging from a thin chain; it was tarnished seven years ago when Vinnie passed it on to me and it still is. It's the only thing I have of Juliet's. I don't know why I kept it. I should have buried it with the rest of the stuff.

His fingertips brush the pendant. It feels like somebody reaching into my chest and poking about in there, messing everything up. I don't know why I don't leap onto his back and claw his eyes out.

I wait for him to say something about it. I wait for the sneer.

"We definitely need to talk to Bill," he says, completely sneer-free. He turns his back on the pendant and faces me. Wait, what? No cutting remark? No "So where's your stash of My Little Ponies?"

"We should get a look around his place," he says.

We? This guy is *so* confusing.

I shake my head. "Bill's not going to want to talk to me anytime soon."

"You piss him off too?"

"Just his front window."

Nate laughs. "Then we'll have to show up when he's not there."

I try raising a single brow. I fail. "And how's that going to help if we can't get inside?"

He grins, leaning against Ian Curtis's face. "Lucky you know a burglar," he says.

Twenty-nine

No. It's not lucky I know a burglar. Not at all.

In fact, I'd say it was unlucky. And this is exactly what I say. To his face.

"I'll wait," he says. "Tomorrow. Eleven a.m. In the alley. You can show up. Or not. Your decision."

He says this to me as I shove him out the front door. He hovers on the front step, hands in pockets and head lowered. I open my mouth but nothing comes out. Frankie Vega: tongue-tied?

He smiles, teeth digging into his bottom lip as he looks at me. "Something you want to ask?"

I hug my arms across my chest, fending off the chill. "Why are you suddenly helping me?"

He shrugs as he turns and walks away. "Nothing better to do," he says.

———

I go to bed telling myself that there is no way in hell I'm breaking into Bill Green's house with Nate Wishaw. I am on probation with Vinnie; I know how close I am to messing up everything. I don't even have to sleep on it: decision made.

I actually get a good night's sleep for once. I wake up early the next day and I'm super perky. My complexion is brighter, my eyes clearer, my conscience is super-duper squeaky fresh.

Frankie 2.0 is here. And she is *awesome*.

I bound out of bed. I shower, brush my teeth, and comb my hair until it's shiny. I decide to wear a dress, which means I need to shave my legs. Back to the shower.

I make small talk with Vinnie over breakfast—mostly veiled attempts to weasel information about her date—all the while checking the clock. Not because I'm waiting for eleven. I want to know when it's five *past*. Or maybe ten past—I have no idea how long he'll hang around. I just want to know when it's *past* the time of temptation.

Not that I'm going.

Not a chance.

I can find out about Bill Green some other way.

Like . . . like . . . like . . . ?

Vinnie dumps her bowl in the sink and searches for a cigarette. "Seeing as though you're in such a good mood, why don't we go see your nonna?"

I crunch on granola. "Sure. That'd be nice," I say. I say it like I mean it.

Vinnie nods with approval. She's beaming. I'm beaming. The toaster is beaming. If Daniel were here, he'd melt from all the warmth and love and Disney in the room.

Buttons scowls at me from his bench-top throne, but I ignore him. Don't piss on my parade, fuzzball.

I wash my dishes and tell Vinnie I need a second. "Just have to get changed."

The dress was kind of pushing it.

"That old guy is staring at me," I whisper in Vinnie's ear. "Make him stop."

She shakes me off. "Quit your complaining. We've been here five seconds."

The old guy with the terry-cloth bathrobe and saggy skin watches me from Peaceful Pines' shared living room. He's holding on to his IV drip like he's Gandalf and it's his staff: you shall not pass! There are a couple of other old people, but he's the scariest.

Vinnie marches up to the reception desk. "Hi, Gloria," she says. "Has she had a good week?"

Gloria has a moustache. It's not even a few wispy hairs—it's a full-on set of whiskers. You really can't miss it, so obviously Gloria doesn't give a shit. Even though I can't stop looking at it, I've developed a serious girl crush on Gloria for being so damn self-assured.

"Not so great," she says with a sympathetic smile. "She's fighting with the volunteers again." Then she turns to me, mouth pinched. "And I hear you've been causing trouble."

"No more than usual."

"You'll drive your aunt into this place if you keep it up," she says, and waves Vinnie on. "Go through. Sofia will enjoy having you two pop in."

As much as I'm crushing on Gloria, she's talking shit. Nonna hates it when we come. Because we never take her home with us. That, and she really hates me.

We leave Gloria and the melty guy in reception and head to room twenty-three. The corridors are narrow and the ceiling is way too low; I know you shrink when you get old, but I can touch the plaster without even standing on my tippy-toes.

My boots squeak on the shiny laminate floor. Vinnie tells me to lift my feet.

As horrible as Peaceful Pines is, Vinnie did a really good job of setting up Nonna's room like her bedroom on Hoddle Street. It's got the crochet blanket her own nonna made for her, photos of all the family (not Juliet, though), and doilies everywhere. Nonna is obsessed with doilies.

When we walk in, Nonna's sitting in her armchair by the window, plaid blanket spread across her knees, a forest-green cardigan draped over her shoulders. She looks older than last time I saw her; smaller, too.

"*E che razza di ora sarebbe questa?*" she says, waving her hand at the clock on the wall.

"I call this three minutes past ten," I say.

Vinnie walks in and starts fluffing things. The blanket, the cushions, the curtains. She can never sit still when we're with Nonna. She has to be straightening and sorting things.

"*Vogliono ammazzarmi,*" says Nonna.

"The nurses are not trying to kill you," says Vinnie. She looks at me as she's pulling the blanket across the bed, making sure it hangs down the same length on either side. "Tell your nonna about school."

"Really?"

Her eyes say, *No, not really.* "Of course, really," she says.

"Well, I'm top of every class," I say, "and head of the cheer-leading squad. They're thinking of erecting a statue in my honor when I graduate."

Vinnie's staring daggers, but it's not like Nonna's actually listening. Even when she had all her marbles she didn't listen. She complained. She moaned. She accused. But she didn't listen.

I sit on the little footstool we bought to help with the fluid in Nonna's ankles. She never uses it.

"You want to play cards, Nonna?"

She pulls a hankie out of her cardigan pocket and holds it over her nose and mouth. *"Ma, chi ti ha fatto entrare, Giulietta?"*

My jaw clenches. "I'm Francesca, Nonna," I say. "Not Juliet."

I shove stuff around on the table beside Nonna, looking for playing cards. She used to play Scopa but now she's a fiend for Patience.

I find a pack being used as a coaster for her cold tea.

"Tell your nonna about that award you won," says Vinnie. She's going through Nonna's drawers, pulling out her clothes and refolding them.

I drag the little card table between Nonna and me. "It wasn't an award." I deal us both seven cards. I used to start with five, but Nonna calls me a cheat if she doesn't feel like she has enough cards. "It was just a best-essay thing. And it was last year. And I've already told her fifty times." It was one of those sympathy awards, actually. Something they give to troubled kids to make them feel part of school, important and smart and like a winner. It's to stop us from going full-on dark side.

Clearly it works.

"I was so proud," says Vinnie, holding up a blue sock and looking around with a frown. "*Così fiero*. You should have seen our girl marching up those steps to collect her award."

"Not an award."

I put a card faceup on the table. Nonna snaps it up and adds it to her hand.

"I wish you'd worn that dress like I asked you to," says Vinnie.

"We had to wear our uniforms."

"But you look so pretty in that dress. *La mia bella principessa.*"

I place another card on the table, this time I try facedown. Nonna picks a card from the pack and puts it on top of mine.

She holds her cards close to her chest, practically in her bra. "Don't cheat."

"How can I cheat if I don't know the rules?"

"You know, I really need to talk to them about the way they fold your clothes," says Vinnie. "Does this sock have a pair?"

"Your turn, Nonna," I say. I haven't had my turn yet but I'm worried about running out of cards.

A bit of pink tongue peeks out from the corner of her lips as she looks at her hand. There used to be a time when Nonna would never have left the house without her hair set and her lips painted with Peach Dreams. Now her hair hangs in limp, gray clumps; she won't let the trainee hairdressers touch her because she thinks they poison her. If they've spent more than five minutes with her it could be true.

She slaps two cards on the table, a seven of clubs and a king. "Pair."

I check the time: 10:13.

"They poison my food," says Nonna.

"No, they don't," says Vinnie. "But I think they might be stealing your socks. I'm going to have a word with Gloria. Back in a sec." She waves the sock at me as she heads to the door. I don't know if that's a warning for me to behave myself or an extension of her anger at the sock-stealing staff of Peaceful Pines. Maybe both.

Nonna laughs and points her cards at me. "*She* steals. *Giulietta è un seme cattivo*."

At least *I* don't stink of pee.

"Hush, Ma," Vinnie says, bustling out the door.

My jaw is clenched so tight the muscles down the front of my neck are starting to ache. "I'm Francesca, Nonna. *Not* Juliet." I drop a five of clubs on the table and pick up a replacement. "Your turn."

Nonna looks at me. Narrowed eyes. "*Ti ho detto di andartene, Giulietta*," she says. "How dare you show your face again."

For the love of Gloria's moustache . . .

I lean in close. "Fran-chess-car."

She waves me away. "I'm not deaf."

I've never gotten the full story of what happened between Nonna and Juliet. I'm pretty sure Juliet getting preggo with me at seventeen didn't help. That and the drugs. And the things she did for money. Nonna didn't want to take me in, but Vinnie won that argument. It's not like it's my fault Juliet didn't put a ring on it.

I lay a card facedown and pick up another.

"Nonna," I say, flicking the edges of the cards still in my hand, "you haven't heard from Juliet, have you?"

She presses her lips together and picks up my five of clubs, sliding it between the cards already in her hand. I wait but she doesn't say anything.

"She had another kid," I say. "You've got a grandson."

She looks at me, frowning.

When I find Xavier, after I'm done beating the crap out of him for lying to me and freaking me out, I'll bring him here to meet Nonna. She'll love him. Vinnie always said Nonna preferred the boys, always smiling at Terry even when he lied, stole, and cheated. When she meets Xavier she'll pinch his dimples and coo at him.

"Do you hear me, Nonna?" She squints at me, lips pressed into a firm, thin line. "She had another kid and she kept him. You always said she never saw anything through. Well, she did. She kept him."

Nonna lays down a card. A knave. I see her throat contract as she swallows. It's hot in this room. Old people always have the heat up too high.

"His name is Xavier. He's fourteen. He's got shit taste in music and he does dumb things like Uncle Terry but he's all right. He's an artist."

I try picturing Xavier in this stale, floral-patterned room. Would he sketch Nonna on the back of a doily? Would he teach her to play Texas Hold'em? Would he chat up Gloria or one of the volunteers? Would he steal Nonna's meds, or her stash of money under the mattress, or the jewelry Terry nicked for her, hidden in an old biscuit tin at the bottom of her wardrobe?

I pick up a card from the pack—seven of swords. "I'm going to ask Xavier about Queensland. When I find him. I've never been to Queensland. Have you? Feels like everyone's been but me."

I lay my seven on top of hers. "Snap."

There's a second of silence—wrinkled-brow, narrowed-eyed

silence—and then Nonna throws her cards at me. "Cheater! *Baro!*"

I hold my hands in front of my face and shrink back as cards fly at me. I guess we're not playing Snap.

"*Baro!*"

She reaches out to claw at my face, but I jerk out of her reach and fall backward off the footstool.

Ouch.

Seriously ouch.

It's not like Nonna doesn't do this every time—mistakes me for Juliet, yells at me, calls me all the bad words she can think of, and then falls asleep, drooling. But it doesn't usually end like this. Me sprawled on the floor; bum aching, face flushed, biting my tongue because I don't want to start swearing and I really don't want to start crying.

"*Ti ho detto di andartene,*" says Nonna. She's got her hands in her hair, pulling at the gray clumps. "You were born bad. I wash my hands of you."

A cry catches in my throat. I keep it back with a hand pressed over my mouth.

And then Vinnie's there. She comes storming over, grabbing Nonna's arm and shaking her. "Don't you dare speak to her like that," she says. "*Non osare!*"

Vinnie grips me under the armpit and heaves me to standing. "We're going, Frankie."

She almost yanks my arm out of the socket. Cards flutter to the ground. Nonna wails.

"I didn't do anything," I say as Vinnie drags me out the door. I'm out of breath as she pulls me along at super-angry speed. "It wasn't my fault, I swear."

Worried, nosy faces appear in the doorways as Vinnie charges down the corridor, me being led like a disobedient dog. There's lots of frowning. Lots of muttering.

"I know it wasn't," says Vinnie, but she's frowning too. Glassy eyes.

There's a burning in my chest. Same as whenever Juliet would drag me out of a shop, screaming and yelling at the girl behind the counter for whatever it was that day: not exchanging the sweater that was stained and that she didn't have a receipt for (maybe because she hadn't bought it at that shop) or because the girl wouldn't admit she'd shortchanged her (because she hadn't).

Everybody would stare at me, even though it was Juliet doing the yelling. Everybody looking at me like it was my fault.

Thirty

Ten forty-five. Not long now.

I lock myself in my room and sort my homework into piles: by subject and then by urgency. The urgent pile topples as soon as I'm done.

I'll make a to-do list. It'll be color-coordinated and I'll pin it above my desk. I'll show Vinnie. No, I'll orchestrate it so she comes into my room and just happens to spy the chart hanging over my desk. "What's that, you ask? Oh, it's just my color-coordinated to-do list. No biggie."

I look at my toppled piles of homework and the half-completed to-do list, tapping my nails against the side of the desk.

10:50.

On the car ride home, Vinnie told me not to worry. "It's not your fault," she said. "It's the dementia. You know that." She kept bashing the heel of her palm against the wheel, the horn blaring at every car that dared get in her way. "Still. Next time I'd better go alone."

I need air. This room is way stuffy.

I climb on the desk and lift the reluctant window with both hands, trying to make as little noise as possible. In a building this old and creaky, making as little noise as possible is a shit-load of noise. I just need more air. That's all.

I stick my head out the open window and gulp it in. The breeze brushes across my face, cooling my hot cheeks. Wow. Never have I appreciated cold air more. They should bottle this stuff and sell it to depressed housewives as a cure for something. Middleclassitis.

10:58.

The cold air is so good I sling a leg out the window and feel about for the ledge. I let go of the sill with my left hand, and reach out for the trellis stuck to the side of the building, leading all the way to the bottom, into the alley.

I need more air. That's all.

The trellis is slippery to touch and covered in ivy, but I manage to get a good grip, good enough to let my right hand go and swing my leg across. I dig my boot into the foothold and grip tight as I swing my other leg.

Spider-Man I am not but somehow I manage to inch my way down to safety with only a couple of yelps and minimal swearing. I jump the last meter but land awkwardly, falling backward with an inconveniently loud curse.

Someone claps me.

I look up and Nate is leaning against the wall beside the bins, grinning. "Nice landing."

"If you want people to stop assuming you're a no-good, burglarizing, stalking creep," I whisper, scrambling to my feet, "then you should reconsider the amount of time you spend skulking in the shadows."

"Hey, I'm not the one breaking out of a house."

I dust my jeans off as he comes sauntering over to me.

He gives me the once-over. "You look even angrier than usual. Something up?"

Oh, nothing. Except that Frankie 2.0 was a dud model.

I shake my head. Behind him I see Jackknife's been back and with a new tag and all. This time the two *k*'s in his name are backed up to one another and the *i* is in the shape of a knife with a splatter of blood for the dot. It's crap—like one of those finger paintings criminals do in therapy. Out of their own blood and feces. Whoever Jackknife is, he's got nothing on Xavier.

"Well, you haven't done anything illegal yet," he says. "You can still chicken out."

I can't tell if he's making fun of me. He's not smiling, just looking at me, head tilted and a little crinkle between his brows. If he starts making chicken noises, then I'll know.

He glances at his watch. And when I say "his" I mean someone else's. "Are we doing this or what?" he says.

You may as well quit fighting it, Frankie. You were born to do this. It's in the DNA. It's what everyone expects. Introducing Frankie 3.0. The most badarse model yet.

I nod, slowly.

"Great. We'll take my ride."

"You have a car?"

"Course."

A text from Cara interrupts my glare.

I feel like skipping school—want to get Spanish doughnuts and talk boys???

I look up at Nate. He's whistling. Actually whistling.

Shit.

I don't like lying to Cara but I think a little white lie is the lesser evil in this case. This is a whole other level of wrong. And I'm not dragging Cara to the same murky depths as me.

Working. :(Rain-check.

I shove my phone deep into my pocket. "So where did you park?"

He looks up and down Gold Street. "Um . . ."

I click my tongue angrily, the way Vinnie does whenever one of the customers says something chauvinistic, homophobic, racist—basically anytime one of them opens their mouth.

"Great. You've forgotten where you parked? Worst. Getaway. Ever."

"Screw you."

He walks to the curb and leans over, peering into the passenger side of the car closest to him. "This one," he says, straightening up and glancing at me over his shoulder.

I look at the car. I look at Nate and then I look at the car again. If I pretend this isn't happening, then it's not, right?

He rolls his eyes loudly. "Something you want to get off your chest, Vega?"

"*This* is your car?"

The bulky station wagon he's leaning against doesn't do Nate's bad-boy image any favors; his black T-shirt, skinny jeans, and black combat boots would be more at home in a black Chevy Impala. Or on a donorcycle.

"Yeah," he says. "This one. Got a problem?"

"No. Except . . . have you been hiding a wife, two-point-five kids, and a job as an accountant from me?"

"Do I look like an accountant to you?"

"No, you're right. You don't look like you can count past five but you do seem to have a child seat in the back there, buddy."

Nate bobs down and peers into the back, his hands cupped on either side of his face. I rest my forearms on the roof of the car and wait for him to reappear with a look of contrition, maybe even defeat. I think about humming a song while I wait—something ironic like "Caught by the Fuzz." But when his head pops up again he's just scowling. I have to give the guy props—still managing to look like Mr. January in the Twelve Most Angry Teens calendar while standing next to a beige station wagon is quite a feat.

"Yeah? And?"

"I'm just wondering why you own the car of a middle-aged man with a paunch and a comb-over."

He gives me a look that signals the fun is over. "So I got confused. Whatever." He walks up to the next car along. A Golf. With a sticker on the back window: *Keep calm and eat organic*.

He waves his hand at the car. "You approve?"

I laugh. "Just open the door."

He looks up at me from beneath his lashes—not in the sexy way boy bands do but in the *I'm thinking about hurting you* way that serial killers do.

"I must have dropped my keys."

I sigh. "Lucky I know a burglar."

He tilts his head. "You don't have a problem with me doing that?"

"It's your car, right?"

He nods. Slowly. "Yeah," he says. "It's my car."

Liar.

I shrug. "So it's not a crime to break into your own car, is it?"

Nate shakes his head, a smile lifting the corners of his lips. "No, it's not a crime."

"What's not a crime?" The voice comes from my left: gruff, tired, suspicious, aching for retirement. Marzoli steps off the curb and into a puddle, his hands cupping the cigarette jammed between his lips while he tries to light it. He shakes the match and tosses it to the ground.

Citizen's arrest for littering!

"You two wouldn't be up to no good, would you?" He leans against the hood of the Golf. The car I was about two seconds away from helping to steal.

Well, *this* is awkward.

"No way," says Nate. "I was just telling Frankie it's not a crime to like Duran Duran. I mean 'Girls on Film,' that's a classic."

I give Nate the mother of all death stares. "Seriously? Duran Duran? Hair spray, tight pants, model groupies in bikinis lolling about on yachts? They're just a few crappy pop songs and a whole lot of wrinkly old men."

"But you told me Simon Le Bon is a better lyricist than Ian Curtis."

"You—"

Marzoli chuckles, smoke shooting out his mouth in jagged puffs. "Nice little double act you got there, kids. Didn't realize you two were so tight. He your boyfriend now, Frankie?"

"Hell no."

Nate gives me a one-fingered salute. "Same to you, Vega."

Marzoli zeroes in on me. "What does your aunt think about you messing around with a convicted criminal?"

I swallow. Bastard. Disappointing Vinnie is totally my kryptonite and he knows it.

"Suspended sentence," says Nate. "And it was expunged when I turned eighteen."

Marzoli's brows shoot up. "'Expunged'? That's a big word. You learn that playing Scrabble?"

"You *implying* I'm stupid?"

"Wouldn't dream of it."

I rap my nails against the car. "You'd be too busy looking for my missing brother to waste your time trading insults with a kid."

Marzoli gives me the pit-bull eyes, but I just fold my arms across my chest and give it right back. "I'm assuming that's why you're here? To let me know how the investigation is going?"

Marzoli gestures over his right shoulder. "Been taking a statement from that place there. They were robbed last night."

It takes all of my willpower not to turn and glare at Nate.

Really? Is it like a compulsion or something? Well, at least now I know why he was hanging round the Emporium last night—apart from stalking me and robbing my ex-boyfriend. "Public service" my arse.

Marzoli tilts his head as he sizes up Nate. "You wouldn't happen to know anything about it, would you, Wishaw?"

Nate scratches the back of his neck. "Nope."

"Cos I'm looking for a kid about your height." Marzoli opens his flipbook. "Six foot, give or take, wearing jeans and a very nice jacket—black, tan suede collar."

You're killing me here, Nate.

I sigh. I can't believe I'm doing this again. "He was with me. Last night, I mean. So I doubt he knows anything." Not *exactly* a lie. He was with me (for a time) and he knows bugger all (about most things).

"You're kidding me," says Marzoli.

I shake my head. "We watched *The Notebook*. Nate cried."

Nate nods but his eyes are on me. Dark. Pissed off. Murderous.

The usual, then.

I smile sweetly back.

"He's just gaga for Gosling. Aren't you, Nate?"

Marzoli sucks on his teeth while he thinks. "*The Notebook*? Is that the one about the moon landing?"

Oh god. This is about to go horribly wrong. Why did I have to be a smart-arse?

"Actually—"

Marzoli holds up a finger to silence me. "Not talking to you, Frankie. Talking to Wishaw."

"No," says Nate. He keeps a calm eye on Marzoli. "It's the one with the old guy in the nursing home and the woman with dementia and he's reading a story from a notebook and then they die."

Silence. I mean, seriously?

Marzoli lets out an epic sigh. It probably causes a tsunami somewhere on the other side of the world. He looks at the car, then at Nate. "This thing yours?"

Nate shakes his head.

"Then quit breathing all over it. And get out of here."

I hurry past Marzoli. The dude actually growls at me.

"I'll be expecting your call," I say. Nate hauls me up the

street by the arm. I shout over my shoulder, "When you've done your job and found my brother."

"I'm sure we'll bump into each other again," calls Marzoli. He's not looking at me, though. He's only got eyes for Nate. "Real soon."

Thirty-one

I step off the bus and right into a massive puddle. Ominous?

"So I got you here in one piece," says Nate, clomping down the steps after me. "I paid your fare and didn't hit on you once. The magic word?"

I step up onto the curb and shake water from my boot. "Fuck you?"

"That's two magic words." He shows me just how many on his fingers—in case I missed it.

"Well, here's one." I also use my finger.

The bus pulls away and we've got a good view of the street. In the yard next to Bill's is my best mate, the little old Italian lady—aka Neighborhood Watch. She's glaring up the street but *not* at us. Good.

Nate leans against the bus shelter, squinting into the glare.

"You look nervous. If you're going to freak out, do it behind that bush."

"I'm just not sure we should be doing this now. Marzoli—"

"I can't help it if Marzoli fancies me. It's tough being this irresistible but I'm not going to let it stop me doing what I do best."

"I bet it's tough work being that conceited, too."

He points in the direction of the hedge. "Freak out behind that bush or tell me which house is Bill's."

I nod across the road. "See the old lady leaning against the fence?"

"Yeah?"

"House to the right."

He nods, eyes flicking up and down the street. They settle on Neighborhood Watch. "Is she a problem?"

I shake my head. "I'm pretty sure she's president of the Bill Green Hate Society. She'll probably give you tips on how to break in." I can't help noticing the boarded-up window in Bill's front door. Oops.

I'm wondering why we aren't both hiding behind the hedge. An old dude with a scraggy dog walks right past, staring at us. I picture him behind the glass as he picks me and Nate out of a lineup.

"Why aren't we doing this at night, Mr. Genius Burglar?"

"Because we want to break in when he's not at home."

"He *could* be at home."

"Which is why I'm going to ring the doorbell first."

"And if he answers?"

Nate fixes a choirboy look on his face and affects a southern

American accent. "Hello, my name is Jeremiah. Have you thought about letting Jesus into your life?"

"So let's do this." I get one boot off the curb before Nate grabs my arm and pulls me back.

"Hell no, you're not going in." His curls dangle in front of his eyes as he shakes his head furiously. "No way."

I get as far as opening my mouth.

"I'm not saying this to annoy you or put you down," he says. "This isn't a male conspiracy. It's called being practical. You don't need to go in there. I'm the one the cops fancy. Besides, have you forgotten what happened when you tried to break into the squat? A house with zero locks?"

He's probably right. Despite being the daughter of a junkie prostitute and despite being suspended from school for extreme violence, I've led a pretty boring life. It's only in the past week or so that things have gotten out of hand.

But here I am, standing outside Bill Green's house wondering if I should have bought a stocking to wear over my head.

And that isn't even the awful, horrifying, don't-look-now part. The horrible part is I am actually, mostly, more than a tiny bit, kind of, in a strange way . . . excited.

So I'm not standing by and doing nothing.

"Fine. What do I do then? Why am I here?"

"You're the lookout," says Nate. "If Bill comes, make a bird noise and I'll get out as quick as I can."

I glare at Nate. A bird noise? What are we, Cub Scouts?

"Actually," he says, walking backward so I don't miss his charming smile, "I just like traveling with a beautiful girl."

Great. I'm the gangster's moll.

I search for a rock to throw at him. Nothing. At least with my head down he can't see that I'm actually grinning.

He walks across the street—making a car slow down so he can cross. The driver leans on the horn and Nate gives him the finger.

Nate waits at the front door for about five seconds, gives up, and approaches the side of the house. The little Italian lady watches him carefully. He pauses in front of the side gate and waves to her, shouting something I don't catch. He's almost smooth enough to pull it off.

The old lady waves her hankie madly and curses him in Italian until he sticks his finger up at her, too.

Not that smooth, then.

Nate reaches for his back pocket as he slides through the gate and out of sight.

The little old lady shakes her head, but she doesn't go running inside her house to call the cops. Seems she's happy to turn the other cheek when it comes to Bill "Fuck Off Back to Greece" Green.

I watch the street for about five seconds.

What the hell am I doing? I step off the curb. Since when do I listen to what anyone tells me?

The old lady straightens. When I get close enough for her to recognize me, I wave. She waves her black hankie back at me. I even get a smile.

She is definitely not dobbing on us.

I hurry round the side of the house, dodging windows and imaginary snipers the whole way. I sneak past a group of bins and find myself crouched on the concrete under a small open window.

I peek over the sill; it's a bathroom.

The window is open enough that all I have to do is slide my hand under and lift. Then I'm pulling myself in, half sitting on the windowsill, praying to Jesus, St. Jude, and the Virgin Mary to keep me hidden from view.

I kick over a dead pot plant.

Shit.

I pause, waiting for the alarms to start. For a yeti-man to come bursting in the room with a sawed-off shotgun. Nothing happens so I swing my left foot in, only just avoiding knocking all of Bill Green's toiletries into the sink.

Nate's right. I don't think I'll talk to my career adviser about breaking and entering as an option.

Out the corner of my eye I spy dandruff shampoo, used dental floss, Old Spice, and a very hairy cake of soap.

Shudder.

I tiptoe over to the door; it's ajar.

Where the hell is Nate?

I slowly open the door and look both ways. "Nate?"

Nothing.

As I creep down the corridor, I hear rattling at the back of the house. It gets louder as I reach the kitchen.

A dark figure appears in the beveled glass of the back door. It could be Nate or it could be Bill Green . . .

I hide round the side of the fridge.

The glass smashes with an ear-shattering crack.

Not Bill, then.

"Shit," hisses Nate.

A black-clad arm reaches in through the broken window, unlocking the door. The door swings open and he steps in, trying to avoid the glass on the floor.

I step out from behind the fridge.

Nate jumps. A sweet little jeté like the seven-year-old girl he is. "How the hell did you get in?"

One to Frankie.

"The bathroom window was open." I look down at the broken glass at his feet. It crunches as he shifts his weight.

"Key was in the lock so I couldn't pick it," he says. "Wait." He narrows his eyes. "Didn't I tell you to stay outside?"

"And I did, for a whole five seconds until I remembered that I don't have to take orders from you."

"So who's keeping lookout?"

"Neighborhood Watch."

Nate opens his mouth to argue but I walk away. "Relax, will you?" I head down the corridor. "This way."

We find Xavier's room at the back. It's not much of a bedroom. There's a mattress on the floor, unwashed sheets, dirty clothes, smelly sneakers, and that's it.

The room stinks of boy. The window is shut and the heavy blinds are pulled across, keeping the light and fresh air out.

"I think he just crashed here every once in a while," says Nate.

There's a stack of papers beside the mattress, including a few books: a school library copy of *The Call of the Wild* and a couple of workbooks. I sit on the edge of the mattress and flip through them, looking for something. Anything.

Nate leans against the wall, hands in pockets. "You've met his old man," he says. "I wouldn't stay here much, would you?"

I open Xavier's English workbook. He's got even worse handwriting than Nate. Of course, in the entire book there's only about three written lines so it's hard to tell. Most pages are filled with drawings—his name in graffiti, sketched faces; I think the pig-woman with the knife through her head is probably his English teacher. Apparently he didn't like her very much.

"Let's look elsewhere," he says.

"We're here to find clues, and that involves more than a boy look."

"Go on," he says. "Clue away."

I scan the room—dirty laundry, no photos, cobwebs—ew. There are little brown watermarks all over the ceiling. I wonder if Xavier tried to make pictures out of them—join the dots. But it's not a clue. Not unless joining the dots spells out something. Maybe Marzoli would know what to look for. Witty observations dripping with sarcasm are about all I'm good for.

But I have to find something because Nate is watching me and he's starting to shake his head.

"All right, Sherlock," I say, "why would Xavier choose to live in a zombie-rat-infested squat over a safe, warm house? Yeah, I've met Bill Green, but I've also been to your place."

Nate's obviously too overawed by my astute observational skills to speak.

I dump the papers. "Why did he stop living with his mum? Apparently those two were thick as thieves."

See? Check out my sarcasm and weep, Marzoli.

"I wouldn't know, *Watson*," says Nate. "But I reckon being impossible to spend more than five minutes with is a Vega family trait. So maybe that explains it."

Touché.

He uncrosses his arms and sits on the edge of the mattress. "Anyway. He hardly ever mentioned your mum," he says. He keeps his head down, fingers drumming a nervous pattern against his thigh.

"Yeah, well, he wasn't real good with telling people the truth."

"You know where I met him? Galaxy."

"That's sort of broad. Could you narrow it down to a country?"

"Galaxy is an arcade. Games and shit. I was there and I lifted a few wallets but by the time I got outside everything was gone. Someone had picked *me*. I turn around and there's your brother. Got my whole stash in his arms and he's grinning."

"You bonded over him robbing you?"

He shrugs. "We didn't bond. I just figured a kid like that would be useful to keep around. And I guess he's not so bad."

I laugh. "Obviously. Why else would you be helping me look for him?"

"Yeah . . ." He picks a thread from his jeans and flicks it onto the floor.

"So we don't care about forensic evidence?"

He nods at Xavier's things. "Found anything?"

"No. I mean, I don't think so." I wave at the table. "Help yourself."

He reaches over me to grab the books. Chlorine, smoke, and the lingering stench of public transport. His arm brushes mine.

He mumbles an apology as he pulls back and dumps the papers into his lap. "So clues, right? Well, I can tell you right away he was failing pretty much everything." He waves a report card at me.

"Unless his school kidnapped him to help maintain their averages, I doubt that's important."

As I look around I realize this is not what I was expecting from my brother's room. Shouldn't it be rotting and full of creepy-crawlies or something? I mean, why else would he choose a squat over this?

Nate is sifting through papers, his face screwed up in concentration.

"How come you live in a squat?" I ask. I lean back, stretching out my legs.

He keeps his head down, eyes on the papers. But he surprises me by actually answering. "My father got sick."

Sick? As in Tate McClelland Hospice sick? Nate scrutinizes Xavier's maths book, nose scrunched up, like understanding algebra is going to nab him a date with a supermodel or something.

"Really sick. He died two months ago."

"Sorry."

He flips a page. "Don't be. He was shitty and he died. Gambled everything we had. Left me with nothing."

"So how come—?"

"Quit prying."

"You're an arsehole."

"So are you." He lets the books fall into his lap and rubs his face. "Sorry," he says. "I shouldn't call you that."

"I've been called worse. Why do you think I gave Steve a new nose?"

"Your sore point is your mum, so I'm guessing whoever Steve is, he said something about her."

He looks at me, waiting to be proved right. "What would you know? You got a mum?"

He flinches. "Nope. Just a shitty dad." Those blue eyes take a wander around my face. Assessing, questioning. The tip of his boot rests against my ankle as his eyes settle on mine and, for once, I don't look away.

"You've got . . ." He reaches out, hesitating, stuttering, his hand inching to the side of my head, fingers brushing through my hair.

I freeze for the longest three seconds of my life until he draws back his hand, a leaf pinched between his thumb and forefinger. "This was stuck in your hair," he says. "You going to make a wish?" He holds the leaf in front of my lips.

"That's eyelashes," I say. The leaf dances with my breath.

His eyes shift to my lips.

I stand. "Besides," I say, too loudly, "you already know what my wish would be. I just want to find Xavier so I know he's okay, and so I can yell at him, punch him, and tell him to get the hell out of my life."

Nate drops the leaf; it floats to the ground. He watches it the whole way. "You're really looking for Xavier so you can tell him you don't want to see him again?"

I kick a pair of Xavier's jeans across the room. "I like to get the last word, okay?"

Nate looks up at me. At first he frowns. But then he laughs. Really laughs. A deep, throaty, free sound that catches me by surprise.

Nate plus boisterous laugh equals topsy-turvy world.

"Are you serious?" he asks when he's done laughing.

"I'm glad I amuse you."

There's a little bit of laser in his eyes as he smiles at me. "You have no idea."

We head to the living room when we've searched everywhere else. I'm not sure what I'm looking for. A signed confession? An if-you're-watching-this-then-the-worst-has-happened video?

"I'm sorry I made you break the law again for nothing."

"No worries." Nate's eyes go straight to the massive TV on the far wall.

Aside from the TV, there's a red leather couch, a coffee table that so came from one of those Italian furniture stores in Footscray, empty takeaway boxes, and scattered beer cans. This is clearly the room where Bill Green spends most of his time. Slouched on the couch watching football in his jocks.

"Xavier did that last job with you because he needed cash fast, right?"

Nate drags loose change to the edge of the coffee table with his finger. He counts it in his hand, then pockets it. There's an MP3 player and he grabs that, too. He stops, just as he's shoving it in his pocket, and looks up.

"I . . . ," he starts.

Our eyes meet but he doesn't say anything more. His cheeks shine leather-couch red.

I sink back into the surprisingly comfortable cushions. "I'll pretend it's not happening," I say.

Nate pushes the MP3 player deep into his pocket and looks around for more. "Hey," he says. "This is mine."

He bends over and when he reappears he's holding a candlestick. Seriously. A silver candlestick. Something that might be used as a murder weapon in a Miss Marple book but not something a homeless burglar would have any use for.

"There's no way that's yours."

"It was mine after I stole it," he snaps. But then his brow creases as he weighs the unlikely object in his hands. "Hang on."

Nothing happens except for more frowning and more silence. "I'm waiting."

"I stole this from your neighbor."

"And?"

"I gave it to Xavier. It was part of his cut."

I look at the candlestick. Have we just entered Cluedo? "You've lost the plot."

"I'm a genius." He waves the candlestick at me. "This means that Xavier came here *before* going to Ted's. It means he paid off Bill with stolen goods *before* he went missing."

I sit forward. "It means Bill lied."

Shit.

Shit, shit, shit, shit.

Shit because I'm sitting uninvited in the house of someone who beats up kids, and shit because it was Nate who found the clue.

I pull out my phone. "We need to call the police."

"And say what?" Nate tosses the candlestick; it lands with a muted thud on the cushion beside me. "'Hi, I've noticed that my missing brother's dad has a stolen candlestick. How do I know? Because I broke into his house and I know it's stolen because the guy who originally stole it helped me break in.'"

"You didn't help me break in, Nate."

"Do you want to get arrested?"

Shit.

He's right, of course, but shit anyway.

I throw myself against the back of the couch and close my eyes. I want everything to fade—to not hear Nate rustling through Bill's belongings, to not have the image of Xavier being beaten to a pulp by his dad stuck in my head, to not hear a car door slamming out front, to not hear the old lady next door yelling . . .

"You're in Australia. Speak English!" Bill shouts, right outside the front window.

I spring off the couch; Nate grabs my arm. "Out back. Quick."

The front door opens as we reach the kitchen. There's a clear line of sight from the front door to the back of the house, so it doesn't surprise me when I hear Bill's gruff voice shouting, "Hey!"

Whatever he's carrying goes crashing to the ground and then all I hear is *thump, thump, thump* as the big hairy yeti-man comes bounding after us, quicker than a man his size should be able to move.

My boots crunch through broken glass as I run out the back door.

I turn left but Nate grabs my arm and pulls me to the right. We don't get far before Bill dives and tackles Nate and both of them go flying to the ground.

It's crazy but I've got just enough sense to notice that despite the mess of his front yard and the rest of his house, Bill Green's backyard is immaculate. Cut lawn, decking, a barbecue, and a DIY area with neatly hung tools and a wood bench. There's even a garden gnome and a rockery. Who is this guy?

Nate and Bill roll around on the grass laying punches into each other. Bill's slow, but he knows how to box. Nate's fast, but Bill's got about a hundred pounds on him. Pretty soon Bill's straddling him.

I grab the first thing my hand touches and swing it round in front of me.

"Oi!" I yell, running up to Bill, brandishing what I think is a welding gun. "Unless you want your head welded to your arse I suggest you get the hell off him."

With his fist raised, ready for the next blow, Bill turns to me. He looks from me to the welding gun in my hand.

"That thing ain't even on, love," he says.

"Then I guess I'll just have to have a think about where I can shove it."

He screws up his brow, remaining brain cells finally kicking into gear. "Hey, I know you . . ."

I wiggle the welding gun at him. "Get. Off. Him."

"You want money? Is that it? Because I haven't got any."

"How come? Xavier paid you back, didn't he?"

"This again," says Bill, sucking on his teeth. Nate's trying to wriggle free but Bill is sitting on him. "You broke into my house because of my shitty kid? Man, that kid's been nothing but trouble this whole year."

He mutters, something about Juliet and women in general.

"Just get off him and we'll talk."

He scowls but starts to lift himself off Nate anyway. As soon as Nate gets the smallest amount of breathing space, he slides out from under Bill. He scrambles to his feet and straight off tries to take a swing at Bill; I grab his T-shirt and he lets me pull him back.

Bill raises both hands and grins. "Don't shoot."

"Tell me everything you know," I say. "Did you hurt Xavier?"

He sighs, lowering his hands. "He came by Friday last week. Said he had a load of silverware to pay me back with but there's no way it was worth what he owed. So I taught him a lesson. Then I told him to get the hell out and only come back when he had the full amount. In cash. I let that kid under my roof— I didn't have to—and he repays me by stealing from me. I'm sick of him and I'm sick of you. Any kid that came from Juliet Vega is a piece of scum—you suck on her tit and you catch it."

Red blots pool in my vision.

My breathing is shallow.

He can't say that about me. He can't say that about Xavier. It's not our fault.

He beat up his own son. He doesn't even care that Xavier is missing; he only cares about his money. He's a racist prick. He's the guy my mother chose over me.

And *he's* calling *me* scum.

I swing the welding gun, but I'm not really sure what happens next. I think I get a good crack across Bill Green's face. Maybe there's blood, but I'm already seeing red so who knows.

Nate grabs me before I can swing again. But it doesn't stop me trying, doesn't stop me fighting him.

Nate's dragging me away—I can hear myself screaming, cursing Bill Green. I pitch the welding gun. I think Bill ducks but maybe it clips him, because he howls.

Have I killed him? I don't care. I'm screaming at Nate to let go. I want to hit Bill again. I want to make him pay.

But mostly I hear Nate shouting at me. "Come on," he yells, fingers digging into my skin. "Come on!"

Thirty-two

Nate screeches to a halt outside the Emporium, double-parked.

I loosen the seat belt but don't get out. This isn't the inconspicuous return I'd hoped for. Speeding? In a stolen car? Officially a burglar?

"Your anger is off the grid," says Nate. He's gripping the wheel, white-knuckled.

This is the first thing he's said to me since we left Bill's. The anger hasn't really left me yet—I'm still breathing hard, the red clinging to my vision.

I turn to him. "I'll try to be more polite next time you're being sat-on-to-death."

"Screw you. Don't blame me for this."

I try to think of something really cutting. Smart, too. But I just call him a twat and it all kicks off—name calling and arm waving and finger jabbing and teeth grinding. The car shakes as I whip round in my seat to tell Nate where he can shove his advice about my anger problem.

Nate shakes his head. "You just don't get it, do you, Frankie?"

"What's to get? Something terrible has happened to my brother and I was *this* close, Nate. *This* close to finding out what."

"He told you everything. He had the silverware, Frankie. You saw it. He wants his money back—he needs Xavier. He doesn't know where he is."

"He was lying."

Nate bashes his hands against the wheel. "You cannot be that stupid."

"You're a waste of space, Nate. You ruin everything!"

I fumble with the door handle but it won't open. I bash my fist on the armrest. "What the fuck is wrong with this door?"

He tries reaching over me but I push him away. I wind down the window and open the door from the outside. By the time I get it open, I'm so desperate to get out, I fall.

Shit.

I scramble to my feet. Lucky I'm never going to see Nate again, otherwise I'd be pretty embarrassed right now.

"Just stay away from me." I slam the door.

"Don't flatter yourself, Vega. I wouldn't want to catch crazy."

"Well, at least I'm not a crappy burglar with shit hair and nowhere to shower."

Nate flips me the bird. I kick the passenger-side door.

"Not my car," he shouts.

"You are the most annoying, most self-centered arsehole I've ever met."

He points to his chest. "I'm self-centered? Why the hell do you think I just broke into that guy's house, Frankie? When it's obvious I've got Marzoli watching my every move. You think I did that for me? You think I did that because I give a damn about your brother?" He bashes the steering wheel. "You have no idea."

I open my mouth but nothing comes out. I don't even get it. Is he saying he did it for me? *Why?*

"You want to call me selfish?" He shakes his head and revs the engine.

Still, I've got nothing to say.

"You're a real piece of work, Vega," he says. "Nice knowing you."

He pulls out right in front of a sedan. The sedan's horn blares; swearwords are exchanged. Tires screech as Nate speeds up Smith Street.

Gone. Over and done with. Out of my hair. Done and dusted.

Good.

Great.

Super.

I should have stayed home. Done my catch-up work. Prepared for The Meeting. Sucked up to Vinnie. Anything.

I turn round.

Shit.

I've got an audience.

There's no applause this time, no black hankie waving and compliments in Italian.

Standing in front of the cracked window of the Emporium, Vinnie's got her mouth hanging open. "Francesca Madalina Vega," she says. "Explain. Now."

And Vinnie's not the only one standing there, arms folded, disappointment drawing her eyes downward.

"You said you were working," says Cara. "You lied."

I can't even move. Two pedestrians weave around me, eyes to the ground. Yeah, I'd kind of like to ignore this too.

"I'm sorry," I say. My voice is weak, which is fitting, because it's a weak thing to say.

Vinnie's red heels start tapping. "What were you doing with that boy?"

Do I have to answer that?

"He's a friend of Xavier's. We were looking for him."

Cara hugs her arms across her chest. "You couldn't tell me that?"

"Any reason why you called him a burglar?" asks Vinnie.

Can I pass on both questions, please?

A couple of women bundle past, elbowing me and scratching me with the sharp corners of their shopping bags. I should move out of the center of the path. I should run away, crying.

I look at my boots, rooted to the spot. "It was a stolen car," I say.

Lesser evil.

Vinnie gasps. It's not a super-loud sound, but to me it's like that time someone drove through the front window of the hairdressers next door. *Bang. Crash. Shatter.* What I'm really hearing is Vinnie's love for me shattering into a billion irreparable pieces. It was already an ugly, mangled thing, stuck together with reels and reels of masking tape from all the times I've broken her trust in the past. How many times can it be reassembled? It's never the same once you break it, no matter how good your arts-and-crafts skills are. And mine are shit.

Vinnie flicks out both hands, fingers spread, pushing the air in front of her like she's shoving an invisible me. "I can't do this," she says. She does a one-eighty and clunks into the shop.

The glass rattles as she slams the door.

I stare at the cracks in the paving.

Juliet used to tell me never to step on them. "Ground opens up and sucks you in," she said. My little legs ached from jumping and running after her, trying to keep up without falling through the cracks.

Oh how I'd love to be sucked into the center of the Earth right now.

"I've been sticking up for you," says Cara. "The shit Steve's been saying. It's all around school."

I wonder if it's hot or cold down there? Lava or ice-cold rock?

Cara's voice is bitter. "And I've spent the past half hour pleading your case to Vinnie, telling her there had to be something important—life-and-death shit—to make you break her rules. To make you lie to *me*."

If I open my mouth I'll start screaming. If I move I'll start throwing punches. So I stand there with every muscle in my body tensed. I'm aware people are weaving around me because every now and then their shadows flitter across the concrete. But I *can't* move.

"I'd ask you where you've been and what you've been doing that was so damn important, but you're not going to tell me, are you?" says Cara. "Do you ever tell me the truth?"

Cara's waiting for me to say something but I'm thinking about a polar bear—my polar bear with the black nose and shiny black eyes.

"I'm going to buy you something nice for your birthday," Juliet said. I was four. I had been four for months. She gripped my hand, dragging me onto the crowded tram and through the mall. We kept bumping into people, trams dinging, rain sloshing. And then there were lights, tinkling piano, and the stench of perfume. Juliet stopped to put makeup on. Smacking her lips and admiring herself in the tiny mirror. A lady in white with the cleanest, smoothest skin I'd ever seen was suddenly beside her. "That's a lovely shade," she said. Did she scrub her skin to get it that smooth and white? "Isn't it?" said Juliet. And then we were moving again, my hand gripped too tight, the lights too bright, elbows, feet stepping on mine, pushing. I asked her to carry me but she told me I was a big girl.

She said I could pick out anything I wanted. She smiled at me, lipstick on her teeth. I went straight for the polar bear. He was white and soft and clean. I called him Harold. I sat with him under a rack of dresses while Juliet looked for her own birthday present.

When we left, Juliet didn't hold my hand so tightly. She walked with her shoulders back and I hurried to keep up, avoiding the cracks in the tiles.

But when we got to the doors, a man gripped Juliet by the shoulder. "Come with me," he said.

Juliet kept shouting: "It's my daughter's birthday." People stared. I was glad when we went into the small pale-green room. No one but the man to stare at us. I hugged the polar bear to my chest.

"Did you pay for that?" he asked. He pointed to the bear.

"Yes," I said. It was a lie. I knew it was a lie. "His name is Harold and he's four years old."

The police came. "His name is Harold," I told them. "He's mine."

I wouldn't stop lying. I couldn't.

Someone bumps my elbow as they pass.

I look up but it's too late. Cara has already walked away.

Thirty-three

There's a hole in the flat again. A Vinnie-size hole on top of a Cara-size hole on top of a Xavier-size hole. There's even a small fissure that's a little bit Nate-size.

Vinnie and I choreograph our movements to avoid each other.

We dance outside the bathroom, eyes down, both going left, both going right, then giving up and scurrying back the way we came. We work side by side but don't talk; the customers order extra loud, trying to cover the silence.

Cara won't return my calls.

I don't even have a number for Nate.

I'm tired of leaving messages on Xavier's phone.

The piles of homework grow and grow until I can no longer pretend I'm not terminally screwed.

There comes a point where you've done all the self-flagellation you can, sent as many groveling text messages as you can, and said "sorry" so many times it becomes meaningless—a word-fart of little consequence. There comes a point where you realize there's actually nothing you can do: you've fucked up. Capital F. Capital UCKED.

I wait for Marzoli to come and arrest me.

He doesn't.

The only call I get is from the school. "You've got a meeting with Ms. Vukovic, Friday at four p.m. sharp. Don't miss it."

Wouldn't dream of it.

Thirty-four

Page fifteen.

There's nothing about Harrison Finnik-Hyde until page fifteen. I guess even rich white kids have an expiration date.

I flip to the crossword, the paper rustling as I struggle to find the edges. It's a tsunami of noise compared to the silence of an empty Emporium. Compared to every second of the past two days.

I don't even know where Vinnie is right now. She left an hour ago without saying a word. Maybe another date. She must be thinking real hard about joining that desert cult right about now.

I don't look up when the door *jingle-jangles*. It always takes people a couple of minutes to decide what they want. I don't want to stand there staring at them while their faces contort with indecision, like I've got nothing better to do than wait until I'm needed, like I don't exist before these people wander in.

Besides, I'm trying to work out what "Unusual dance per-mit creates big mess" means. Eleven letters, last letter is a *t*.

"This some new kind of customer-service trick?" says a fa-miliar gruff voice.

Okay. So there's any number of reasons why Marzoli and his snot-nosed sidekick have wandered into the Emporium. Not all of them end with me being hauled off to jail.

Quite a few do, though.

Marzoli drops a twenty on the counter between us, right over the top of the crossword. "I'll have the usual. Peters will have the same."

"Does that include the usual side of contempt?"

"That's very humorous." Marzoli tries to smile. Nine out of ten for effort but a mere point-zero-zero-five for the frankly shocking execution.

I grip the electric knife and start carving strips from the lamb spit. My hand shakes.

"You doing the crossword?" Peters peers at the paper upside down and screws up his nose. "Man, I hate those things. How's anybody supposed to know what . . ." He swings the paper round right side up. "'Unusual dance permit creates big mess' means. Total gibberish."

"Ms. Vega is a crossword whiz," says Marzoli. He says it like an accusation. "So I guess you're home sick from school again?"

"I'm taking a break. Got to wait for the other kids to catch up."

The meat's a little pink. Most times I'd fry it on the hot plate but today I dump it straight onto the flatbread. I carry it over to the counter and start piling on the salad—two scoops of jalapeños and extra chili sauce.

Marzoli *harrumphs*, nudging Peters with his elbow. The guy's still leaning over the newspaper, mouth hanging open for extra concentration. "Huh?"

"I think Miss Vega might want to hear the news about her brother." Marzoli leans against the bain-marie and watches. The pit bull is out in force.

I fold up their kebabs and slide them over with trembling hands.

"Xavier Green's sister, eh?" says Peters. He whistles. The I-wouldn't-want-to-be-in-your-shoes whistle. He's got a chalky stain on his tie. Toothpaste. Or actual chalk, like they use to draw round dead bodies.

I grip the counter. "You got news?"

Peters rips into his kebab. Guess he wasn't watching me make it. Marzoli lays a hand on top of his but doesn't pick it up. "Your brother's house got broken into two days ago. His father's place: Bill Green. You know him?"

I shake my head. Small, jerky movements. I always feared Vinnie's wrath above everything else—now I'm not so sure.

I yank the crossword out from under Peters's elbows and grab my pen. Unusual dance permit creates big mess . . .

"I'm just thinking it's a hell of a coincidence," says Marzoli. He picks up the kebab. Sniffs it. "Your brother goes missing and then his dad's house gets broken into."

I tap my pen against my lip. "I'm sure it had nothing to do with Xavier."

"Yeah?" Marzoli coughs as he tries to swallow his first bite of the Frankie Special. "Why's that?"

"As far as I know, Xavier hasn't been living in that house. He's been squatting."

Marzoli and Peters exchange looks. "Well, I think the

government will be interested to know Mr. Green is claiming welfare for a dependent he doesn't have," says Marzoli.

I keep my gaze focused on the crossword, voice as even as I can make it. "Maybe whoever broke in was worried about him. Maybe they were looking to make sure Bill Green hadn't done anything bad to him."

Marzoli nods slowly. He hasn't gone back for a second bite. "Bill Green thinks Xavier's run away. Says he owes lots of money and, like his mother, isn't real good at facing up to responsibility."

Peters shrugs. "Sounds like a solid story."

But Marzoli frowns. I'm pretty sure these guys rehearsed this before they came in. I'm also pretty sure we're getting to the heart of their little performance. The music is swelling and the camera is panning in for a close-up. It's Oscars clip time. "Then again," says Marzoli, "Bill Green could have been confused. He'd recently been assaulted."

Peters whips out a large, glossy photo from his coat pocket. Boo-ya! He pushes it across the counter at me. "Sure you don't know this man?"

Somehow I don't run screaming from the room. Even though my knees wobble and my heart sinks, I stay upright.

Just.

I shake my head. Marzoli *tsks*.

The photo has obviously been taken at an emergency room. Bill Green's got a black eye, a swollen cheek, and a nasty cut on his brow—like someone introduced his face to a welding iron. He's staring murderously at whoever's taking the shot. It could have something to do with the fact that he's wearing a hospital gown and the chill air is probably freezing his puny yeti-balls off.

I'm in so much trouble.

I stare at the picture, waiting for Marzoli to whip out the handcuffs.

He leans over the counter, garlic and jalapeño breath wafting my way. "Mr. Green's not being real cooperative. Guess he doesn't want the police looking round his house. The doctor called it in, but when we tried chatting to Green about it he got all tight-lipped. He reacted when we showed him a picture of Nate Wishaw, though. He looked real angry."

I bite down hard on the inside of my cheek. Really hard.

"And he didn't look too happy to hear your name either." He flashes me a mouthful of crooked teeth.

I lower my eyes to the crossword. Unusual dance permit creates big mess.

I will get this.

I will not be stumped.

Eleven letters, last letter is a *t*.

Marzoli sighs. "Between you and me, Frankie, Bill Green's not the best of characters and I'm not real worried what happened to him. In fact, I couldn't give a shit. I'm more interested in getting hold of Wishaw, a boy who seems to spend a lot of time in other people's houses, uninvited."

I stay silent, afraid of opening my mouth and word-vomiting incriminating things.

Unusual dance permit creates big mess. Big mess? Try: "Frankie." Try: "my life."

"Let me outline my position, Frankie." Marzoli dumps the barely touched kebab on the counter. "I see kids like you all the time. Nobody to show them how to do things right. You're smart but you don't apply yourself. You get in fights. You get mixed up with the wrong crowd—kids just like you. Broken families. Tough lives. They're the ones who understand you, right?

"But your aunt has done a good job with you. Don't let her hear me say that but it's true. With the start you got in life, it's a wonder you turned out as well as you did. Don't throw all that back in her face, Frankie. Don't protect a criminal—you think he can find your brother? He's stringing you along because he needs your alibi. He'll dump you in the shit the second it suits him. You think he won't squeal on you when we haul him in?"

He taps the photo of Bill Green. Fingers thick, stubby.

"I figure I've got two choices," he says. "I could spend my time looking real close at what happened at Bill Green's house or I could focus on Wishaw. Forget everything else." He pulls out a mug shot of Nate and dumps it right on top of Bill's photo. "What do you reckon, Ms. Vega?"

I stare at Nate's photo. The angry glare, the scowl, the couldn't-give-a-fuck tilt of the chin. But so lost. Let down. Acting out.

I hate him.

I hate that I don't hate him.

I hate that I can't ignore what he did for me.

I shove the mug shot toward Marzoli. "Fine," I tell him. "The truth is it was Reverend Green in the library with the candlestick."

The kindly-old-man routine fades as Marzoli presses his cracked lips into a firm line. We have a brief staring contest before he stuffs the photo back in his coat. Peters chews his kebab. Loudly.

"If you happen to run into Wishaw," says Marzoli, "tell him I'm looking for him."

He picks his kebab off the counter, garlic sauce dripping out the open end. He looks just about to leave but then he pauses.

"Ten across, Frankie," he says. He jabs the paper. "'Unusual dance permit causes big mess'? 'Predicament.'"

He smirks as he walks out the door.

Thirty-five

Vinnie's still not talking to me but when I wake up Friday morning, there's a note pinned to the fridge.

DON'T FORGET SCHOOL CALLED—MEETING WITH VUKOVIC TODAY. FOUR P.M. DO NOT BE LATE. DO NOT TAKE YOUR ATTITUDE. WEAR UNIFORM. PRACTICE GROVELING.

Subtle.

It's too loud to concentrate in the office because a couple of the homework club kids are cleaning out the stationery cupboard, making paperclip chains to whip each other with. Square-Tits doesn't say or do anything about it.

My fault for getting here late, I guess.

I hit Steve because I was temporarily insane.

I was possessed (but I'm okay now).

I slipped and accidentally broke that kid's nose.

It was a political statement. You can't expel me for express-ing myself.

I scribble out everything I've written, accidentally ripping the paper.

I didn't plan on being late. But I walked the long way here, trying to clear my head of the rotting chipmunk carcass stuffed in there, and got distracted by my own pity party. I mean, what's the point? I'm past forgiveness with Vinnie. What else matters? I've missed so much school now that the idea of going back and trying to catch up just seems . . . vomit. It's not like I was going to get into uni anyway, not with my lazy-arse marks.

So when I rocked up half an hour late, Vukovic was waiting for me, sitting with her palms facedown on her antique desk, a steaming mug of coffee in front of her. Not the only thing steaming.

"I've been waiting," she said.

"That's bonus free time for you," I said. "To do whatever it is that you do outside of school. Actually, what do you do? I'm betting it's got something to do with horses."

"I take my job very seriously," she snapped. "You should take your future seriously."

"I said I was sorry."

"Sorry only works the first few times, Frankie. But you keep making the same mistakes."

I thought hard about climbing across Vukovic's desk, grab-bing one of her stupid horse pictures, and throwing it across the room. It would have smashed through the window and sailed into the quad. It might have landed on someone's head. Ava Devar's, if I was lucky.

I didn't do it. But I thought about it. In graphic detail.

"I called you in today because I'm not sure I can trust that you'll say the right thing at the meeting on Monday," she said. "When the board calls on you to explain your actions."

I didn't say anything. In my head I was busy doing the conga around Ava Devar's lifeless body.

"So I'm asking you to write a statement. I suggest you take this seriously. I don't think you understand how close you are to losing your place at this school." She waved me toward the door. Dismissed. "Doreen at reception will set you up with a pen and paper."

So for the second time this week I'm being made to write something and I've got an audience while I'm doing it. If Square-Tits looks down her nose at me one more time I'll insert my pencil up it.

She clears her throat loudly and reaches for the Wite-Out.

I check my phone but Cara hasn't responded to my latest text.

I raise my hand. "Miss? Reception lady? Can I go to the bathroom, please?"

"Have you finished your statement?"

I look down at the page full of scribbles and crossing out. "Yes."

She laughs. "You can't leave until you're done. Really done. Ms. Vukovic's rules."

The glass doors open and in walks Steve Sparrow. He's got a bucket and sponge in one hand, his school bag in the other. His white shirt is soaked through. He dumps the bucket in front of reception and shoves in his earphones.

"Done," he says. "It's child labor. Wait till my dad hears about this."

Square-Tits's nails *clickety-clack* against the keyboard. "Sit," she says.

"What?"

"Sit." She points a narrow silver nail over his shoulder at the chairs behind him. *My* chairs.

I sink lower and let a curtain of black hair hide my face.

Steve coughs "bitch" and turns around. He takes about two steps before he sees me.

"Shit no," he says. "You can't make me sit near her. She's psycho."

Square-Tits points again. "You're in enough trouble as it is, young man. Take a seat and wait for your father to get here."

Steve does a massive loop around the room, shuffling with his back against the wall, keeping his eyes on me the whole time. He lowers himself into the chair farthest from me; there are only three chairs to pick from and I'm in one of them. He presses his white earphones in deeper.

"Keep your hands to yourself," he says. He dumps his bag on the chair between us.

I start my statement again: *Steve Sparrow is a prick. I did the world a favor. The end.*

Steve beats his palms against his thighs. He can't sit still. He keeps shifting in the chair—every time he shifts, the whole bank of chairs wobbles. "What are you even doing here? Didn't you get expelled?" he says.

I scribble out "the end": *If you let me back into this school I promise I will make it my life's mission to hurt, annoy, piss off, and maim Steve Sparrow. The end.*

"You're such a freak," he says.

Square-Tits shushes him. The homework club kids giggle from inside the stationery cupboard.

Steve loops his finger in circles beside his head. "Freakie."

I grip my pencil tight in my fist. This is so going to end badly.

"I'm not even supposed to be here," says Steve. "Your stupid lesbo mate dobbed on me, but I didn't do it. My dad is going to sue these bastards."

He says "bastards" loud enough to earn a *tsk* from Square-Tits.

Don't get sucked in, don't get sucked in, don't get—

"Dobbed you in for what?"

He scowls at me—the bruising on his face has turned all sorts of crazy colors and shapes. It looks like one of those ink-blot tests, the kind that reveal how crazy you are. "Why are you talking to me, freak?"

"Because you won't shut up."

"You shut up."

I scribble out "maim" and write "kill."

Steve unzips his bag and gets out his pencil case. He rummages through it loudly before pulling out an oversize marker. He zips up the bag and plonks it on his lap. He's got a half-finished drawing on the side.

We sit in silence.

The homework club kids are pretending the rulers are light-sabers and they're Jedi. There's a loud slap as one of the Jedi gets whacked. There's giggling and sucking in air, trying to breathe but laughing instead.

The marker zips and hums as Steve slides it across the rough schoolbag fabric, blacking out a letter. *E*, I think.

I scratch out everything I just wrote. Half a page of scribbled-out bullshit. Vukovic is not going to like it.

I hold my pen against the paper but nothing comes: I have nothing to say. I could tell them about Ava and that first day of school. I could tell them about every one of Steve's insults. It gets boring after a while, though—slut, whore, freak, whore, diseased whore, freak, weirdo, whore, blah, blah, blah. They wouldn't like all the swearing so maybe I shouldn't tell them. I could tell them about Mark and Ava behind the science block. Bill Green, Xavier, Juliet . . .

I don't write a thing.

How messed up is that?

Even Steve's got something to say. Something he's prepared to display on the side of his schoolbag. He's got his tongue sticking out and he's totally focused. The *E* is almost completely blacked-in now. It's the last letter in a single word. In the middle of the word, two *K*'s stand back to back, the top of each of them is a bloodied knife, dripping.

"Holy shit!"

"Shhhh." Square-Tits frowns at me.

I cover my mouth and swear again. "You're Jackknife?"

Steve's eyes go wide and he looks as though he'd like to jump across the chair between us and shove his marker down my throat. "Are you high? What the hell are you on about?"

I point at his bag.

He dumps it at his feet. "You're full of shit."

"I've seen your stuff."

"Stop talking to me."

"I live in the flat above the Emporium. The alley beside the shop?"

He clicks the pen lid on and off as he stares at his feet. "I told you, shut up."

I throw my head back and laugh. "Man, I could get you in so much trouble."

"You don't have any evidence. No one would believe you."

I wipe my eyes. "Yeah. I know. I'm not going to. I don't care what you do." I pull the lid off the pen and write: *Because I felt like it*.

"Don't tell my dad," says Steve, and it's the first time I've heard him say anything without a sneer in his voice. He takes out one of the earphones. "What do you know about it, anyway?"

I draw smiley faces over the top of both *i*'s. "I know you covered a much better piece with your stupid tag."

"You're full of shit. No way is that Skid-Mark guy better than me."

"X Marks."

"Whatever."

He shoves the earphone back in and squeezes his hand into his pocket, turning his music up. A fuzzy, screamy, drummy drone.

The smiley faces get pigtails and a sombrero each.

"He's been doing it longer than me, is all," says Steve. He sinks down in his chair.

I give one smiley face a cigar and the other angry brows.

"He's my brother," I say, drawing a distinctly middle-finger-shaped poof of smoke wafting from the cigar.

Steve yanks out an earphone again. "What?"

He watches me drawing. Maybe he's wondering how I can be related to Xavier if I'm such a shit artist. It looks like poo, not smoke, wafting from the cigar (which also looks like poo).

"You don't have a brother," he says. The sneer is back.

"Correction. I didn't have a brother until two weeks ago, when I learned I have a half brother. My mum, as you've pointed out more than once, is far from a nun. So it's possible I have many half brothers, but X Marks—Xavier—is definitely one of them."

"I don't understand half the shit you say," Steve says. "But it's cool X Marks is your brother. His stuff is pretty awesome."

Well, how about that. Steve saying something that doesn't make me want to maim him. Shame it's about Xavier.

"Pity he's a lying, thieving prick." I scrunch up the paper and shove it deep into my backpack, way down the bottom with all the pens, receipts, maths homework sheets, and muesli bar wrappers that live there.

The homework club kids hurry out of the stationery cupboard, rubbing the red marks on their arms and grinning at each other. "Done, Miss," they say at the same time. Square-Tits waves them into the office, where she gives them another mind-numbing bunch of busywork. They'd be better off wandering the streets, joining gangs.

"I saw him the other day," says Steve. He's not grinning or sneering. He's serious. He shrugs. "Doing a piece along the river. There's this awesome wall, ripe for it."

I gape at him; he doesn't look like he knows he's just dropped a life-altering piece of info.

"When?" The armrest digs into my stomach as I lean over it.

"Maybe a couple of Sundays ago? Some black-and-white thing. Not his usual but pretty good, I guess."

"What time?"

"Dunno."

"Was anyone with him?"

He shrugs.

"You don't know who was with him or you don't know if there was anyone there?"

"Chill, Freakie," says Steve. "I was just passing but I saw him with—"

A loud voice barks Steve's name from the front entrance.

Both of us jump in our seats. Steve stands as his dad marches over to us.

"I didn't do it," says Steve. There's a clink as his dad boots the schoolbag at Steve's feet. Fred Sparrow grips his son by the shirt, lifting him and pushing him up against the wall.

"Do you know who I had to cancel to come here?" says Sparrow.

Behind reception, Square-Tits holds a hand to her mouth. She doesn't say anything, though. She doesn't even get up.

Steve's blinking his eyes heaps. "But I didn't do it."

Sparrow pushes Steve in the chest as he lets go of the shirt. "Defacing school property? The same damn thing every time. You're a waste of space."

As Sparrow bends, grabbing Steve's schoolbag in the middle, he glances at me. I'm not sure he recognizes me but he sneers anyway. Talk about resting bitch-face. I open my mouth—there are twenty different smart-arsed things I could say but I don't say any of them. The bag strap catches on the armrest and Sparrow yanks it hard to free it, rocking my chair.

"We're going." He doesn't even look at Steve as he says it.

Steve watches his dad march out, the glass door rattling as he slams it shut behind him. Steve stands there, hands balled into fists by his side, breathing hard.

Nobody says anything.

Steve pushes his hair out of his eyes, sniffing loudly. Then he looks at me. "What the fuck you staring at, Freakie?" He sounds like a five-year-old.

I shake my head. Twenty different things I could say.

He walks away, punching open the doors.

Square-Tits gawks at me.

I don't know if I sit there for half an hour or half a second, but eventually I get up and walk to the reception desk.

"You have something for me, Fran-chess-caaar?" She holds out her hand.

I place the pen in her palm.

"And the—"

I walk away.

Thirty-six

I ring the front doorbell.

There's a tumble of thumping and shouting as Cara's brothers rush to answer the door.

Lawrence gets there first, elbowing Aaron as he flings it open.

He looks excited for all of about three seconds and then his face crumples. "It's only Freakie," he yells.

Aaron shoots me a glare. "We're waiting on pizza," he says.

"Take a look in the mirror," I tell him.

Lawrence grabs his gut and laughs. "Oh my god. Burn."

Aaron kicks Lawrence in the shins. "Shut up. At least I don't have a pizza arse."

"Do not!"

Cara appears halfway down the entrance hall, coming from the living room. Her smile is wiped the second she sees me.

I've seen her give that look to Ava about a billion times and it's always made me laugh. Because I wasn't on the receiving end. Because she was giving that look to Ava out of loyalty to me. Having her death stare turned on *me* is a massive kick in the guts.

"You two, get back in the living room," she snaps. The twins are kicking and punching each other. Cara boots one of them up the behind, I can't tell which from here. "What did I tell you?"

"You said you're a loser."

"You said we could read your diary. Oh wait, we already did."

She kicks out, but they're already running for the living room, snorting with laughter.

"Boys, huh?" I say with a plastered-on grin.

Cara juts out her chin. "What do you want?"

Okay, Frankie. You never expected this to be easy. Just do it. I shift my weight and chew on my lip.

"I'm here to say sorry."

"You said that already. I wasn't impressed the first time."

"I know. But this time I'm saying sorry with Spanish dough-nuts." I hold out the paper bag. It's almost completely translu-cent, the fat having seeped through the paper. Most of the sugar is shuffling round the bottom of the bag.

"And I've got another lead. About Xavier. I thought we could go together. I'm not really supposed to leave the house without asking Vinnie first, but if we hurry . . ."

She leans against the door frame and watches me, arms folded, paying no attention to my bribe. She's kind of frowning, kind of pissed off, kind of worried.

"What's the name of the guy my mum's dating?" she asks.

"Huh?" I open the bag to make sure the doughnutty smell can waft seductively up to her nose.

She blinks, slowly enough that her eyes are closed for a couple of seconds. Blotting me out of her vision, I guess. When she speaks there's a pause between each of her words. "What's the name of the guy my mum's dating?"

"Your mum's dating someone?"

"What happened to Paul at work a week ago?"

"Your older brother?"

She nods. Again, it's slow and deliberate. "You know, six foot, shoulder-length black hair; you've met him about a hundred times."

"I don't know what happened to him."

"How about me? Do you know how my date with Truc went?"

"You had a date?"

She looks away. "Exactly."

I shuffle from foot to foot. Waiting. I don't think this is going very well.

"You don't know anything because you haven't asked," says Cara.

"I've been distracted but—"

"Yeah, Frankie. I know you've had a shit time of it, but seriously. Get over it. We've all got sob stories. Yours isn't even the worst one around."

I step back. I guess the depth of her anger has caught me off guard. Even when she's standing on the top step and I'm at the bottom, I'm still taller. So how come I feel so damn small?

"You could just tell me stuff," I say. "You don't have to wait for me to ask."

She laughs. "If I waited I'd be wetting myself in an old

people's home before you took an interest in my life. But it isn't even about that." She folds her arms. "I can get over the fact that you're self-absorbed. You always have been. I can even forgive you flaking on me over a boy but I don't think I can get over you lying to me. You lied to *me*. I thought we were in it together."

I lower the doughnuts, my cheeks burning. How stupid am I? This isn't like the time I spilled Coke on her favorite T-shirt after borrowing it without asking first. That took me ten Spanish doughnuts and two English essays to fix. And here I am with a bag of doughnuts—cold now—and a bunch of half-arsed excuses.

"I mean, you're not even going to tell me what you and that burglar were really doing, are you?"

I grip the bag tightly. The only sounds are passing traffic, a really loud cartoon blaring from inside the house, and Lawrence and Aaron screaming insults at each other. The perfect sound track to a perfect moment.

"I'm so bored with this. You never tell me anything. You won't even tell me why you hit Steve and I'm supposed to be your best friend."

I drop the doughnuts at her feet and stick up my finger. I've never done that to Cara but there's a first time for everything. "Screw you," I say. "I don't need this." I stomp on the doughnuts.

"Real mature, Frankie."

I charge down the front path and wrestle with the front gate. "If everything about me is so damn annoying, then I don't know why you even bother."

"That makes two of us."

I finally win the war with the gate, slamming it shut behind me and stalking up the street. I don't look over my shoulder even though all I want to do is go running back, begging for a second shot. A third shot. A gazillionth shot.

"Call me when you've had a personality transplant," Cara shouts. The front door slams shut behind her.

I hurry up the street, holding myself together for half a block.

That did not go according to plan.

That just took a shit on top of my best-laid plans.

I crouch in the middle of the footpath and cry. I've just made things about a thousand times worse, haven't I? I can't even really wrap my head around how bad I've just screwed up. Bigger than any number of Spanish doughnuts can fix.

I go to the river without her. Which is stupid because it's getting late and even stupider because I'm on the world's strictest curfew.

Why am I still looking? Because I'm worried? Because I care? Or maybe I just need to find him so this will all make sense, so I can show Cara, Vinnie, Nate: *See? It was worth it. I've found him.* The scary part is I know exactly why I'm still looking: the sick feeling in the pit of my stomach won't let me stop worrying that something bad has happened.

The concrete wall runs for a good chunk of the path along the river. All the way along the right-hand side, leading up to an overpass. Steve was right—it's perfect for graffiti, and about fifty million graffiti artists have worked that out already. The path cuts under the bridge and that's where I'm headed until I stop dead in my tracks.

I almost don't see him at first.

I was walking with my head turned, trying to spot Xavier's piece. X marks the spot.

But Dave's impossible to miss, his long puffer jacket and his shock of white hair.

"Don't cheat me," he says.

The sound of his voice brings the bile up from my stomach.

He's under the bridge, pacing back and forth. I step off the path, behind the hanging branches of a tree.

Some twitchy-looking guy is standing in front of him. "Nah," he says. "Nah, I wouldn't. Not you, Dave. I've got the money."

"So go and get it."

Twitchy kid runs his fingers through his hair. "Can't you just spot me a gram?"

Dave hisses and then there's a flash of something silver, something metal, and the twitchy kid is backing away, hands out front.

"All right," he says. "I'll get it."

My hand goes to my neck. I back away too. Slowly.

"Get me my money, shithead," says Dave.

The twitchy kid runs. As soon as he's out of sight, Dave lets out a roar. He turns, beating his hands against the concrete wall. He's muttering; nothing intelligible, nothing I want to hear.

When the knife-wielding psycho is having an episode, that's your cue to run, Frankie.

For once, I listen to my brain.

Thirty-seven

When I walk through the front door of the Emporium, Vinnie's serving a couple who are all over each other.

"Out," she says.

The couple give me freaked-out possum eyes. They probably think I'm some kind of crazy person, banned from every kebab joint in Melbourne.

I start backing up. "Okay."

"Not you. Them." She jabs a nail at the couple, one at a time. "You two," says Vinnie. "Out. Now."

My bum bumps into the edge of a table as I back up.

The couple don't stop to argue, bushy possum-tails between their legs as they scurry out. That's another shit review for Terry's Kebab Emporium.

Vinnie marches over to the front door and flips the sign. *Closed.*

Hey, at least she's talking to me again.

Vinnie's got one hand pressed to the Closed sign, the other on her hip. "Take one guess where I had to go this afternoon."

"Another 'appointment'?"

That's right, Frankie. Poke the bear.

She thumps the heel of her palm against the door. The glass rattles. "You better think twice before giving me some smart-arse response," she says. "I've been down at your school being made a fool of again."

She turns round.

"I can—"

"You wander in late and act like a spoiled brat when you get there? You're given yet another chance to defend yourself and you throw it away?"

She leans against the counter, like staying upright is a challenge. This is Vinnie—Vinnie who could run a marathon in stilettos and pick up a date at the end of it. I swallow the great lump of bitterness in my mouth.

"They don't trust me to speak in front of the board so I have to write an essay on why I'm such a screwup. You think that's a genuine chance?"

"Someone in your position, Francesca, takes every chance thrown her way. What are you waiting for? A golden bloody ticket?"

I grab the thing nearest to me—a napkin canister—and throw it to the ground. Just to hear something crashing. Just to make a noise. "What am I supposed to write?"

For the first time in my life, Vinnie looks afraid of me.

I hate myself for it.

"What do I tell them, Vin? That I'm some psycho freak who doesn't know how to control herself? That I rearrange some guy's face just because I don't like something he says? Who does that?"

Vinnie stares at me, brow furrowed and mouth open. I hate it when people say "her lips formed a perfect O" because they just don't make that shape. Not perfect. It's distorted, ragged, deflated.

She shakes her head, voice quiet. Too quiet. "You're going to lose everything you have if you keep acting like this. Everything."

Joke's on you, Vin. Pretty sure I've already lost everything.

"Well, that's what we Vegas do, right?" My whole body is shaking, rattling. "We rid ourselves of whatever doesn't fit. Whatever isn't fun or exciting or useful anymore. We dump it at the Collingwood Children's Farm and fuck off to Queensland."

"Don't you—"

"Or maybe that's just me. Because she kept him. Did you know that?" I grip the side of the table, hold myself upright. Just. "Thirteen years she kept him and could barely make it through four years with me. I'm the common denominator, aren't I? It's me people run away from. Juliet, Xavier, Cara, Mark, Nate, you."

I can't take it anymore. Can't stay here and look at her face, at her disappointment. I can't hear her say the words that are surely coming: *I'm sorry, Frankie. Sorry I ever gave you a chance in the first place.*

I turn, my foot kicking the canister along the ground. *Crash. Clang. Bang.*

Everything's a blur but somehow I make it out of that place. Somehow I run up the stairs and into my room. Somehow I make it behind the closed door before the tears start.

It was grandparents' day at school. I guess I was six. Maybe seven. Vinnie had found the note scrunched up in the bottom of my bag the night before.

"What's this?"

I looked at Nonna chopping tomatoes in the kitchen. "Nothing," I said.

Vinnie flattened out the note against the coffee table. "Like hell it's nothing. Ma," she shouted. "Ma, *vieni qui!*"

Vinnie held out the note for Nonna. She wiped her hands carefully on her apron and squinted at the note.

"*Sono troppo occupata,*" said Nonna.

"Too busy?" said Vinnie. "Doing what?"

I went to sleep to the sound of them arguing. But the house was silent when I woke up. I found Vinnie in the kitchen making my lunch.

I gripped my stomach and groaned. "I'm too sick to go to school," I said.

She walked round the end of the bench and placed the back of her hand against my forehead. "Get your uniform on. You feel fine."

I wasn't feeling fine when I got to school. Gray hair, yellow smiles, look-at-me-Grandma shouts echoing through the playground.

Vinnie grabbed my hand and walked me to where my class was lined up. I looked up at her as I stood in line, my little fingers squeezed in her grip.

The girl in front of me stared at Vinnie. I wanted to kick her but I couldn't reach, and Vinnie wasn't letting go of my hand.

Mrs. Ibrahim came over. "Ms. Vega," she said. "Are Francesca's grandparents coming today?"

Vinnie stared back at the girl in the line until she turned around with red cheeks.

"I'm here," said Vinnie. "It's aunt and niece day."

If I gathered all my memories like that and tried to bury them in a time capsule in the backyard, the Earth would bulge and the old willow tree would fall down.

As I lie in bed, facing the wall, I listen for sounds of Vinnie returning to the flat. I wait for stomping through the apartment, the pantry door squeaking, kettle boiling, toilet flushing, tap running, and lights clicking off one at a time.

It never comes.

I fall asleep to the sounds of silence.

Thirty-eight

It's blacker than Satan's bile when I wake. I don't know if it's Sunday night or Monday morning. Maybe the world exploded while I was sleeping and there's no such thing as Monday anymore.

I can't get back to sleep, so at six I get up, shower, and sift through the clothes on my floor—the sniff test isn't a scientific approach, but it's effective.

I struggle into jeans and scan the floordrobe for a top.

It's one of those nothing-to-wear days. Everything's a fat top, a lumpy-arse jean, a wobbly-thigh skirt.

I think about finding the dress Vinnie liked and putting it on. Maybe even the pink skirt Nonna Sofia bought me. My "keep," "donate," and "burn" piles never really found their way off my floor so now they're all part of one big pile and I have plenty to choose from.

A black sweater will do. Forget the holes; it doesn't matter.

The apartment is cold. Feels empty. For about three seconds I freak out that my nuclear bomb/meteor/alien invasion theory was correct and I'm the last person on Earth, but then I press my ear to Vinnie's bedroom door and the sound of her snoring steadies my heartbeat.

Kind of.

Vinnie hates me. Cara hates me. Nate hates me. And it's Meeting Day.

I tiptoe to the front door. Buttons is perched on the sideboard in the corridor. He doesn't run or hiss or flash me his arse. He just looks me over, eyes half-closed, a steady purr. Great. I'm so pathetic even Spawn of Satan pities me.

I let the front door click shut behind me.

Outside it's gray. Art-house moody lighting. Like that shit film our media teacher tortured us with—three hours of black-and-white, some girl wandering round a mansion looking worried/upset/hungry. It was French—'nuff said.

I wrap my coat tighter around me and hurry to the back of the yard because I have something important to do.

Willow branches slapping my face marks the spot.

I left the trowel stuck in the ground beside the trunk so I grab it—the handle is freezing. Why couldn't I have done this at three in the afternoon? Why couldn't I have done it in summer? On a tropical beach?

I crouch and drive the trowel in. I'm glad this time it's kind of dark so I can't see how many worms I kill.

How many wriggly lives have you got to ruin before you take a good hard look in the mirror, Frankie?

Dirt goes flying as I scoop the trowel in and out. This time I don't have anything to add to my time capsule. I'm digging it up so I can throw it away. The necklace, too. And the kitten statue. Every damn scrap of useless crap. The time capsule really was a dumb idea and I don't even know why I did it. Stupid Daniel. Who wants to be reminded of stuff in twenty years' time that they don't even want to think about now?

I've decided to get rid of all my shitty memories, less-than-perfect actions, regrets, and epic failures. It's a fire sale—get in quick for a bargain.

As I'm digging I hear a creaking noise behind me.

You'd think I wouldn't be surprised by Nate just turning up anymore. But I freak out so much I overbalance and almost fall backward.

It's not so dark that I can't see him, leaning against the fence, arms behind his back. He's not out of place in this French-art-house film of a morning.

I'm pretty sure the back gate was locked. No such thing as a locked-room mystery when Nate's around, though. Agatha Christie would have hated him.

"What the hell? Why are you here?"

"The Fitzroy pool," he says. "I know the guy on the morning shift. He sneaks me in. It's where I shower."

I stare at him.

"You asked," he says.

I guess that explains the chlorine smell. Not why he's in my backyard at six thirty in the morning.

"I took a walk," he says. "Ended up here. What's your story?" I offer him a smile, just a small one. Because no one else I know wants to talk to me.

"I couldn't sleep. I have this thing today. Kind of important." I drop the trowel. He's watching me. Intently. "You know when a country invades another country and the UN has a meeting to decide if they're going to bomb the shit out of everyone to stop the bad country from bombing the good country? Well, it's kind of like that."

"So which are you?"

"The bad country."

He laughs, just a small one. With his head down. "Well, I'd better tell you something before they bomb you," he says.

I wait for him to go on, but we end up just standing there, staring at each other.

Forgive me for assuming that was the kind of sentence that has a swift follow-up. Never assume, Frankie.

"I broke a guy's nose once," he says before I can chime in with something stupid.

"Only once?"

"And two teeth."

"Not bad. It's not exactly breaking a nose, cracking a jaw, and causing PTSD with the collected works of Shakespeare, but you can join the Teenagers with Violent Tendencies club. I'm president, so I can guarantee you membership."

"It wasn't just some guy." Nate takes a step closer, his boots squelching in the mud. "It was my dad."

"Did he deserve it?"

"He deserved worse." He smiles, lopsided. "It's how I got my first black mark. A fine and community service but it's on my record."

"Which was expunged."

"Big word."

"I know. I must have picked it up somewhere. From someone pretty smart. For a dickhead."

He brings both arms around from behind him. He's holding something thin but square. Like a big piece of cardboard.

With a drummer boy on the front. *An Ideal for Living*. The album is a bit damp around the edges from being shoved deep in a bin but I'm sure it's still worth a few grand.

"*You* stole it? I left it *in* with the rubbish. With the rotting tomatoes, spoiled meat, and congealed fat. How did you—"

"Saw you dump it."

"You were watching?"

"No, I was hiding because the cops were sniffing around."

"And you took it because?"

He shrugs. "It's worth a shitload."

Oh. Not what I was expecting, but hey.

I drop the trowel and reach out for the vinyl. "Four and a half grand. Sure you just want to hand this over?"

"I'm guessing it's worth more to you than me."

There's a second or two when we're both holding on, one corner each, and then he lets go and it's in my hands.

Hey, drummer boy. You've caused quite a bit of trouble, did you know?

He takes another step closer. "I'm sorry about what I said to you."

"So you should be."

A wayward curl covers his left eye. It makes him blink.

"I mean, me too," I say. "Sorry."

"So you should be."

I reach up and brush the curl aside. It's almost a cool move, except my hand trembles and my uncut nail scratches his forehead. So not cool at all. He doesn't move, doesn't even blink.

"You should go," I say. I wrap my arms around the vinyl to stop any further embarrassing compulsions. "I can't get into any more trouble or Vinnie will kill me. That's not hyperbole, you know. For real. Kill me. Do you even know what 'hyperbole' means? It's when—"

Nate cuts me short by kissing me.

Really kissing me.

Vinnie's-romance-novels kissing me.

Me-running-through-a-field-of-daisies-on-planet-Hot-Guy-with-the-music-swelling-to-a-moving-crescendo kissing me.

He pulls me close, both hands holding the sides of my face. His lips are soft—soft like Harold the polar bear's fur and the guinea pigs and the silk blouse Vinnie wore when she collected me from the police station, me with the note in my pocket from my deadbeat mum. Soft like all the things that ever made life better.

He kisses me, hands sliding down my shoulders, fingers digging into the flesh of my arms, his teeth grazing my lip, his breath mixed with mine.

But I just stand there, clutching the vinyl, arms folded. I'm like a big, dead, wet fish.

Because I mean . . . so . . . just . . . wow. How did this guy become *the guy*? I try to process this totally unexpected wowness.

While he's kissing me.

Kissing. Me.

Until he's *not* kissing me because the whole dead-fish vibe overwhelms him and he steps back. He looks as confused as I feel.

"I don't know why I did that," he says after a whole lot of frowning and staring. "I'm sorry I did that."

I stare at him wide-eyed. I've lost my words—maybe they're still prancing around planet Hot Guy while the rest of me is here on planet Majorly Embarrassing. I blink as my brain picks itself off the floor and my body unfreezes.

Okay, so I have processed the wowness and I have reached a conclusion: it must happen again.

"Actually," he says, "I'm not sure why you didn't kick me in the balls for doing that."

I reach out, my fingers through his bramble of curls. "That makes two of us."

He smiles. It makes me smile.

He steps in again, hands sliding up my arms, across my shoulders, fingers brushing up my neck.

"Would you hit me if I did this?" He leans forward, nose gently brushing my cheek.

I tilt my head toward his. "Maybe."

He laughs. His lips pause against my skin.

"You're not going to kiss me again, are you?" We're so close that when I speak my lips brush his chin. It's weird how you don't know how much you want something until it's right there in front of you, centimeters away.

"I was thinking about it," he says. He grips me around the waist and pulls me closer.

"Is it just to shut me up?"

"Partly."

"What's the other part?"

He lowers his head, and . . .

My phone rings.

Shit.

He steps back to give me enough room to squeeze my hand into my jeans. He clears his throat.

"It's not me," I say. "It's my phone."

I don't recognize the number. Bill Green. Or Marzoli.

Either way, it's too early for a call. A tremor runs through my chest: It could be good news. Or very, very bad news.

"Sorry," I say. "Sorry, Nate. Only be a sec." I press the phone to my ear. "What?"

"That's rude." It's a girl.

"Sorry, no. I thought you were—do I know you?"

The voice on the other end pauses. She exhales loudly. "You're looking for Xavier."

"Maybe. Who are you?"

"Who are *you*?"

Nate gives me an eyebrow raise and for the first time I don't want to slap him for it. Well, not completely.

I go back to the phone. "If you don't tell me your name, I'm hanging up."

Nate reaches out, his fingers brushing my hips. Maybe I'll hang up anyway.

"Fine," says the girl. "But I saw your poster. Thought you'd care."

Nate squeezes the tips of his fingers into my waistband and draws me closer. "Get off the phone," he says.

"I do care."

"I know you do," says Nate.

"Shut up."

"You're so rude," says the girl.

"No, not you shut up. Him shut up."

"Who?"

I push Nate away.

"I'm Xavier's sister, okay? I *am* looking for him. What do you know?"

"Shit. Hang on." There's rustling, heavy breathing, and

movement. A door closes. "Sorry. Mum just got up. I have to go."

"Wait—"

"Meet me at Bellini's." Her voice is harried, whispered. "Eight a.m."

"Who *are* you?"

"Reenie." Another door closes and her voice drops even lower. "I'm his girlfriend." Her voice catches. "I mean, I *was* his girlfriend."

"But—"

She hangs up.

Thirty-nine

"What's this chick look like?" Nate's hair falls across his face as he inspects his boots.

I shrug, too preoccupied with maintaining a sane exterior to answer. It's peak hour in my head: thoughts, memories, and freak-outs zooming about. I keep checking the time, thinking about Vinnie and the note I should have left for her, worrying about Cara never speaking to me again, angsting about Steve Sparrow's broken nose, about being late for a meeting that will apparently decide my future, and why Reenie said she *was* Xavier's girlfriend, not *is*. But what's really holding up traffic is the kiss. That kiss.

I look away when Nate catches me staring and I suddenly can't stop looking at a tram rambling past. Seriously, it's the most fascinating thing I've ever seen because, you know, living in Melbourne means I hardly ever see a tram.

The tram's brakes screech and the bell dings as a four-wheel drive turns in front of it. I hope no one inside took a tumble—then again it's the 86 and probably full of hipsters. They'll land softly on their beards.

"So how are we going to know which one is her?" Nate asks.

I cup my hands and peer through Bellini's window. It's gloomy: lots of wood, maroon walls, low lighting, and taxidermy animals popping up in strange places. Like a meerkat holding the tip jar. "I think she might be the girl in the school uniform sitting on her own."

Nate peers through the window, his breath huffing up the glass, shoulder brushing against me. He jerks back, grabbing my arm.

Maybe the guy doesn't like meerkats.

"Your school meeting's in an hour, Frankie," he says. "You don't have time for this."

"What?"

"It's a bad idea. I can get you to school. I'll steal a car."

"Speaking of bad ideas."

"Seriously."

"I know. Seriously."

He looks at me. Pleads with his eyes.

I laugh. "What the hell's gotten into you?"

He frowns at Bellini's window. The guy has a meerkat phobia.

"I'm just . . . I don't know. You don't need me here, do you?"

"Need you? Hell no." I pull him with me toward the front door of Bellini's. He digs his heels in but whatever last-minute freak-out he's experiencing is no match for Stubborn Frankie. "I'll keep it super quick. And I won't even throw a welder at her."

I only score a grimace as he pushes open the door, waiting

for me to scoot in under his arm. "Five minutes? Promise?" he says.

"Relax," I tell him.

As soon as we get inside he grabs my hand and squeezes. He doesn't look me in the eye. "Are you sure this is important? This could stuff up your chance at school."

"Have you been having secret meetings with Vinnie?"

A guy, about twenty, shoves a couple of menus under our noses. "Two?" he says, somehow making a three-letter word drag on for a whole minute.

I point to Reenie, tucked in the back corner. A dead fox prowls the shelf behind her head. "We're with her."

Nate swats the menus away.

"Two coffees," I say.

"What kind?"

"The coffee kind."

I push Nate toward Reenie and the fox; she watches us approach from beneath false lashes.

I should be nervous about meeting this girl—about the things she has to tell me—but all I can think is: How the hell did my brother land *her*?

Plump, black-skinned, hair shaved close to her head, full-lips, and a high forehead. I swear I've seen her in a fashion magazine. She's *gorgeous*.

I stumble to a halt in front of the table. Her look says, *Yeah, and?*

"You Reenie?"

The seat across from her slides out as she kicks it. "I was supposed to be at school five minutes ago."

"So was I." I try smiling as I sit opposite her but it feels like my face might crack. Nate drags a chair from another table with a screech, a thud, and a scowl.

"So what did you have to tell me?" I lean on the table and regret it instantly—the surface is sticky.

Reenie spoons sugar into her coffee. "Sorry, who are you?"

"I'm Xavier's sister. Like I already said." God I wish that fox would stop grinning at me from behind her head.

"Not you." She points her spoon at Nate. "Him."

He clears his throat, eyes on the coaster he's twirling under his thumb. "Nate."

The waiter arrives with two long black coffees, plonking them on the table in front of me and Nate. "Your coffee," he says, putting the "aggressive" in "passive-aggressive."

Reenie leans forward. "Xavier owes people money. I don't want to dump him in it."

At least she said "owes," not "owed." I take an angry sip of coffee. Or is it black sludge? "I know he did. But I only met him three times and I'm too poor to lend anyone money."

"Then you're lucky," she says. "God, that's gross." She spoons three more sugars into her coffee, bashing the side of the cup as she stirs. "He owed me shitloads. That's why we broke up."

I check the time. "So this info you have on Xavier . . ."

"You don't look like him."

"We only share a mother. And we never actually shared her. He hogged her." My phone vibrates against my thigh. "Sorry." I pull it out and reject the call without even daring to acknowledge the name flashing on the screen. Ten past eight. "Do you know something about Xavier or not?"

Nate leans into me, whispers in my ear. "We can just go."

"Wait a second," says Reenie. "How did *you* know him?"

Nate suddenly only has eyes for the big-screen TV on the back wall. There's a soccer match on so maybe he's into sports. Or maybe he's casing the joint. "We robbed a few flats together. Well, I did the robbing; he was the lookout. Did a shit job of it too."

I kick him under the table. Why is he being a jerk all of a sudden? I mean, why is he back to being a jerk?

Reenie narrows her eyes. "Did you say your name was Nate?"

He points at the TV. "Did you see that? Fucking offside. Bullshit."

I unstick my forearms from the table and lean forward. "You said you know something? About Xavier? It's kind of why I'm here."

She keeps her eyes lowered as she turns her coffee cup round and round. She doesn't say anything.

I check the time again: 8:12. "This is kind of important. The last anyone saw him was Friday two weeks ago. He paid his dad some of the money he owed and got beat up. He might have been spotted by the river on Sunday, but I haven't verified that. I broke the guy's nose who told me so I'm not sure he can be trusted."

Reenie looks up. "That's not true."

"It is—I used Shakespeare."

"I mean it's not true the last anyone saw him was that Friday. *I* saw him later than that."

My coffee sludge is going cold but I wait, unmoving. "When?"

"I saw him that Sunday. We'd already broken up but we were still hooking up, you know. He was all excited. Said he'd found a way to get all the money back he owed and then he was going straight. For you." She looks at me, eyes shining. "Said he was going round to his mum's and then he was gonna tell you."

Can't. Even.

I grip the table—the room starts to spin.

Nate tenses beside me.

Reenie rolls her eyes and keeps talking. "All about his stupid fantasy. How the three of you are going to live together and be one big happy family. I've met your mum, though. He took me to see her in that home and she's a leech. She might be dying but she'd still do anything for a hit. You'd think all the drugs she was hooked up to in that place would be enough for her. I mean—"

Reenie doesn't shut up—her mouth keeps opening and closing. But I've got the world on mute.

Hearing your mum's dying has that effect.

Hearing she's somewhere in this state, in this city, within visiting distance.

Dying.

Nate grips my thigh tight but I can't even feel it. All I can think about are pink shoes. I'd forgotten about them. Forgotten the whole thing. Now I just want to clamp my hands over my ears and scream because I can't stop remembering.

The day before the children's farm there was lots of screaming. Juliet was throwing furniture round. Bill was there, shouting too. I watched from the couch, cartoons blaring but not loud enough to drown them out. I had these pink shoes on. They were new and Juliet had actually paid for them—a gift for me. I hadn't taken them off—I'd slept in them.

"Do something about it," Bill was yelling.

"I haven't got anything," Juliet was shouting back. She threw the kettle at his head. I stared at my shoes, feet dangling off the edge of the couch. They were shiny, a little button in the shape of a heart on the elastic strap and lights on the heels that flashed whenever I moved.

Next thing I knew she was kneeling in front of me, blocking the cartoons. "I need these, Frankie Bean," she said. She grabbed my feet and starting pulling at my shoes, twisting them and dragging me half off the seat. I screamed but she told me to act like a big girl. She told me she'd get them back for me. She promised.

Bill took the TV and then they were gone. I got left on my own a lot so I didn't really panic. But I cried about those damn shoes. I cried the whole time they were gone. At least Juliet and Bill came back happy—no more screaming.

". . . Frankie?" Nate's shaking my arm. I blink. Someone's phone is ringing. Why don't they answer it?

"I'm fine," I tell him. I growl.

He looks down at the table. At my phone. Ringing.

I reject the call without checking to see who it is. I know who it is. It's 8:20.

Reenie's looking at me, brown eyes wide and questioning. The fox is too, grinning at me through the mood lighting.

"Frankie," says Nate. "Do you want to—?"

I shove my phone to the side and lean forward. "So you didn't hear from him after Sunday?"

Reenie shakes her head. "And he told me he was going to call. I had a basketball game the next night, a really important one, and he said he was going to call and ask me how it went. He always calls after my games."

"But you were broken up," says Nate. "Maybe he—"

"Hey! That's how I know you." Reenie jabs a finger at Nate.

"The time Xavier took me to meet his mum? You were there. Your dad's in the same home, isn't he?"

The bottom drops out. *Smash.*

Nate turns to me. Desperate eyes. "She's full of shit. Let's get out of here."

"Screw you," says Reenie. "Xavier introduced us. I remember you being a jerk then, too."

"Listen, kid," says Nate. "We didn't come—"

I stand; my chair goes flying back. "Well, that was a big fucking waste of time." I search through my pocket for cash.

"So rude," says Reenie.

Eight twenty-three.

I dump the cash on the table, swatting Nate's outstretched arm. I stick my finger up at the dead fox because I don't know what else to do.

I hurry around the tables, clipping my thigh on the back of a chair as I weave. I'm walking like I'm drunk.

Nate calls after me, the sound of cutlery and dishes crashing as a tray goes tumbling. I don't stop.

"Wait," he calls when I'm already outside. I'm jogging down Smith Street, through the early-morning crowd: suits carrying takeaway coffees, students struggling home from a big night out, and Homeless Eddie rambling to himself. He isn't really homeless. He has a home; it's just that we're standing right in the middle of it, which is pretty rude of us. He owns the whole of Collingwood. Ask him, he'll tell you.

"Frankie!"

I jerk to a halt as Nate grips my arm. I shake free of his grip and slap him. The sound cracks. People walking by gasp.

"You knew?"

Nate holds his cheek with one hand, the other reaching out

for me. "Xavier said he was going to tell you when it felt right. He didn't want you to know she'd kept him when she'd dumped you. He thought you'd hate him for it. I didn't think it was for me to tell you."

Homeless Eddie shuffles toward me, asking if I'm okay. He holds one arm high, wrapping it around the back of his neck as he hovers a meter away. He doesn't know anyone at the Fitzroy pool.

"I'm okay, Eddie."

"Please," says Nate. "I didn't lie, I just . . . He went missing and . . ."

"I already know that Juliet kept Xavier longer than me. I didn't know she was here. That's something you could have told me."

As the icy wind bites through my jacket to my skin, a realization creeps into my mind. One of those insights that come about five minutes too late—usually because you're so focused on something else that you don't see what really matters until too late.

"You said your dad died two months ago."

Nate shoe-gazes while Homeless Eddie starts humming, loudly.

"But I *saw* you go to the hospice a week ago." I grab hold of Nate's chin and force him to look at me. "Did you go to see *her*?"

"I was asking about Xavier. For you."

"You arsehole." I hit his chest. Not hard. Not hard enough.

"So you keep saying! She lied to me, though, didn't she? Said he hadn't been there for ages."

"That's what she does. She lies. Everybody does."

Eddie keeps on mumbling "Everybody does" over and over.

Nate grasps my arm and pulls me in close. "I thought I was doing the right thing. I thought you hated her. You've already got this weight on your shoulders—you try to hide it but I see it. I didn't want to give you another reason to hate yourself. And I didn't want you to hate *me*."

But I can't even look at him.

I shrug free and walk away.

"Where are you going?"

"Where?" shouts Eddie.

My phone is vibrating in my pocket but I ignore it.

"To get my shoes back."

Forty

The day after Xavier first contacted me I was in the school library, hiding in the corner with the classic literature. No one would find me there. I needed time to pick through what was left of me—I wasn't Frankie anymore. I was in pieces, blown apart by a bombshell called Xavier.

She's my mum too.

She's my mum too.

She's my mum.

There was this moment I couldn't get out of my head. A memory that had always been hiding in the periphery—but I kept shoving it back. Shoveling the shit on top and forgetting about it.

I couldn't forget about it anymore.

Before my mother took me to the children's farm, I stood in the doorway of her bedroom while she swayed in front of her full-length mirror, a hand rubbing her tummy. It was sticking out, like she'd overeaten. She was looking at herself in the mirror and smiling.

She caught me watching her. I shrank against the frame but she said, "Come here, Frankie Bean."

I went to her. When I got close enough, she wrapped her arms around me and pulled me in tight, my cheek pressing against her thigh.

"It's going to be so brilliant," she said. "Can you feel it, Frankie? Everything's brand-new."

And we smiled at each other.

Sometimes I forget that we smiled.

Sitting in the library on my own, I came to know what that moment really meant. The lie behind it. Both of us smiling but for different reasons. The truth of it wrapped tight around me, suffocating.

And that's when Steve showed up.

That's when I looked up and saw his mud-gray Vans a foot away, laces undone, black at the ends.

He opened with "What's up?" but it went downhill from there. He didn't exactly ask me out—he didn't have dinner and a movie on his mind—but he made a pass so I told him to shove it.

His cheeks burned red as he glared at me. "Who do you think you are?" he said. "Some guy paid your mother for sex. So do I need to pay you? How about five bucks? No wonder she dumped you."

I'm not sure who I was hitting when I swung that book but it felt good. I think I was tired of taking punches; I wanted to hit back.

I wanted someone other than me to be the one who was always hurting.

The Tate McClelland Hospice is all clean lines, lots of white and a shade of gray-green that's probably called Frost Ivy or Scandinavian Moss. The place is hushed; nothing but a stream of murmuring and faint beeps echoing off the shiny tiles. It smells like bleach mixed with vomit.

My boots leave a trail of mud pellets as I thud toward reception, a set of inner doors sighing calmly as they close behind me.

A woman with a tight bun and the face of a cat's arse heads me off before I can reach the desk. Her soft-soled shoes squeak across the floor.

"Who are you?" She holds a semitransparent clipboard to her ample chest.

It takes all of my strength not to punch her in the face.

"I'm here to see Juliet Vega."

Cat-Bum purses her lips as she checks her watch. Nine o'clock. On the dot. "You're early. Visiting hours aren't until ten."

Too early. How about that?

"I'm her daughter."

She laughs—a single, throaty "Ha!" "She doesn't have a daughter. She has a son."

Maybe it's all the white, sighing doors and frosted glass having a calming effect on me, but I continue *not* to hit the woman, which is a huge surprise to me.

"I don't carry my birth certificate around but I *am* her daughter. And if you know Juliet Vega—which I'm assuming you do—then you'll know that no one would admit to being related to her unless it was absolutely necessary."

She tilts her head and lightly raps the clipboard against her chest. Thinking music.

Sure. Because I've got all the time in the world.

I look over her shoulder at the TV in the waiting room behind her.

It's the news.

On the screen four people are standing in front of a blue curtain. A gray-haired cop in uniform is looking proper and stern and like you'd be happy to leave your baby in his care. He's standing next to Harrison Finnik-Hyde's parents.

The mum's got her hair set. That's what Vinnie calls it when she puts rollers in her hair overnight and then in the morning she's got these perfectly set waves. There's more of a honey hue to her hair than last time she was on TV. Maybe she saw herself and didn't like it. Sometimes you can't tell until you see a photo of yourself. Harrison's dad is looking unhappy and happy at the same time. Frowning and smiling. Lights are flashing. Cameras.

Standing between them is Harrison Finnik-Hyde.

Thinner, red-eyed, eyes down, nervous. Both his parents have their arms wrapped around him.

His mum hasn't taken her eyes off him. "We're just so happy he's come home. We're not even mad," she says.

"Kids make mistakes," says his dad. "I don't think he even knows what running away has done, how much trouble he's caused."

"We're never going to fight again." The mother's voice breaks.

My nails dig into my palms.

"Listen," says Cat-Bum, "I can't—"

"Paula?" A crisply white woman leans over the reception, crooking her finger at Cat-Bum. "IV for Mr. Rodriguez?"

Cat-Bum's eyes roll back into her head, the most exaggerated eye-roll I've seen outside of my own mirror. When they're done rolling, her eyes settle back on me.

"Room seventeen. Morning's best for Her Majesty anyway."

She swivels on her heels and squeaks away.

My mother sits in a chair by the window, her body bent to one side, her head jutting left. Her arms, fingers, and legs are sort of curled, like they're seized up. Like a dead bug, all crispy and hollow. Left out in the sun too long.

I stare at her. My mother.

This place is a fifteen-minute walk from the Emporium. Fifteen minutes. I should have asked Cat-Bum how long she's been here, how long I've been fifteen minutes from her. I wish I could ask Xavier.

Her head jerks toward me, her eyes rolling around to find me.

"What do you want?" She talks like there's an egg in her mouth.

I stay in the doorway. The room is small and painted Scandinavian Moss. There's a photo of Xavier by her bedside; everything else in the room is medical—drips, silver trays, pill bottles, straps, monitors. It's not like my mother was ever surrounded by personal things—she sold everything she could—but I remember her being surrounded by *stuff*—junk and men.

My fingers stay pressed to the door frame. "Do you know me?"

Every part of her body seems to want to bend left; only her eyes remain straight on. They're yellow-tinged and watery. "Should I?"

I take a step in, but I keep one hand on the door frame. Just the tips of my fingers. "Is that your son? In that picture?"

"Who the fuck are you?"

She doesn't remember. It's the disease. Whatever the hell she has that's killing her. Probably a cocktail of diseases. They're eating her brain. She probably doesn't know what day it is. It's all the drugs she's taken.

"I'm Frankie." I drop both hands to my sides. "Francesca."

She tries to shift her body higher, her chest puffing out and her elbows digging into the back of the chair. I'm not going to feel sorry for her just because she's sick. My mother who used to show me how good a dancer she was in the middle of the street. She would pirouette, her leg knocking groceries from the hands of people stupid enough to walk close by her. She would say, "Look at me, Frankie Bean. Look how your mother dances." It's a strange kind of dance she does now.

"I had a daughter called that," she says. "She's dead now." She collapses back into the chair, no higher, no straighter than before.

I teeter on the spot and squeeze my hands into fists. I want to rub my eyes, try to rub away the red inkblots pooling there.

"I'm not dead."

I have this dream, all the time. Sometimes it comes to me in the daytime. Sometimes I think about asking Daniel what it means but I don't really believe in all that dream analysis bullshit. Or maybe I already know what it means.

It's dark. Then I see a sliver of her profile, a crescent moon of human flesh. I feel her hot, urgent breath on my neck and my oversize nightie twists around my body. My mother's hands reach for me but it's as if I'm made of water. She slips through me and then I can't see her, not even the sliver of moon. In my dream it's dark and someone is sobbing, but it's not me.

The armchair squeaks as her body jolts. "You want money? Is that why you're here?"

"I want Xavier."

When she laughs, spit dribbles down her chin. "Another disappointment," she says. "I was cursed."

Well, how about that, Nonna? Like mother, like daughter. I come from a long line of curses.

I close my eyes and picture Daniel's sleepy smile. *How does that make you feel, Frankie? Did that hurt your feelings? You can't bottle everything up, Frankie. How much room do you think you have in there?*

It makes me feel like shit, Daniel.

"He's missing," I say.

When I open my eyes she's not even trying to look at me anymore.

"Haven't seen him."

"Sunday. Two weeks ago. He came here."

More dribble. This time she just kind of gurgles. If she's trying to say something, I don't hear it.

I walk to the bedside and pull a tissue from the box there. I stop for a second to look at the photo. He's younger. Thin. Too thin. He's holding up a painting of the sun and three stick figures in front of a house.

My mother's eyes follow me as I walk to her side. She tries to jerk away but she has no control. She can't run away from me now. How about that.

I stand over her, wiping her chin clean.

"Did he talk to you about the money?"

"Money?" She licks her lips.

"He owed heaps. Thought he could get it back somehow."

"No idea."

"Sunday. Two weeks ago. What happened?"

She pushes her back into the chair, head rolling to the side. "I didn't take his money. He was waving it under my nose but I didn't take it."

"Did he tell you where he got it from?"

"I didn't ask. He didn't give me any. What do I care?"

"He's in trouble. He's . . ."

Her yellow eyes roll to the side, to the little buzzer on the table beside her. "Get out," she says. "I don't want no ghosts in here."

I drop the tissue and grab her arm. "I am *not* dead."

I grip her so tightly. Her skin is waxy and dry. It would be easy to break her arm. All I'd need to do is squeeze.

"You ran away," she says. "I called the police but they said—"

"You left me behind. You dumped me." I spit out each word and squeeze her arm tighter. I don't think she could reach for the buzzer even if I let go of her. "Why did you leave me?"

"You were holding us back. Bill said."

"Bill mattered more than me?"

"I didn't like the way you looked at him, you little tart."

"I was four."

"You were *my* daughter."

"And you were supposed to be my mum."

How does that make you feel, Frankie? Did that hurt your feelings? You can't bottle everything up, Frankie. How much room do you think you have in there?

I don't have any room, Daniel. But I'll have a clear-out. Keep, donate, burn. I'll burn Juliet, donate my anger to medical science, and keep Cara and Vinnie. I'll burn the pink shoes and keep a Vixen Rampage kiss on my cheek.

"You were supposed to love me," I say.

My nails dig into her flesh. I could break her: One bone for every time she broke my heart. One bone for every day she made me live without her.

How does that make you feel, Frankie?

Actually, Daniel, it makes me feel good. Grateful. Thankful for the feel of a silk blouse against my skin, for a pair of soft hands on my cheeks and the words "Don't you worry, baby, your Aunt Vinnie's got you now." Thankful for all the bedtime stories about a raven-haired princess who stormed the castle and slayed the dragon. Thankful for so many "I forgive yous" and the early-morning raids to get me to school on time. Because every day my mother made me live without her was a day spent with Vinnie.

I wasn't dumped. I wasn't lost. I was found. I was loved.

I could break my mother.

But I don't.

I drop that waxy, flaky arm and step back.

"I'm not your daughter," I say. "You're right. She's dead."

She jerks her head to watch me. Her mouth opens but it's only dribble that comes out.

I look at the woman who gave birth to me. The hollow shell. The dried bug. She isn't my mother; she's an impostor. In the end it's so easy to walk away.

"Where are you going?" The chair creaks; she gurgles and groans.

I grip the door frame. I'm walking away. I am.

"He stole it." She swallows around her words. "The money. Some drug dealer. How stupid do you have to be?" Her laughter turns into a coughing fit.

I close my eyes. The realization lands in my heart with a heavy, choking thump.

Oh, Xavier. What did you do?

I push off from the frame and run. It doesn't matter that I hear my mother calling, "Don't leave me alone!"

I'm not walking away. I'm running.

Forty-one

Beneath the overpass, the walls are covered in graffiti but only one piece belongs to Xavier and it's unfinished.

The whole area stinks. Stagnant river water, bird shit, and years of drunks using the walls as urinals.

I walk the narrow bike path running alongside the water; above me, the bridge yawns across the Yarra. The bridge foundations are on my right, forming a high, graffiti-covered wall; water drips down the pylons, little trails of green, brown, and gray. Pigeons coo from the bridge beams above, daring me to look up.

I hurry past Xavier's unfinished piece, hardly able to register it. The path is clear. Nothing in the scrub alongside it.

But this is the place. This is where I saw Dave, hiding under the overpass like a troll waiting for passing goats. This is where Steve saw Xavier.

It's still. Cold. Quiet.

I walk out from under the bridge to where a thick carpet of green covers the bank; at the top, a narrow dirt road leads to the children's farm.

I wade uphill through the knotted undergrowth, keeping close to the side of the bridge. My boots rip a path through the creepers; I watch my feet but can't stop thinking how nearby children are playing with guinea pigs, their parents looking on with dopey smiles, cameras flashing. Maybe if I close my eyes and breathe quietly I'll hear their laughter, their squeals of delight.

I kick something. Something black, square, about the size of my hand.

I bend, pick it up—a wallet, gritty with dirt and leaves. My heart beats hard, pulsing in my ears. I stay crouched, hands trembling as I flip it open. No money, no ID. A couple of receipts, damp and hard to read—a corner store, an ATM statement, something . . . I don't know.

I can only make out one word.

Galaxy.

I drop the wallet and shoot to standing, body tense. Rigid.

All I do is breathe.

In.

Out.

I stare at the wallet. *Galaxy, galaxy, galaxy* . . .

And then I move. So fast. Everything's a rush. I swipe at the undergrowth, vines pulling tight against my forearms. I don't stop, I can't stop. I have to find him.

There has to be more. Some sign. Some hope.

My jeans are wet through, heavy and damp. Uphill. Tangled. Stumbling.

I have to find him.

I have to tell him I get it. The kind of person who steals four and a half grand just to buy a gift so he'll be liked is someone who doesn't know what it means to be loved.

That kind of person is lonely.

Is crying out for help.

Is lost. I get it.

I reach the top, knee-deep in a tangle of green. Where the bridge meets the road there's a gap, a concrete cave about two meters high, five meters deep, a floor of dirt. A troll's cave.

It's dark inside.

But I can see. The smallest hint beneath the dirt. Not quite covered. Not deep enough.

I fall to my knees, choking off a cry, my hand covering my mouth.

It's not possible.

It can't happen like this.

I end up on all fours, clawing at the dirt. I don't have to dig deep.

Brown hair, gray hoodie, high-tops. That's what I find.

Bright blue high-tops so I know it's him.

I call Vinnie.

Dirt catches in the cracks of my busted screen as I search for the number, shaking.

"It's me," I say when she answers.

There's silence. I breathe loudly. Rasps in every intake of breath.

"I waited," she says, voice cold and flat. "Waited at home, waited when I got to the school. I waited—"

"He's dead."

Silence again. Different this time. How many kinds of silence are there?

"Dead. I found him. I found . . ."

I look at him; I can't stop looking at him. There are splashes of paint on his bright blue sneakers. Yellow, purple, white, red. Lots of red.

I shove my fist in my mouth and drop to my knees.

She doesn't ask me to explain, doesn't ask who, just where: "Where are you?"

I force an answer and then I wait. I sit at his feet and wait. I can't leave him, because he's been alone for too long and I'm not going to do that to him now.

I listen to birds.

I hear the river.

Traffic in the distance; a gentle hum.

It's peaceful. But it's wrong.

Nothing can be right until she gets here.

When she does, she scoops me up and hugs me tighter than she ever has, tighter even than thirteen years ago when the silk of her blouse against my cheek made me shudder with relief. She doesn't say anything and I'm glad for it. In her arms, my edges feel defined again. For a moment I am contained, real, and whole. Almost whole.

She tries to lead me away. I tell her I can't but she says it's going to be okay, that we're not leaving him.

I let her guide me to the edge of the river where we wait, me in her arms. It's not right—nothing's right—but it's better. It's better because she's here.

That's how we are when the cops arrive.

"Goddamn mess," says Marzoli. He points, starts barking instructions.

My arse is wet from the damp grass; dirt so far under my nails it'll stick around for days. I cling to Vinnie and she makes gentle noises. Ducks surf the river current, pushed downstream toward the children's farm.

Behind us there's a glow of red and blue from the police cruiser parked on the grass. Someone says something about a stretcher.

I bury my head in Vinnie's shoulder and tell her I'm sorry I missed the meeting. She says not to worry, it's nothing—but it doesn't stop the shame. The reality of what I've done—what I've missed—hits me hard all at once. I missed the Most Important Meeting of My Life. The Your Future Is Decided Today Meeting.

Who am I going to be now?

I'm nobody's daughter.

Nobody's friend.

Nobody's sister.

Vinnie pulls out her cigarettes. That new-pack rustle. She clears her throat. "Your pop-singer fellow didn't go to uni."

I lift my head, look at her. "Ian Curtis?"

"Remember? You told me. Average at school, no uni. But he changed music. Changed lives."

"He killed himself, Vinnie. At twenty-three."

She lights a cigarette. "Shouldn't have done that, should he? Because he's still got my niece dancing like a maniac to his mopey bloody songs thirty-odd years later. Point is, the good stuff lasts. He should have lived a happy life till he was ninety-three—just think what he would have created if he'd lasted that long."

"Xavier was an artist too," I tell her. "The good stuff."

She looks at me for an age. "Well, there you go. Maybe thirty years from now there'll be Xavier fangirls running about the place."

I rest my head on her shoulder and imagine what people will think when they see Xavier's creations. How many of them will stop and stare? Who will smile, who will tilt their head and gaze with wonder? They might be painted over by some dumb punk next week, but they could change someone's life while they're here, couldn't they?

"Some people just have it in them," she says. "Nothing can stop them. Not school, not lazy-arse parents, not broken hearts. Nothing." The ducks quack. They agree. "I'm sure your brother was looking forward to getting to know you and making something of himself. He had that taken from him, but you, you've got it all ahead of you. And just think what a smart girl like you could do. Endless possibilities."

I close my eyes. "Did you know guinea pigs aren't actually pigs?"

"Is that right?"

"They're not from Guinea, either."

"I didn't know that. How'd you get to be so smart?"

"One word. Six letters. 'Scrambled vein can be changed into first part.'"

"I don't know what the hell you're talking about." She squeezes me tighter. "My baby girl: the crossword goddess."

I *am* the crossword goddess.

And I'm somebody's niece.

That's a start. That's a really good start.

A sharp noise turns my head.

Two guys in white jumpsuits are on either end of a stretcher, gumboots tearing through the tangled undergrowth as they pick their way downhill. A long black bag, matte plastic and smaller than you think it should be, is strapped to the stretcher.

They head toward Marzoli, smoking, leaning against a pylon. Behind him is the unfinished painting of a boy, his arms raised, captured right in the middle of beating the large drum strapped to his chest. It's almost the same as my album cover, except for the face. It's Xavier. And he's grinning, like he's never felt so alive.

Epilogue

We sprinkle his ashes in the river. Vinnie, Cara, Nate, and me. The smiling drummer boy watches us. I guess he approves.

It's strange, doing this when we don't have answers, when Dave is still missing and no one can tell me anything more than "We'll keep looking."

Marzoli says helpful things like, "TV makes it seem like all crimes get solved, when most of them don't," and, "At least you get to say good-bye to him. How many families never get that?" In some ways I understand what he's saying, in other ways I want to cut off his nuts and feed them to a Doberman.

I know it was Dave—I'm certain of it—but I don't know if he meant to do it. One punch, they say. Massive trauma to the back of Xavier's skull from when he landed on the concrete.

One punch. Anger does crazy things to people.

Believe me, I'm kind of an expert.

Which is why I've decided to bring a little more forgiveness into my life and let some of that anger go.

The school can't forgive me for breaking Steve's nose but I forgive them for being a bunch of arsehats. Vinnie says good riddance to bad rubbish—I can finish my high school diploma at another school anyway. And I will. I told her I'm still going to be the person who makes up the crosswords in the paper and she told me, "Princess, you can be whatever the hell you want."

Except maybe a cop.

Cara forgave me. Turns out it's written in the BFF handbook: no matter how mad you get with your BFF, if they grovel and buy you more Spanish doughnuts than you can eat, you must forgive them. Besides, she needs me to hold the ladder while she paints an obscene statement about Truc on the art block later tonight.

I've decided it's time to forgive Mark, too. Sadly, I lost his number in a massive bonfire so I can't call and tell him he's forgiven. Shame about that.

Then there's Nate.

He took me on a tour of the city last night, showing me all Xavier's pieces so I could take photos. So Xavier can live forever.

The last one we found was a sea of all-seeing eyes but my favorite is his final piece—Xavier the grinning drummer boy.

Nate wrapped his arms around me as I gazed at the wall of eyes and I asked if he was sure he wanted to be with me. "I might not be very open," I said.

"That's okay. I'll try to stop breaking the law, but I can't guarantee I won't piss you off," he said.

"Then I might hit you. Repeatedly."

"I might laugh at your angry face."

I hit him. He laughed.

"I might fall in love with you," he said, and kissed me.

I guess I forgive him.

Daniel reckons that more than anything I'm supposed to forgive myself. I told him, "Bullshit. It's Juliet I blame for skipping out on me," but he just flashed me that knowing smile and started taking notes in his little book. In green ink.

I don't forgive Daniel.

But I'm working on forgiving Juliet.

Most important of all, Vinnie forgave me—for Steve, for The Meeting, for being a world-class brat. I had to promise to clean out the meat tray for the rest of my natural life, but I don't mind. I think I might be able to be a crossword goddess *and* stink of garlic. I'm starting to think I can have it all.

The way I see it, my aunt is the queen of Collingwood so the world is my oyster. Or maybe something less slimy. Churros. The world is my churros.

When I've scattered Xavier's ashes and cried and been hugged, and laughed and told them everything I know about my stupid, beautiful, talented, messed-up brother, Vinnie pulls out a small scrap of paper. It's old, torn halfway through the center, curled at the edges and yellowing.

She holds it out for me. I take it, unfold, and read.

It's a handwritten note—just Vinnie's name and a telephone number.

"I kept it," she says. "I don't know why."

I nod. It's kind of all I can do. I feel Cara's arms around my waist and Nate's chin on the top of my head as I hold out my hand and let the note go.

The wind catches it and it flies away.

Nothing gets buried anymore.

Acknowledgments

BFG-sized thanks go to the ever-helpful, ever-supportive Line Tamers—Rosey Chang, Marie Davies, Cathy Hainstock, and Sarah Vincent. Without your advice and copious read-throughs, *Frankie* wouldn't exist. Mocktails all round.

Massive thanks to everyone at Flatiron, especially Sarah Dotts Barley for taking a chance on a story about a troubled girl from Collingwood. Also thanks to my Australian publishers: Jane Godwin, Lisa Riley, Michelle Madden, and all the team at Penguin.

Thank you to Sari Smith, Kirsty Murray, Toni Jordon, and Penni Russon for your wisdom and inspiration, and for kicking me up the behind when I needed it most (I'm looking at you, Kirsty). To the gang at Writers Victoria—the supportive community and well-timed vegan cupcakes you provided gave me the strength to keep going. Thanks to Alexis Drevikovsky and

Kate Larsen for being more awesome than any two people should be allowed. I am especially grateful for the support of the Grace Marion Wilson Trust for its 2014 Glenfern Fellowship. Thanks to Tomas Drevikovsky and Jaclyn Crupi for fixing my terrible Italian and to Cheryl Pientka, agent extraordinaire.

And finally, big love to my wonderfully forgiving friends and family, especially Peta "Pooh Bear" Dempsey and my too-amazing-for-words mum and dad. Sorry for all the last-minute cancellations and months of MIA. Love you.